Cold Shoulder Road

Joan Aiken

Delacorte Press

Published by
Delacorte Press
Bantam Doubleday Dell Publishing Group, Inc.
1540 Broadway
New York, New York 10036

Library of Congress Cataloging-in-Publication Data

Aiken, Joan.
  Cold Shoulder Road / Joan Aiken.
      p.   cm.
  Summary: As they search for Arun's mother, Is Twite and her
cousin Arun are grateful for their ability to communicate telepathically
when they find themselves in a series of dangerous predicaments in-
volving the evil Dominic de la Twite and his Silent Sect.
  ISBN 0-385-32182-1 (hardcover)
  [1. Sects—Fiction. 2. Adventure and adventurers—Fiction.
3. Extrasensory perception—Fiction. 4. England—Fiction.] I. Title.
  PZ7.A2695Co   1996   95-22176
                                                          CIP
                                                          AC

The text of this book is set in 12-point Cochin.
Book design by Susan Clark
Manufactured in the United States of America
April 1996
10 9 8 7 6 5 4 3 2 1
BVG

Cold
Shoulder
Road

Every night, around nine o'clock in Cold Shoulder Road, the screaming began. It came from the end house in the row. It was not very loud. The sound was like the cries of the gulls that flew and whirled along the shingle-bank on the seaward side of the road.

People who lived in the road (there were not many of them) took no notice of the screaming. It's the gulls, they thought, or the wind; or, they thought, Whatever it is, it's no business of ours.

Only one person felt differently, and she lived next door to the house from which the screaming came.

Night after night she clenched her hands and stood trembling by the window.

Something has got to be done, she thought. Something *must* be done.

At last she did it.

One

On a chilly evening in late spring, many years ago, the schooner *Dark Diamond* was feeling her way through the narrow passage known as the Downs, between the coast of Kent and the Goodwin Sands. Nothing could be seen, nothing could be heard, save the creak of ropes and the wash of water along the side of the ship. Fog lay like thick white wool over the English Channel. If there were lights along the shore, half a mile away, they were hidden behind the misty blanket.

"But likely there's none," observed Captain Podmore on the bridge, gloomily peering ahead and rubbing his bristly chin. "That tarnal great flood-wave what came a-raging down this coast last January—that drownded a many souls along the Essex and Kent shores. And swept away a many houses. Folk is still hard at work putting all to rights— those as wasn't drownded. They do say the naval boatyard at Deal was a right hurrah's nest—stove-in vessels perched atop of house roofs; and they found one thirty-three-gun frigate a couple of miles inland at Womenswold, lodged in the crotch of a big old chestnut tree. It's still there, I've heard tell; nobody can figure out a way to get it down."

The two passengers on board the *Dark Diamond*, who were standing with Captain Podmore on the bridge, looked at one another anxiously.

"Your mother, Arun—" began the girl.

"Nay, nay, I know what you're a-thinking," Captain Podmore said hastily. "You're a-thinking that Mrs. Twite might ha' fared badly down at Folkestone town. But don't you be frit, Arun my boy, you can surely set your mind at rest. Folkestone did none so badly. That turble flood-wave bore on south'ards, on towards France, arter it scraped Dover. Towns west o' Dover didn't get it nigh so hard. And, farther down the Channel, past the Island, it were naught to write home about."

"That's the Isle of Wight?" asked the girl.

"Right, Missie Is. That's why the old *Dark Diamond* come through without a splinter off her gunwale." He patted his ship affectionately. "We was hove to in Poole Harbor, and never felt no more than a ripple."

"Up north it was dreadful," said Is. "The whole town of Blastburn was flooded out, and the coal mine filled with water."

"Aye, because the doddy fools thought fit to build their town low down inside of a cave. What could they expect— do there come a high tide? And what's befallen that Channel Tunnel the Folkestone people spent years a-building, I wonder?"

"Did they finish the Tunnel, then?" asked Arun. "They were still hard at work digging it when I ran off from home."

"Aye, 'twas finished and working—unless the tidal wave stove it in."

"Do people ride through to France on horseback, then?" asked Is.

"Nay, nay, lass, they've a wagon-train that runs through, once a day. You can fit a tidy-sized coach in one o' they wagons, and they have horse boxes too, and folks does the crossing inside o' their own carriages. They don't even get out. Twenty-six miles to Boulogne, it be, and that-ar old train does the crossing in only one hour, will you credit it?"

Captain Podmore spat vexedly over the side of his ship. "And the worst of it is, that-there Tunnel is putting honest Free Traders out of business."

"Why, Captain Podmore?"

"Why, up to five years agone, there was a big cross-Channel trade in smuggled goods—any brig sailing these waters, you could lay your sweet life she'd be half full of run brandy, or 'baccy, or French kickshawses. But now all these cargoes, they comes through by Tunnel. Taking the bread out of our mouthses! There be a new tribe of folk running the business—the Merry Gentry, they calls their-selves. O' course *I* don't have owt to do wi' them," he added hastily. "Very nasty coves they are to tangle with, 'tis said. Hang you up by your heels from a lamppost as soon as kiss your hand. To make an example, d'ye see? So folks knows better than to meddle with their comings and go-ings."

"But aren't there police or customs officers at the entrance to the Tunnel, at each end, to oversee what comes through?"

"Oh, aye," said the Captain. He winked. "They has a gate at each end, like a portcullis. And a chap at the gate to lock all fast when the train has run by. And other coves in King's uniforms a-poking and a-prodding at folkses' bags and bundles. But, lord bless ye, there's a deal of contraband still goes through. A coin in the hand is worth two in the bank, and a blind horse knows which side his hay be buttered on. Mammoths' tusks, they do say, is the prime article these days."

"*Mammoths' tusks?*"

"*I* wouldn't be a-knowing," said Captain Podmore virtuously. "Sea coal and a drop o' Highland Malt is all *I* ever carry. But 'tis said they dug up a deal of those old, frozen long-ago elephant critters up in the steppe-lands near Muscovy and Hell-Sinky. Loads o' they tusks are a-coming south, through Norroway and Jutland and the Lowlands and Normandy; and now, the word goes, they runs 'em through the Tunnel."

"But what in the world do folk want mammoths' tusks *for?*" asked Is. "Diamonds, now, I could understand—"

"They carves 'em into snuffboxes, lassie. Sneeze-coffers. Or into false teeth," added Captain Podmore. "All the crack, sneeze-boxes made from mammoth tusks are. And rich folks nowadays has sham teeth screwed in when their own has worn out. Flying in the face of Nature, if you ask me. Anyhow there's a mighty deal of rhino to be made in the trade, so 'tis said."

6

He peered forward, for Dover Light was now faintly to be seen ahead, and most of his attention must be given to navigation.

"But don't you fret about your ma, Arun my boy," he went on after a minute. "Folkestone town be set mainly on the cliff. That way the folk stayed high and dry."

"Yes," agreed Arun. But still he sounded worried.

It's because he ran away from home, Is thought, and never wrote to his mum in years. And now he feels bad about it.

"Hearken, young 'uns," said Captain Podmore, when they had passed Dover and were putting in toward Folkestone. "Ye'll not think me disobliging if I don't take ye right into harbor, but get my man Sam to row ye to the foot of the jetty steps?"

"Of course we don't mind," said Arun, a little puzzled. "It was very kind of you to bring us all the way south from Stonemouth. But why—why don't you plan to go into harbor here?"

Captain Podmore laid a finger alongside his nose. "What the eye don't see, the heart don't glather over," he said. "They be mortal sharp, they Preventive chaps around Folkestone, and there were a little bit of bother over French strums—"

"Strums?"

"What you'd call periwigs, for the Mayor and Corporation, what never paid a penny of Duty. I'd as lief not show my nose in this port until they've other matters on their minds—let alone cut queer whids with the Merry Gentry,

who are powerful strong along this stretch o' the coast, so
'tis said—"

He stared ahead into the foggy dark and called softly,
"Ease her to stabb'rd, Sam!"

"The *Mayor and Corporation*? Well!" said Is, shocked.

"Eh, well, when it comes to smuggled goods, missie,
even the highest in the land ain't too toploftical. That's
why the folkses that fetches the goods gets to be so
powerful strong. Now bring her to, Sam! And step
lively, lower a dinghy, but don't let me hear one dunt or
scrunch."

So, after whispered farewells and thanks, Is and Arun
found themselves, ten minutes later, at the foot of the drip-
ping, slimy stone steps that led up to the seaward end of
Folkestone Pier.

Captain Podmore gazed after them anxiously and solicitously from the ship as they began the steep climb.

Then, behind them, silent as a moth, the *Dark Diamond*
drifted away southward, toward Hastings.

Ahead, as they walked quietly along the pier, Arun and
Is could see a few lights, scattered up and down a high
rampart of black land that began to show up against the
paler night sky.

The air felt bitterly cold and dank. A gusty wind chewed
at their elbows and ankles. Nothing could be heard but the
slop of waves along the stone jetty.

"Whereabouts does your mum live, Arun?" whispered
Is.

"At the east end of the town." Arun pointed with his

right hand, forgetting that she could not see it in the dark. "In what they call Frog-Hole Lane."

"Rummy kind of name."

He shrugged. "Scruffy kind of neighborhood. Not very friendly. Its other name is Cold Shoulder Road. You see, that's where the Sect first settled, when they came over from the Low Countries."

"The Sect?"

"I told you about them, didn't I? My mum and dad belonged to a Sect, the Silent Folk. They don't allow any talking, not by anybody. Except the Elder, and he speaks only when it's needful. Like, maybe, talking to folk who don't belong to the Sect. And, of course, when he preaches on Sundays."

"Nobody talks *at all*?" said Is, aghast. "But that's crazy. How the pize do you find out anything you want to know?"

"By making signs. Or, if it's too hard for signs, you write on a bit of paper. Or a slate. I used to do a lot of that when I was a kid."

"But what a fubsy way of going on! Now I come to think, your dad did say summat about it." But, after a moment's thought, Is burst out laughing. "Hey, though, it wouldn't matter to *us*, would it?"

Is and Arun were able to speak to each other by using thoughts instead of words. They did not always choose to do so. But sometimes an idea crossed over more quickly if it did not have to be translated into language. So their talk was often a patchwork of words and silences during which thoughts flashed back and forth between them like shuttles on a loom.

"That was why I ran off from home, d'you see," said Arun. "I couldn't stand all that silence. My dad used to wallop me if I asked a question. Or else I'd be shut up in my room. And that was only a cupboard."

"Your dad was sorry after you ran away," said Is thoughtfully. "He was *real* sorry, later on, when he lay a-dying."

"It was too late then, wasn't it?"

Arun's tone was impatient. He was peering ahead, into the gloom. "Can you hear music, d'you think?"

"No. Did your mum wallop you too?"

"No. She didn't. But she'd never cross my dad. She always did what he told her. Dad would never allow what the Sect called *flightiness*. Even fetching a bunch of primroses into the house—he'd say that was flighty. I—I sometimes thought my mum would have *liked* to bring a bunch of primroses into the house. Or dandelions."

"D'you reckon she stayed with the Silent Sect after your dad died? How many of 'em are there?"

"Forty or fifty. Most had come over from Dunkirk. Some joined in Folkestone. They're a-saving up to collect enough cash to shift the whole Sect over to New England by and by, get themselves a plot of land there, and build a village."

"Maybe they'll have gone already?" suggested Is.

"Not very likely. They are mostly weavers, or basketmakers, or joiners, or chimneysweeps—those trades don't make enough to save more than a few shillings a week. Dad was a chimneysweep and cobbler. But he never saved much. He was out so often, roaming about."

"Well," said Is, "*I* think it's a scaly notion, choosing not to talk to folk. Why did we ever *invent* words in the first place, if we ain't to be allowed to use 'em?"

"Song and dance was even worse," Arun said. "My dad joined the sect partly because he couldn't stand Uncle Desmond and his music. Dad said they were the Devil's tunes."

Is sighed. "It's true, *my* dad really took the bun when it come to wickedness. A proper rat, *he* was. But that's not to say his music is wicked. That's plain foolishness. Hey!"

She stood still, grasping Arun's arm. Then she said, "You're right, someone is a-playing music. And that's one of my dad's tunes they're playing—'The Day Afore May-Day.'"

"Maybe there's a fair," Arun said. "Or a market."

They had by now reached the inner end of the jetty and turned right along the harbor front. A thin slip of moon was rising, and it was possible to see that, though not destroyed, the town had suffered in the flood. Bits of the seawall were missing, a number of houses had boarded-up windows or stove-in doors; chunks of masonry lay here and there on the muddy, sandy roadway.

Another few minutes' walking and they could clearly hear the sound of music ahead of them: a tune intended to be cheerful was being played slowly and dolefully on a crumhorn.

"Ah, it *is* a fair." Is peered ahead at the cluster of little booths and market stalls in a space where the houses fell back from the sea front. "Rabbitty little set-out, though, ain't it? Still, maybe one of 'em will have summat we could buy your mum for a fairing, Arun?"

"My mum?" he said, astonished. "Take my mum a present? Why? My mum never had a present in the whole of her life. The Silent Folk don't give each other presents. They don't hold with such doings."

"Well then, it's high time she *did* get given summat, even if it's only a new milk jug," Is retorted, thinking of all the presents, small but welcome, that her aunt Ishie and her sister Penny had given her.

But when they reached the meager little row of stalls it became plain that there was no great choice of goods to be bought. Most of the things on sale were food—rows of silvery herrings, a handful of withered apples, cabbages, a pot or two of honey, and some loaves and pies. There were, too, old clothes, a few household wares, some wooden whistles, pipes, and tops.

A skinny old man, sitting on a box, played tunes on his crumhorn, but so slowly and wearily that even the liveliest ones sounded like funeral marches.

The stallholders were gloomily stamping their feet and rubbing their hands to keep warm. There were very few purchasers—half a dozen shadowy figures shuffling from one stall to another, inspecting the goods for sale. Nobody seemed to be buying much.

Then Is, looking up over the market stalls, saw something very strange. There were houses up above, scattered over the hillside, and, higher still, a stretch of roadway crossing the grass. Now along this passed a figure so singular that Is rubbed her eyes, wondering if she had been mistaken. What she saw seemed to be a person astride of two large wheels—nothing more—and tugged along by the pull of a large pale-colored kite, which flew above and ahead in the windy moonlit sky. The person—the wheels—the kite—all passed so swiftly that, a moment after, Is thought she must have imagined the whole thing.

For how could a person ride on two wheels?

Pulled by a kite?

Arun lingered by a stall, looking at the pipes and whistles on it.

"I used to *long* so for one of those," he murmured. "I don't suppose—"

"Oh, come on, Arun, do," said Is impatiently. "Your ma won't want a whistle! How about a fourpenny pie?"

As she spoke, Is felt a sudden startled movement beside her, as if someone were about to grab her arm. She looked round to find, at her elbow, a person even shorter and smaller than she was herself (and Is was not tall), a stumpy, thickset little boy, clasping a bundle of hazel branches, which he could only just carry.

Their eyes met for a brief moment—his were large, round, and pale—and then he scuttled off hastily into the crowd.

"Those pies don't look too tasty," said Arun.

"Well, there ain't a lot else. And we may be glad of one ourselves, if we don't find your mum—"

"Don't find my mum?" said Arun crossly, feeling for

pennies in his breeches pocket. "Why shouldn't we find her? She's not one to gad—"

As he bought the pie and the stallkeeper wrapped it in a bit of greasy paper, Is noticed the little boy again. Or was he a girl? It was hard to decide.

He had now stopped in front of a stall that sold brooms and brushes; without speaking, he held up the bundle of brushwood he carried, showing it to the man behind the table. The man took the bundle, inspected it carefully, nodded, and passed over a few small coins. Clutching them tightly, the boy ran to a fish counter, where he pointed silently at the herrings. Three were handed to him in a cabbage leaf; he paid for them and scooted off at top speed into the darkness.

Wonder if he's one of Arun's Silent Folk? thought Is. Wonder if he *can't* speak, or won't speak? Come to think, if they're never allowed to say a word, it's a blooming marvel their kids ever learn to speak at all.

"This way," said Arun, who was now walking at impatient speed; and he turned inland from the sea front, threading among a crisscross of little streets which had plainly suffered from the flood, for their cobblestones were heaved out of place and lay in piles ready to trip passersby. The ground between the cobbles was muddy and slippery; a sour smell of salt, wet rope, and rotting wood hung in the air. A few shadowy animals—dogs? wolves? slunk in and out of gaps between the houses.

"Now we turn right, this is Cold Shoulder Road." Arun gestured to a little tumbledown row of weatherboarded houses, joined together by a common roof, which ran the length of the lane. "Our house is the last but one, down at the end."

Beyond the last house rose a bushy, brambly hillside, and above that, cliffs were outlined against the sky.

Is, who had grown up in the spacious woods of Blackheath Edge, felt a little sorry for Arun, obliged to spend his childhood in such a dank, muddy little street. Still, at least open country must be nearby—supposing his parents had allowed him to go off into the fields, or climb the cliff?

"And the sea's just over the road, after all," she said, half aloud.

"What's that? Come along, I'm freezing," snapped Arun. He was striding faster, almost running. Waves of worry came from him.

When they reached the last house but one, Is could see that its door, unlike many in the row, must once have been painted white, and had a brass figure 2 on its crosspiece, tarnished by sea air.

Arun banged nervously on the door with his knuckles. Then, as there was no answer, he rapped again, more loudly.

But there was still no response. He tried the door. It was locked.

Now a black cloud slipped across the slender moon.

"Seems like there's nobody home," said Is, after a fairly long pause. She added hopefully, "Maybe your ma might have gone out a-marketing? To the fair? To get herself a fish for supper, likely? Or to visit a friend? Do you think?"

"No I don't!" said Arun. "She never went out. Dad did the marketing. And she wouldn't stir out at night. Not unless it was to look after a sick person."

Is could hear the worry and uncertainty in his voice.

She thought: His dad died. Now, maybe, he'll find his mum has died too. Poor Arun. It's hard for him. But what *we* need, right now, is a bite to eat and somewhere to doss down.

Aloud she said, "Did your mum use to keep a key anywhere? Like, under a brick?"

A note of hope came back into Arun's voice. He said, "Yes, she did, come to think. Round at the back. You have to go past the end house, and there's a path all along behind the back gardens."

They walked on past the last house in the row. Its windows were dark. In fact, there had been very few lights all along Cold Shoulder Road. Which seemed odd, thought Is, for it must be early still, not more than about nine o'clock.

She shivered as two large drops of icy rain fell on her cheek.

"I sure hope she did leave a key. Maybe she's round at one o' the other houses, chewing the rag with a neighbor."

"I tell you, she never —"

Arun shoved open a small paling gate and made his way gingerly along a narrow, slippery garden path between cabbages that had shot up tall and then fallen over. They smelled strong and rank.

16

By the back door of the house there stood a wooden rainwater barrel, set up on two piles of bricks. Arun knelt and poked his hand into the gap between the bricks, then let out a grunt of satisfaction.

"Here's the key, inside of a jam pot."

"Not before time," muttered Is, for rain was now falling steadily, and a low rumble of thunder came from over the sea.

The key from the jar opened the back door, and they walked through into icy cold and damp, thick, stuffy dark.

"Smells like a sardine factory in here," muttered Is. "And the floor's ankle deep in mud—watch how you step! Where does your mum keep her candles, Arun?"

"On a shelf under the stair."

He crossed the room and felt in the accustomed place, but let out a yelp of disgust.

"Shelf's all mud and slime. Like fishing in a basket of eels."

"Reckon the flood got into the house, waist level at least," said Is, feeling the stairs, which rose straight out of the kitchen. "And no one's troubled to clean up since. Best have a look upstairs, had we?"

She tried to speak in a cheerful, matter-of-fact voice, but secretly she had a frightening notion of what they might find up above.

"Ma always did keep a bedroom candle and some lucifer matches in her room," Arun murmured. "I'll just take a look up there."

He slipped past Is on the narrow stair and went up. She

followed close behind, hoping strongly that the upper floor of this little house might be less damp and wretched than the downstairs.

A rumble of thunder overhead accompanied them as they climbed; it was not a full peal, but sounded like people shifting bits of furniture about the sky so as to make room for something bigger.

"Lucky we're under cover," Is remarked. "It's raining stair-rods out there. Hark!"

They could hear the rain lashing on the roof.

Arun said nothing. There were two doors at the stair top, each side of a tiny landing place. He opened the right-hand one and walked into the room beyond, Is still keeping very close behind.

As they entered the room a mighty, scalding-yellow canopy of lightning swept over the whole sky. Next moment a tremendous crash of thunder, just overhead, it seemed, made the whole house rattle.

"Croopus!" gasped Is. "That was a close one!"

But she spoke with huge relief. The flood of yellow light had revealed a neat bedroom, with bedcovers tightly tucked, clothes hanging on a hook, candle and matches on a chair by the bed. Nobody was here. No ill or dead person— which was what Is had feared—lay stretched on the bed.

"I just can't understand it," Arun was saying in a puzzled voice. "Where *can* she be?"

"Maybe she went on a visit? You got aunts—uncles—she got family of her own?"

Is knew nothing about her aunt Ruth, Arun's mother,

save that she had married Arun's father, Hosiah Twite, brother to Desmond Twite, Is's own father. And that the pair had belonged to this Silent Sect.

"Her parents were dead," said Arun. "We've only got family on Dad's side, and who'd want Uncle Desmond?"

He was trying to light the candle. Slowly the flame grew, and soft shadows flickered across the small room.

"The Twites ain't all bad," said Is. "There's Dido. She's a real one-er! And my sis Penny's not so bad, so long's you take her the right way—"

Arun was carefully carrying the candle across the room. "I'll have a look in Dad's room—"

His voice came from the top of the stairs.

"Where did you sleep, then?" asked Is, following behind.

"There's a little clothes closet off Dad's room. I slept in there on a cot-bed—*blister* it! What in the name of—?"

There was a loud thump and a crash.

"What's up?" called Is.

"There's *things* piled all over the floor—bits of board—I gashed my shin—oh, curse!" He tripped again, and only just managed to save himself without dropping the candle. "Watch how you go!"

"Rum stink in here," said Is. "Paint, you reckon?"

Another terrific flash of lightning suddenly lit up the room in bold black and yellow. Arun and Is let out simultaneous gasps. For what dazzled their eyes was not only the lightning, but also the contents of the room: all around the walls, and on the bed, and stacked three deep over the floor, and on the single chair, and on the clothes chest, were piled squares of wood about the size of chair seats, and these were all dashed and splashed with wild, brilliant color.

"What in creation's name *are* those things?" gasped Is as they were plunged back into dark, lit only by the candle's shadowy gleam. She picked up one board and held it near the flame.

"It's a picture. Of flowers. But *what* flowers! Glorious me! I never saw anything *like* it! Not in my whole life. And there's hundreds of 'em."

"In the closet too," said Arun, investigating.

Several more lightning flashes gave them a chance to decide that all the paintings had been done by the same person. They were nearly all pictures of flowers.

"There's jars of paint here, in the corner," said Is. "And brushes. D'you reckon your mum did these, Arun? Was she fond of flowers?"

"Well, she was," he said doubtfully. "If she were out in the lane, and she'd see a dandelion on the bank, most often she'd stop and look at it. Just for a minute. But my dad was the real one—he knew a lot about plants. He'd walk all over the county, times when business was poor, or even if it wasn't, and he made a map showing where all the rare ones grew, Jacob's Ladder and Green Man and the Monkey Orchid. But he never told people where they grew. And Ma never went with him."

"Could your dad have painted these?"

"Never!" declared Arun. "He used to say pictures were the Devil's likenesses. He'd never do *anything* like this. And he'd never allow Ma . . . not when he was alive. No, this couldn't be Dad's work."

Is felt inclined to agree with Arun. She had, by chance, been present as her uncle Hosiah Twite lay dying of cold and wolf bites. He had seemed a sad, defeated man, certainly not capable of producing pictures like these, which blazed with color, which twisted and writhed and swarmed with strong, bright, wild interlocked shapes.

"Then it must have been your mum what painted them. But where can she be now?"

"If only I knew!—We can't sleep in here," said Arun. "There's no room for a mouse. We'd best drag out the mattress from underneath and lay it on the floor in the other room. I'll have that, and you can have Mum's bed."

"Maybe she'll come home yet—yes! Hark!"

Rat-tat! on the front door.

"Maybe she lost her key," said Arun with a huge gulp of relief. He ran down the stair. There was no key in the locked front door. He opened the window beside it, with a struggle, and called hopefully, "Is that you, Ma? Go round to the back, we've no key for this one."

When he returned to the kitchen, his candle flame revealed the sorry state it was in, mud and slime all over the brick floor, mold and mildew on the surfaces of chairs, table, and sinkboard. But on the dresser he found two more candles, and lit one of them before opening the back door.

Surely this can't be Arun's mum? thought Is, gazing with some dismay at the woman who came pushing into the kitchen. She looked like a weasel, with a thin, pale face, wispy gray hair escaping from under a shawl, and a lot of teeth, which looked as if they were made of china.

"Mrs. Boles!" said Arun.

"There! I made sure it must be robbers when I saw your light!" cried Mrs. Boles aggrievedly. "That or yer ma come back. I never thought as how it would be *you*, Arun Twite! Given up for lost, *you* were! And your dad walking to London town seventeen times, a-searching for you, and yer mum crying her pore eyes out—when *he* wasn't there. Caused a peck of trouble, *you* did."

She stared at him accusingly, out of eyes that were red-rimmed with gin, not tears.

"But where *is* Ma?" demanded Arun.

"Ah! There's plenty as 'ud like to know that! Vanished clean away, she done—clean as a whistle. Shot the moon! Not but what they all of 'em went, those mumchance beggars as calls 'emselves the Silent Sect—*I'd* give 'em silent! I daresay their thoughts is as nasty as anybody else's, *if* not nastier; special that one as calls hisself the Elder—Dominic de la Twite, fiddle-faddle! Plain Twite's his moniker, ask me!"

"The Silent Sect have gone from Folkestone?" exclaimed Arun. "Did they go to America, then?"

"Nah, nah! Only just up the road to Seagate town. Made the neighborhood too hot to hold 'em here, I reckon, and there was plenty empty houses going free up there. Seagate's welcome to 'em, says I. Not but what your Ma was a decent body, when you got her alone; nursed me through a nasty case of gordelpus, she done, once. But as to where she'd got to—well, a nod's as good as a wink to a dead donkey."

She crossed her arms and stared at Is and Arun. "Oo's the gel?" she demanded. "She've a look of you, Arun—but you never 'ad no sister, did you?" Her eyes gleamed with curiosity.

"She's my cousin, Is Twite. My uncle Desmond's youngest. But when did my mother go, Mrs. Boles? You say she *didn't* go with the Sect, to Seagate?"

"Nah. Like I say, she went afore they did. Days afore. And there's some as say she abducticated little Abandella Twite, time she went. And was a-going to use the kinchin for wicked magicking, some do say. There's plenty, Arun Twite, as said your mum is a witch, that she got rid of you, first, and then done in your pore dad. In fact, if it weren't for me, keeping a neighborly eye on the place, this house woulda been burned down, weeks back."

"What?" Arun gaped at the woman, quite stunned. "For a start, who in the wide world is Abandella Twite? I never heard of such a name. And why should my mum abduct anybody? She's the very *last* person . . . And, as for her being a witch, that's just clung-headed. Why, Mum wouldn't hurt a fly! I've seen her pick up an ant, when she saw one crossing the kitchen floor, and carry it safe outside."

"All I knows is," said Mrs. Boles, "there's folks around this town as don't scruple to call your mum a wizard. Acos she used to go and nurse sick folk, and mostly they got better. That ain't natural. And you'd best look out yourself,

Arun Twite—anyone as is connected to the Silent Folk, hereabouts, they can be in for a peck of trouble."

She leaned close to Arun and whispered, "With the *you-know-who*!"

"I don't know who," said Arun, puzzled, stepping back. Mrs. Boles's breath stank of gin, old potato peelings, and fish bones.

"The Emjee!" she whispered, and nipped through the back door, pulling it to behind her with a spiteful slam.

"The Emjee?" said Arun to Is. "What in the world can she mean?"

She shook her head.

"We'll find out in the morning. Let's eat the pie and go to bed."

They went to bed as the storm rumbled away inland. Is wondered if the rain was falling on Arun's mum. And on those two queer figures—the stumpy little character with pale eyes like silver pennies, and the person riding on two wheels and drawn across the hillside by a kite.

I must have just *thought* I saw him. But how could I invent such a thing?

Finding no answer to any of her questions, Is fell asleep.

Two

"We had better get hold of Mrs. Boles and ask some more questions," said Is next morning. She and Arun had breakfasted scantily off a loaf that Is had gone out and bought in Wear Street, and they were now making a rather hopeless attempt to clean the filthy kitchen with brooms and rags and pails full of seawater, scooped from the high tide, which chomped and frothed beyond the shingle-bank on the south side of Cold Shoulder Road.

"Mrs. Boles is a horrible woman," said Arun. "There's lots of things missing from the house—Ma's workbasket, and the pink mug my granny Twite gave me when I was born, and all Dad's fishhooks and lines. And the clock. I bet she took them—"

"Hush! Here she comes now," warned Is as the garden gate clicked.

Mrs. Boles, seen in daylight, was no great improvement on last night's version: she had pale gray skin, scanty gray hair done up in curl papers, and a well-used apron tied over layers and layers of grimy clothes. She was holding the pink mug.

"Took it for safekeeping," she explained. "Ah hah! Getting the place a bit straightened up, are ye?" she said with an indulgent glance at their efforts. "Well, it does look a mossel better, I give ye that. You been trying your best. Not but what my best advice to you is leave here right soon —there'll be nowt but trouble for you in this town. Like I was telling ye last night—"

"Mrs. Boles, what is the Emjee?"

"*Hush,* will ye!" Mrs. Boles's eyes—still very red-rimmed —shot nervously hither and thither. She laid a skinny finger on her lips. Then, dipping the same finger in Arun's pail of seawater, she drew ten letters in the thin layer of sand on the brick floor.

M E R Y J E N T R Y

"Merry Gentry? But what have *they* got to do with my mum?"

"*Quiet,* boy, will you? You want them to come and poke you headfirst in a bog-hole on Romney Marsh? And me as well?"

"No, of course not; but why—"

"She took and went off with the Handsel Child!"

"She did what?"

"Y'mum. Stole the Handsel Child."

Arun was beginning to look frantic.

Is said quietly, "We don't know what the Handsel Child is, Mrs. Boles. We never heard of it. We have only just come from a long way off—Blastburn, way up in the north country. You'll have to tell us about the Handsel Child."

But this Mrs. Boles seemed quite unable, or unwilling, to do. She clapped a hand over her china teeth, stared haggardly at each of them in turn, gulped, and muttered, "Well, *I* don't know, I'm sure. Don't know—How'm *I* supposed to tell ye? I wish now I'd gone off with my Meena—that I do. And then—and then there's all y'mum's pictures—I'm sure I—"

"Did my aunt Ruth paint all those pictures?" Is asked with lively curiosity. She thought how very much she would like to meet a person who painted flowers in such a way. She had been up before breakfast to take another look at them by daylight.

"Oo else woulda done so, gel?"

"Did you watch her painting them?"

"Mercyme! Not on your Oliphant! *I* don't want to turn dropsical—or come down with hot pulpitations." Mrs. Boles made the nervous gesture with her fingers of someone warding off bad magic. "Oo else woulda painted them if not Mrs. T.? Pictures don't paint theirselves. Nobody else 'as bin in the 'ouse—only the skinny lady, and she didn't stop—she come axing questions after y'mum took and scarpered—"

"The skinny lady? What skinny lady?"

"Come axing for y'mum. She'd come here times afore—I remember her around Michaelmas a-colloguing with y'mum. Tallish and sharpish-looking and bony as a hostrich; I showed her where the key is kep'—'case she might want to take the pictures—dunno if I done right—but she never stopped—"

Mrs. Boles's voice dribbled away. She peered warily at her two listeners. Is wondered what other people she might have let into the house, and what they might have taken from it.

"You goin' to get rid o' them pictures? Take them outa here?" Mrs. Boles asked hopefully.

It was plain that she feared and disliked the pictures, seemed to believe they had magical properties, might do her harm.

"Mrs. Boles, will you *please* tell me about my mum and the Handsel Child?"

But this threw Mrs. Boles into a gibber of terror.

"Na, na, me boy, na, na, I dassn't do that. Mid as well chop out me own tongue, right here on the kitchen floor! Na, you hatta find some other body to ax about that. Ax—lemme think—" She visibly racked her brain. "Owd Mr. Crockenden—nay, he won't do. Miss Tinpenny—won't do, she's so deaf you hatta shout. Mrs. Barefoot, in High Street. The dentist feller—no, he's gone—*I* got it! You go see his cousin, the owd Admiral, Admiral Fishskin."

She nodded at them triumphantly.

"He'll be the feller to help ye. He's a reel wonder, the owd boy, riding on his wheel-shay, flying his kite. *He'll* tell ye all ye need to know. And, like as not," added Mrs. Boles, a brilliant idea striking her, "he'll have some knobby notion what to do with y'mum's pictures. For they shouldn't stay here. Ah, a great owd boy for pictures, the Admiral be! His house is full of 'em. I should know, I useter do for his lady —in the place, cleaning and such—afore she took and died, afore the Admiral retired. Pictures all up and down the walls, 'e 'as—'undreds of 'em."

"Flying his *kite*?" asked Is.

"But why should the Admiral —"

"Thought a deal of y'mum, the Admiral did," went on Mrs. Boles, "acos she nursed 'is missus. Now I gotta go." She retreated hurriedly through the back door, wiping her hands on her grubby apron. Absently she picked up the pink mug and took it with her.

"Where does the Admiral live?" Arun called after her.

"Up the East Cliff!" she hissed, removing herself even faster. "A big new 'ouse with a fancy garden sticking out on props."

So, presently, Is and Arun abandoned the rather hopeless task of trying to clean the kitchen, and set off for the East Cliff.

"Folkestone is built over seventy hills," Arun told Is as they toiled up a steep slope, between grassy banks dotted all over with little hawthorn bushes.

"I can see that," she panted, turning to look at the town lying scattered behind them, like a handful of dice dropped over a crumpled landscape of gullies and hillocks. Behind it frolicked the sea, blue and cheerful this morning under a frosty sun.

"Do you remember this Admiral? Admiral Fishskin?" she asked Arun.

"Only just. He hadn't retired when I was at home. But sometimes he'd come into Dad's shop, between cruises, I suppose, and chat. Dad would just sit quietly, nodding and listening. Do you think the Admiral would really have some notion of where my mum has got to?"

"How can I tell?" said Is doubtfully, remembering that strange apparition on wheels. "I don't see why he should. But it's worth asking."

"I *can't* understand it!" burst out Arun after another five minutes' steep climb. "*Why* should my mum go off? Why wouldn't she leave a message for me, at least, if she did? To say where she was going? She always used to do that. If she went out to nurse a sick person, she'd leave a note on the dresser. Or in the teapot—"

"The teapot wasn't there," Is reminded him. "Maybe Mrs. Boles took it. Anyway, Arun! How long is it since you ran away from home?"

"I dunno, exactly." He began to count on his fingers. "First I went up to London and sang songs in the street— and made friends with Davey. Then I went up north with Davey—then I was in the mines—then I ran off from there —and then I was out of my wits for a spell, because it had been so horrible in the mines—"

Is nodded. She had worked in the northern mines herself and knew what they were like. And she knew that, for a while, Arun had believed he was a cat, so as not to have to remember the bad things that had happened to him and his friends. Particularly his friend Davey.

"Four or five years, I suppose," he said at last. "Since I left Folkestone."

"Well," said Is, "why should your mum ever expect you back? She must have thought you was gone for good and all. Dead, maybe. And your dad was dead—why should she trouble to leave any message? Specially if she didn't want folk to know where she was gone? Anybody might get into the house and read the message—or swipe it. Maybe Mrs. Boles did that."

"Mum would have hidden it in a secret place," Arun said stubbornly.

He seemed hurt to the quick by his mum's faithless behavior.

Is sighed at his unreasonableness. Then she said, "Look, there's a baker's cart. Reckon he oughta know where this Admiral lives."

The baker's boy proved well informed.

"Up to the very top, along the chalk track, and it's the big red-brick place, all planted about with nut trees and poplars. With a garden that sticks out on a platform over the cliff edge."

Indeed, East Hill House was readily recognizable. The neat garden looked newly laid out. And at least half the garden extended out on a platform supported by girders. This platform—just like a regular garden—had grass on it, and gravel paths, and large earthenware pots containing plants and bushes.

"Coo!" said Is. "Looks mighty drafty out there! Suppose them props were to give way? *I* wouldn't fancy picking daffodils outa those pots."

"I suppose the Admiral must have known what he was about."

They approached the house by a tidy path. Flowers bloomed in rows; not a leaf was out of place.

So it was quite a shock, after they rang the bell and the

door was opened by a smallish, oldish, round-faced man, with a bald head and a bad limp, to find that the inside of the house was unbelievably untidy, with its floors and contents coated in what looked like seven years' dust. And mixed objects of every conceivable kind piled all over the floor.

"Admiral Fishskin? Yes, certainly I am he," the small man told them in a soft Welsh accent. "What is your business, pray?"

He had on a gray morning coat and a gray waistcoat and white trousers. His cravat was very neat. His eyes looked in different directions. They were large, round, like pale pebbles. He wore rimless glasses.

Arun now seemed unsure of how to begin, so Is said, "Arun here is looking for his mother, Mrs. Ruth Twite. From Cold Shoulder Road. I dunno quite why, but the neighbor, Mrs. Boles, seemed to think you might have a notion where she'd gone."

"Oh, dear me. Mrs. Twite. Well, now, indeed. And you are her boy, Arun Twite? You left home, I seem to recall, some years ago. Yes, yes. And now you are back. And naturally you wish to find your mother. My goodness me."

The Admiral reflected in silence for a moment or two, while his confusing eyes moved slowly back and forth between Is and Arun. Then he said, "At this time of the morning I generally have a mug of grog. Will you join me?"

Taken by surprise, they nodded. He nodded gravely in return, then led the way across a hall filled with sundials and orreries, along a wide passage piled knee deep on each side with books and newspapers. There was a narrow gully in the middle. The walls of the passage were hung with pictures, five or six deep, mostly ships and seascapes. Open doors of rooms revealed more articles of every possible kind, piled in amazing disorder.

They entered a large kitchen, which was quite as messy and chaotic as the one in Cold Shoulder Road, though plainly here there had been no flood. There was a smell of many bygone meals: stale food, rancid fat, sour milk.

"Take a seat, pray take a seat," said Admiral Fishskin, dipping milk with a mug from a pail that stood on the floor. The milk was then transferred to a pan that had been used many times for the same purpose and never washed. The pan was placed on a big iron range, which glowed and kept the room stuffily warm. Cobwebs thick as clotheslines stretched from wall to wall above and lined the corners of the room. Various kites, of many different patterns, hung from hooks.

Is and Arun looked about them warily, then moved some pots, plates, baskets of eggs, letters, golf balls, sides of bacon, strawberry nets, and bunches of turnips from a pair of chairs and, finding nowhere else to put these things, set them down on the floor.

"That's right, that's right, make yourselves quite at home," said the Admiral absently, pouring dark brown liquor from a potbellied bottle into the hot milk. "There, now, that should put a bit of red into your noses." And he handed them a mug apiece.

The drink was boiling hot and amazingly powerful. Is,

after one sip, unobtrusively poured hers into a thick mat of cobweb that screened the top of a log basket.

"Now then—hmm." The Admiral took a swig of his own drink. "Yes: your good mother. She was most distressed when you ran off, my boy—most distressed indeed. And so was your father."

Arun's mouth set in an obstinate line. "I had to go," he mumbled. He set his mug down on the floor.

The Admiral looked at him with his large, odd eyes, and waited.

"They planned to apprentice me to Amos Furze the wigmaker," Arun went on, after a moment's silence. "Making wigs! I'd have been obliged to keep quiet, twenty-four hours a day, hold my tongue, like the rest of the Sect. And make wigs."

The Admiral nodded slowly.

"Hard discipline, that," he said. "Silence—yes. Yes, indeed. Good in its own way—but certainly does make conversation *devilish* difficult. I used to talk to your father, when I took him my boots to repair—or sometimes I could persuade him to play a round of golf with me; he was a first-class golfer—but speak, no, he would not. At the most he'd write replies to what I said in a notebook. I'd ask him about his wanderings round the countryside . . . sometimes he'd write a note on a scrap of paper. Got some of 'em still lying about, I daresay—" The Admiral gave a rather doubtful look round the cluttered room, but instantly seemed to abandon any notion of hunting for one. "And your mother the same. Capital nurse she was. Looked after

Maria—m'wife—when . . . But—no use. Then, after Maria died—and after your father died—Mrs. Twite would sometimes come to me for advice. Write down a question on a bit of paper. Troubles with neighbors, y'know. Prickly folk, that Sect of yours."

"Not mine," said Arun. "I left. Didn't agree with it."

The Admiral shot him a sharp, pale glance. "Well, well—nobody here was sorry when they moved up the coast to Seagate," he remarked.

"But my mum didn't move with the rest of them—Mrs. Boles said."

"No. Well. Affairs are a bit topsy-turvy in the town. Y'see—"

The Admiral looked from Arun to Is, carefully and attentively. "You've just arrived here from some way off, that right? Don't know how matters stand here?"

"Up north, we were," said Arun, nodding.

"So you've not been in Folkestone since the Tunnel opened?"

"It is open, then? It's being used? It wasn't harmed in the flood?" Is cried with lively interest.

Admiral Fishskin snorted. "No. No harm came to the Tunnel in the late flood. *Most* regrettably! The Tunnel entrances, both here and in France, are so far inland that they were not affected by the tidal wave. And the Tunnel is sunk so deep beneath the seabed that it was not damaged. A pity! A pity!"

"You don't like the Tunnel, sir?"

"Huf! It is a disaster. Why, pray, was this Island surrounded by sea, if not to protect it from Continental influences of the most pernicious kind? In the old days there would be a bit of Free Trade—a few pipes of brandy and such matter were fetched over from France, a few pairs of silk stockings—but now this scandalous group has been formed, these Merry Gentry as they style themselves— Merry Gentry! Murky Devils, *I'd* call them!—bringing goods through the Tunnel in outrageous quantities—positively outrageous, I assure you—and the whole countryside is being held to ransom. It is a positive reign of terror!"

"Are the Merry Gentry something to do with the Handsel Child?" Is asked.

"Indeed they are, my girl." The Admiral sipped his drink thoughtfully. Arun surreptitiously kicked his over so that it leaked away into the black, greasy matting.

"The Merry Gentry, you see," went on the Admiral, "keep a hostage, a child, what they call a Handsel child, as a surety for the good behavior of the people who live in these parts."

"Good behavior?"

"So they will not dare to lay information with the Excise Men."

"You mean, so they won't blab on their neighbors?" said Is. "But who *are* the Merry Gentry?"

"Ah! Nobody knows, my child," said the Admiral. "Nobody has the least idea. Or, if they do, they take care not to say. When the Merry Gentry ride out at night to collect a load of smuggled goods from the Tunnel, they blacken their faces with tar. Or wear black hoods. And their leader always wears a white mask and a big, broad-brimmed white hat. So nobody can ever see their faces or recognize them."

"But what about this-here kinchin, the Handsel Child?" Is asked, as the Admiral came to a stop. "Where does he come in?"

"Ah, well, there are supposed to be two Handsel Children. In the first place the Merry Gentry took a hostage. He was a little boy of four or so called Sam Ringwould. It was thought they took him out of the country, shipped him off to France maybe. Well, then, unfortunately, both his parents died in the flood, so nobody missed Sam very much. And a man from the local people around here said it was unacceptable that one side should have a hostage and the other side should not. (It was your father, by the bye, Arun my boy, who said this, when he came back from one of his field trips and heard what had transpired; he wrote his opinion on a sheet of paper and stuck it up outside the Bluejackets' Rest, where everybody would be sure to see it.) And, it seemed, the Merry Gentry agreed that his idea was a fair one, for, only a few days later, a completely unknown child was found sitting on the harbor front, one foot shackled to a bollard and a note pinned on its back: 'This is the Gentry child given for a Handsel.' "

"But—!"

"But—!"

Both Is and Arun exploded at the same time. Is went on, "Couldn't the child say where he had come from? Whose he was?"

"No. He was very small. Only about two, or thereabouts,

I believe. He could not speak, knew no words. And has never learned any since then. It is thought he must be dumb."

Now where, Is thought, where in the last day or so have I seen a child who didn't speak?

Arun was asking, "Who took charge of the child? Where does he live?"

"The head of the Silent Sect—a man respected in the locality—he took the child into his home. His sister cared for the child. They adopted it as their own."

"So now the kid has moved with the Sect to Seagate?"

"In fact, no. That is not the case. The child vanished. Disappeared, out of Mr. Twite's house, a few days before the move to Seagate."

"*Mr. Twite's* house?"

"After the Reverend Amos Furze went to New England," explained the Admiral, "the Silent Sect elected as their new leader a man recently arrived in this country from the Lowlands. His name is Dominic de la Twite. Naturally I asked your mother if there might be any relationship between this person and her husband. She thought not."

"Fancy his being called Twite, though," said Is thoughtfully. "It ain't a common moniker. What sort of cove is he, Admiral, sir?"

Admiral Fishskin considered.

"Not just in the common way. A big man. Tall, very handsome. Keen eyes. Impressive presence. *Godlike.*"

His voice was disapproving.

"Godlike?" said Arun.

"His eyes," went on the Admiral, "are a particular shade of blue gray. I would never choose a man with eyes that color to be my first officer. No indeed." He folded his lips together and shook his head. "Twite's sister, though," he added after a moment, "is a woman of great capacity."

"The Twites are a dicey lot," sighed Is. "Slice 'em where you like."

Arun said, "And folk think *my mum* went off with the kid? But why in the world would she do that?"

"So far as I know," said the Admiral, "there is no shred of evidence to support such a wild story. Except, of course, that they were both lost to view at the same time."

"How old would the kid be now?"

"Five, or six, maybe."

"A boy?"

"I am not sure. I never laid eyes on the young person."

"And what about the second kid? The one the Merry Gentry took? Whose was that? And where was it taken?"

"Ah, it is said that it was taken through the Tunnel into France. Where the organization is known as Les Gens Aimables. No doubt it remains there."

"Whose kid was it?"

"I have a notion," said the Admiral vaguely, "that it was some connection of your neighbor Mrs. Boles. But people are very reluctant to talk, as you will find. And I may not have the facts correctly."

"Mrs. Boles certainly don't wish to talk."

"Ah, well, she has reason," said the Admiral. "Her husband, Ern—who, I fear, was a sad, drunken fellow; a lamp-lighter, he used to be, in the town—one night he boasted, when in his cups, in the Bluejackets' Rest, that he knew a clever artist who had seen all the members of the Merry Gentry and could draw their portraits. Dear me, that was *not* a wise thing to do."

"What happened?" Arun asked as the Admiral fell silent.

"He was found, three days later, in Shadoxhurst Forest. His hands had been clipped together in a green ash tree that had been split and pulled apart and then allowed to spring together again. He was dead."

"How horrible!" cried Is. "Had he died of hunger?"

"No," said the Admiral. "The wolves had got him. A quantity of wolves (as you may know) have contrived to slip over from France and squeeze between the bars of the Tunnel gate. You must always keep a sharp lookout for wolves at night in the countryside. Or even here, in less well-lit parts of the town."

At that moment something black and furry, and about the size of a football, came sliding down, on a silvery thread, from the soot-grimed ceiling.

Is and Arun both started violently, then stared, petrified, as this creature, which had two very bright eyes and a lot of legs, toddled across the floor, climbed up the Admiral's white-trousered leg, and settled itself cosily in his lap.

"Rosamund, one of my spiders," said the Admiral, strok-ing the creature, which appeared to enjoy this, but all the time watched Arun and Is with brilliant diamond-colored eyes. "I brought back her great-grandmother from the Larboard Islands on my last command. Such beasties make capital watchdogs. Rosamund keeps my house safe from intruders. And from mice, also."

I'll lay she *does*, thought Is, who did not care for spiders. She scowled at Rosamund.

"Sir—would you have any notion at all of where my mum might have gone?" asked Arun, trying to keep his eyes away from the spider.

"There, my boy, I regret I cannot help you. But if some notion should ever come into my head I will, of course, communicate it to you at once. You plan to remain in Cold Shoulder Road?"

They nodded glumly.

"I do not think that is a good plan," said the Admiral. "I fear that you may have difficulties with neighbors. Mrs. Boles, alas, is not a sensible woman, and her husband's fate overthrew what wits she had. Also I believe her daughter ran off to America. I should not be surprised if it were Mrs. Boles who had been putting about all these unkind tales concerning your mother and the child. Also, the Sect were *never* popular in this town. It might," the Admiral went on thoughtfully, "it might be better for you to transfer yourselves to Seagate. There are numerous empty houses in that town, after the late disastrous flood. And I can always send messages to you by the baker's boy. Or indeed, come myself."

He cast a glance at a mechanism that Is had been staring at, on and off, ever since she had noticed it. Half covered with a waterproof sheet, it stood in a shadowy corner: a spindly affair, made of metal, with two large wheels, one somewhat bigger than the other, which were connected by various rods and a revolving chain; between the wheels and attached to the bars hung a triangular piece of wood, covered with leather, which might, perhaps, be intended for a seat.

"I invented the device," said the Admiral proudly. "When becalmed, years ago, in the Sea of Sargasso. I call it my Dupli-gyro. I sit, you see, on that leather crupper, place my feet on these small bars—which rotate, causing the wheels to do likewise—and I thus proceed at a quite remarkable velocity, I can assure you."

"Doesn't it fall over sideways?" asked Arun, fascinated.

"No, my boy, because the velocity maintains its equilibrium. As when you bowl a hoop, you know, or spin a top."

"Yes, I see."

"I have made a number of them," said the Admiral in a tone of satisfaction. "But this one is the best. I can propel myself to Seagate and back on it in little over an hour. So—my dear young people—I strongly advise you to transfer to that charming little place."

Seems like everybody wants us to leave Folkestone, thought Is, who now knew what it was that she had seen gliding across the hillside the previous evening. I shouldn't care to ride on that thing, she thought. I reckon the Admiral is a spooky old gager, with his spiders and his Dupligyro.

"Sir—Admiral," she said. "Mrs. Boles wants us to stow Arun's mum's pictures somewhere safe."

"Pictures?" The Admiral at once looked very interested indeed.

"There's a whole scoop o' pictures upstairs in Arun's house. We think his mum musta painted 'em."

"I should be most curious to see them!" declared the Admiral. "Are they landscapes? Still lifes? *Portraits?* Are any of them portraits?"

"They're beautiful pictures," said Is. "They aren't like anything else at all that I've ever seen. Stunning, they are. Ain't they, Arun?"

But Arun did not seem to want to talk about his mother's pictures.

"Are there many?" A greedy light flashed in the Admiral's eye.

"You just bet! A whole room full."

"Well," said the Admiral, in a tone of gracious consideration, "I do not see why they should not be stored—as a purely temporary measure, you understand—in my dene-hole cellar. Fortunately it is very spacious. And dry. And, I confess, you have made me quite curious to observe these works!"

"A dene-hole?" said Is doubtfully. "What's that?"

"Dene-holes are very well ventilated," the Admiral assured her.

"But what is a dene-hole?" asked Arun, rousing himself out of a longish, moody silence.

"Made by prehistoric folk some time between the Stone Age and the Bronze Age. (That is to say, many many thousand years ago.) Chipped out of the chalk, you know, by flint knives. Their habit, those long-ago folk, was to dig out quite a network of caves. Indeed, I have never explored these ones very far. My lame leg, you see, prevents me." He patted it, causing Rosamund to turn on him a reproachful glare. "And also—I must confess—I am not partial to enclosed places."

"How can we shift all the pictures, though?" said Is, puzzling. "There's a mortal lot of 'em. We'd need a wagon."

She hoped the Admiral would suggest sending his carriage. Instead he said, "I have a trolley. On which I am used to wheel my golf clubs. That would serve, no doubt?"

"Let's have a look at it."

So, first tipping Rosamund onto the floor (she retired sulkily up her web again), he led them through a back door into a spacious conservatory, filled with a mad clutter of garden tools, golf clubs, fowling pieces, fishing rods, baskets, hip baths, and boots.

Among these articles stood a large trolley, made from heavy sail canvas stretched over a metal framework and mounted on grooved wheels that had solid tires made from thick rope.

"A very handy device," pronounced the Admiral, surveying it with approval. "I designed it myself. The wheels, as you see, will run over the turf of the golf course without injuring the grass. And this same factor will enable you to transfer your mother's works of art by night, without arousing the unwelcome attention of neighbors."

"At night? You think that would be best?" said Arun.

"Undoubtedly, my boy. I fear that an angry crowd, if

they saw you, might reduce the pictures to shreds—and, possibly, you too. I most *strongly* advise you to shift them tonight—then to remove yourselves from Folkestone without further delay. Now I will show you the entrance to my underground store."

He walked through a door into a kind of garden room next to the conservatory, which contained wheelbarrows, wicker furniture, many more kites hanging on hooks, and several more Dupli-gyros in various stages of construction. A well-like cavity occupied the center of the floor, and a ladder led down into it.

"At the foot of the ladder, down below," said the Admiral, "you will find a circular series of rooms, cut in the chalk. There will be ample space to store the pictures, nobody will disturb them, and your minds can be at ease. I will instruct one of my gardeners to leave a lamp and matches here tonight, at the top of the ladder."

"Won't you be here, sir?"

"Most unfortunately," said the Admiral, "this evening I must attend a meeting of the Folkestone and District Association of Magistrates and Justices of the Peace. But very likely I shall return before you have completed your task. How many loads of pictures do you suppose there will be? At a rough estimate?"

Arun and Is eyed the trolley, comparing its size with the roomful of pictures.

"Three, maybe," said Arun.

The Admiral's eyes brightened noticeably at the thought of so many pictures.

"Capital, capital. In that case I may very likely be home before you have done, and can invite you to a little hot supper afterwards. Goodbye, then, my dear young friends, for the present. You need not reenter the house; this path will lead you round the house to the gate, and you may take it tonight."

Isn't it a bit rum, Is thought, that the Admiral gets us to store the things in a place where he don't care to go himself? Wouldn't you think there'd be a space somewhere in that great house of his?

But then she recollected the state of the house, the number of things already stored in it. Maybe there wouldn't.

Waving a brisk hand in farewell, the Admiral turned back into the conservatory. Pulling the trolley behind them —it ran very smoothly—Arun and Is followed a path among the shrubberies. On their way to the gate they noticed five or six men at work in the gardens.

"Queer he keeps his garden so spange when the house is such a mux," Is remarked as they reached the gate.

"He's a rum old cove and no mistake. Did you like him?"

"Oh—tol-lol. I didn't like *Rosamund* above half. Creepy sort o' pet to keep."

"Still, I reckon we could use one like her in Cold Shoulder Road," Arun said gloomily.

Indeed, when they arrived back at Arun's home they were discouraged to find that a piece of paper had been nailed up on the back door that said in large red letters:

GIT ART YORE NOT WONTED

Thoughtfully they parked the trolley in the back garden among the sad cabbages.

"Hope that means you're leaving!" A man strolled along the back path, leaned on the fence, eyed the trolley, and spat.

"None o' your affair, I should think!" retorted Is, carrying out a pail of dirty seawater and emptying it close to his feet.

"Ho? No? But what about Miz Twite making off with the Handsel Child? You know what? The Gentry stuck up a sign saying they'll take a whole lot more kids if that one's not brought back. And already Tabitha Howe had her youngest took."

"Well *we* didn't take the little perisher," snapped Is.

"No, but his mum did," said the man, spitting again, with a nod toward Arun. "Her and the one with the cat. Two of a kind, ask me."

"Hey!" Is called after him. "What d' you mean, the one with the cat?"

But he made no answer, and was soon out of sight.

"Arun," said Is, "I've a notion—dunno if it makes sense, but you never know—Hey, Arun! *Do* listen!"

"Oh, what?" he said impatiently. "Don't bother me, there's a good girl. I've a splitting headache. To tell truth, I've had just about enough of it here."

Is studied her cousin with dismay.

When she had agreed to travel south with him on the *Dark Diamond*, her plan had been to stop for a night with Arun and her aunt Ruth in Folkestone and then make her way northwestward to her own home with her sister Penny and cat Figgin in Blackheath Woods. By now she was longing to rejoin her own family.

But the arrival in Folkestone to the mystery of the empty, wretched house had given this plan a decided check. Is felt that she could not leave Arun with such uncertain prospects. He did not seem fit to face them on his own.

"Oh, what's the use of it all?" he burst out, flung down his scrubbing brush, and strode off to the shingle-ridge. There, between two upturned fishing boats, he sat down heavily and stared out to sea.

He seemed quite overthrown by all these happenings.

I only hope he won't want to go back to being a cat again, thought Is, deeply worried.

She was fond of cats—particularly her own cat Figgin— but she did not feel it would help matters just now if Arun should choose to eat nothing but fish and stop speaking to humans.

She, too, left off scrubbing—really it did seem a waste of time if they were not going to stay—and went slowly upstairs, where she stared for a long time at Ruth Twite's amazing pictures.

Seen in daylight, they were like an explosion. Vermilion red, black, olive green, lime yellow, sapphire blue, peony pink. Solid shapes and thick black lines scrambled and rioted and twisted.

"Croopus, Auntie Ruth, you musta had a whole lot of fun painting 'em," breathed Is, staring at each in turn. She studied all the ones in the bedroom, then pulled out the ones from the closet that had been Arun's room and looked at those.

Some of them were almost recognizable as flowers: arum lilies, honeysuckle, anemones, bee orchids. Others were wholly unfamiliar.

Maybe Aunt Ruth just made 'em up, Is thought, studying some green, black, and salmon pink star-shaped flowers the size of horse's hoofs, which were being visited by giant bees.

At the very back of the closet, under the last pile of pictures, she found a slip of paper. It was grubby and dusty, folded into a concertina shape, tucked under the skirting board.

Is carried it over to the window, for she could see faint writing on it.

She read:

> Carry my heart to the steps of the sky
> Carry it high
> Throw down the blackhearts, we must be free
> Springy as wicker
> Sleek as the sea
> We must be free
> We must be free
> Now we must bring out the blind to see
> The dumb to deliver their ABC
> Blow wind my heart to the roof of the sky
> Lark and lapwing fly with me
> Peewit and plover, come fly with me

> Lies and silence are gone for ever
> Fear and envy are gone for ever.

"Well!" said Is.

The lines were in Arun's handwriting, but in a childish script that was rounder and larger than his present style. They must have been written years ago, before he left home.

There was writing on the other side of the paper as well; she turned it over and read *Somewhere in the woods.*

Is pondered over this for a long time. Then she slipped the paper into her pocket (she wore breeches like a boy, a habit she had acquired from life in the woods, where it was often necessary to run very fast or climb trees to escape the wolves). She left the house, shutting the kitchen door behind her, and found her way to the steep and narrow High Street.

The town was very silent. Few people were about. The ones who were eyed each other suspiciously and had nothing to say. Is received many hostile looks, and some muttered remarks were flung after her.

"Who's that little skellum?"

"One o' those Silent Folk, maybe."

"We don't want her sort round here."

Ignoring these comments, Is bought two hot fagots at a ham-and-beef shop, and, at a baker's next door, two large slabs of thick, pale pudding studded with large, flat raisins. These things she carried to the shingle-ridge, where she found Arun sitting in exactly the same position.

"Here," said Is, "have a bit o' dinner."

Arun silently accepted the food and ate it. He was already beginning to take on the look of a cat, Is thought, sighing; his eyes were slitted and his cheeks were drawn in. But perhaps that was just lack of food. He seemed very hungry.

"We gotta find some way to earn a bit o' blunt," Is remarked when the meal was done. "That was my last brown. You got any mint sauce?"

"Not much." He turned out his pockets and produced a sixpence and a few pennies.

"How did you go on for cash when you was living in London?"

"I sang songs in the streets."

"Make 'em up?"

He nodded listlessly.

Is knew that he had not sung any songs, or made up any new ones, since his time spent in the mines, and the death of his friend Davey.

"You make this one up?" she asked, passing him the scrap of paper.

As he read the lines, a faint spark of interest and recognition came into Arun's eyes. He frowned and looked about him as if he urgently needed a pencil to make some improvements.

"It's not much good—hopeless, really. Must have been when I was ten or eleven. I can just remember writing it—"

"What about what's on the back?"

He turned over the paper. Then he said, "But that's

Mum's writing. How can she have got hold of this? Where did you find it?"

"Tucked way in, right at the back of the closet—where you slept. Under all them pictures. As if she meant it to be found."

She paused, as he still intently studied the single line of writing; then she suggested, with caution, "You think maybe that's a message? From your ma?"

Arun flung down the paper impatiently.

"If it is, what's the use? 'Somewhere in the woods'? What good's that?"

"She dassn't make it any plainer," said Is, "case somebody else come across it."

Somewhere in the distance a cat mewed. Is turned her head sharply.

But the cat—she saw it in the distance, rubbing its back against the keel of one of the upturned fishing boats—the cat was not her own dear Figgin. It was a fat black-and-white animal with pale eyes. Still, she threw it a piece of fagot.

Turning back to Arun, she was dismayed to see what looked like a tear pushing its way down his dust- and salt-caked cheek. Angrily he rubbed it away and pinched his lips tight together. But it was plain that he was in very low spirits, very low indeed; this return to an empty house had upset him badly.

"Maybe we should ax about in the town?" Is suggested. "We ain't seen no one yet. We might meet some old pals of yours. Maybe arter your dad died your mum made friends we don't know about. She might ha' said summat about her plans to one or another. How about that?"

"I don't see the point," said Arun listlessly. "Ma never had friends. Dad said a wife's place was in the home. How could she talk to folk, anyway? You know she wasn't allowed."

"Still, I think it's worth axing around a bit," Is persisted.

"Suit yourself. . . ." Arun drew his arms round his knees and rested his chin on them. "I'm tired. I didn't sleep last night."

Is sighed and left him. She had slept badly too, but now she felt restless and longed for action. She set off for the center of the town, clumping around the steeply climbing High Street. On the way she noticed various notices stuck on doors and lampposts.

IF THE HANDSEL CHILD IS NOT RETURNED WITHIN 20 DAYS, PUNITIVE MEASURES WILL BE TAKEN, said one. Another said A REWARD IS OFFERED FOR INFORMATION RELATING TO THE WHEREABOUTS OF TABITHA HOWE, AGED 7.

Small shops faced each other across the High Street—fishmongers, bakers, chandlers, gin shops, barbers, cobblers. Toward the top of the hill the shops were of a higher class—there were drapers, hatters, even a circulating library with books and papers and notices on a board. The two about Tabitha Howe and the Handsel Child were displayed here too.

Few people were about. Of those she met, Is asked, "Did you know a Mrs. Ruth Twite?"

Sometimes people said, "Why do you want to know?"

"She's my auntie."

Some spat and looked angry. "She was one of that Silent lot. Think themselves better than their neighbors. Went off to Seagate. Good riddance. Some said she was a witch."

Some asked, "How is it that *you* talk?"

"My dad didn't belong to the Sect."

"Mrs. Twite used to do nursing," somebody said. "She nursed old Mr. Lillywhite when he was took bad. You could ask his widder."

"Where's she live?"

"Next to the paint shop."

Aha! thought Is. Maybe that's where Aunt Ruth bought her paints.

"Is you Mrs. Lillywhite, beg pardon?" she asked a plump old lady carrying a jug of milk, who was about to climb an outside flight of steps alongside the paint store. At the foot of the stair stood boxes and barrels and pans of brilliant powders and liquids.

Bet this *is* where Aunt Ruth got her stuff.

"What did you say, my dear? I am a little hard of hearing." The old lady cupped a hand round her ear.

"Is you Mrs. Lillywhite? I wanted to ask about my aunt Ruth Twite," Is bawled.

A man passing on the other side of the street halted and looked up attentively.

Mrs. Lillywhite shook her head vigorously. "Come up if ye like, love. But I can't tell ye anything to signify."

However, once she was back in her small room—which was kept neat and clean as the inside of an eggshell and held little beside a bed, a table, chair, and about forty blooming geraniums, all different colors—Mrs. Lillywhite said, "Ah! She were a right one, your auntie! I was sorry when she had to go. Looked after my old man like a hangel, she did. But she was one as had to do what she thought right."

"Did you know her well, then? What *did* she think right? Did she talk to you, Mrs. Lillywhite?"

"Used to fetch along her bit o' slate, and we'd have a chat, once in a while, her writing, me talking. And a good cup of tea. She liked that, did your auntie." The old lady was able to hear Is better in the silence of her room.

"When did she go? *Why* did she go?"

Mrs. Lillywhite looked vague. "A fair old while back, it was. As to a week or so, I couldn't say. 'Mrs. L,' she writ on her slate, 'there's summat terribly wrong. And I can't stand it no longer.' Those were the words she writ down. 'I gotta do summat,' she writ."

"But what was the trouble?" cried Is, deeply interested. She wished Arun were there.

"Ah—that, dearie, I can't tell ye. 'Twas summat to do with her Sect. That Reverend Twite, as he calls hisself. Twite, blight! I'd give him Twite. A powerful good thing it is they've all gone to Seagate. Better if they went right away to Ameriky."

"My aunt Ruth, though—*she* didn't go to Seagate?"

"Not as I thinks on, dearie. Going with her friend, I bleeve she was."

"Friend?" Is pricked up her ears. "What friend?"

"A lady. A lady with a funny name. Cashy? Minty? Pinky?"

"Not Penny?" cried Is, electrified.

"Penny—ay, ay, that might ha' been it. Skinny kind o' woman—had a rare sharp way with her."

"Had she a *cat* with her?"

"As to that, dearie, I couldn't tell ye. I only saw her the once, in Cold Shoulder Road, a colloguing with yer auntie."

"I'll lay it *was* my sister Pen," muttered Is with deep satisfaction. "The very minute we've dropped off Aunt Ruth's pictures with the Admiral, I'm agoing to make Arun come with me to Blackheath Edge, to Penny's and my place."

She was talking mostly to herself, but Mrs. Lillywhite caught the words. "You going to do what? Leave y'auntie's pictures with the Admiral? Admiral Fishskin? The dentist feller's cousin? The old 'un up top o' the cliff as flies the kites?"

"Yes, why not?" demanded Is, suddenly caught by some note of warning in the old lady's voice. "He's straight enough, ain't he? The Admiral?"

Mrs. Lillywhite shook her head doubtfully. "A rare rum bird, he be, the owd Admiral. Like a magpie. Once he latches on to summat . . . I dunno. They say that house of his is like a jackdaw's nest, since his wife passed away. Got treasures there from all over. Locked up at night like a prison, they do say."

"Well," said Is, "we ain't putting Aunt Ruth's pictures exactly in his house. In a cave, they're going. Safer there, he said they'd be, than in Cold Shoulder Road, where Mrs. Boles says the neighbors are ready and raring to burn the house down."

"An' I don't say she tells a lie. Though I dessay lies comes easy as breathing to Winnie Boles."

"Better in a cave than all burned up. Have you seen my auntie's pictures, Mrs. Lillywhite?"

"Ah," said the old lady thoughtfully. "I have, then. Right purty, they are. She give me one—" nodding toward a bit of gaily painted board lodged among the geraniums. It blended in so perfectly with their dazzling hues that Is had not noticed it.

"Ay, that's one of hers, sure enough."

"Real naffy they are; real nobby," said Mrs. Lillywhite. "I tell her, she oughta show them to some genelmun in Lunnon town, they fare to make her fortune. But, 'No, Mrs. L,' she writ on her slate, 'I does them for the good feeling I get. Not for money.' But—mark you—what she done that was even cleverer—to *my* mind—was her likenesses."

"Likenesses?"

"Folk's faces; y'auntie Ruth is a rare hand at that. Maybe," said Mrs. Lillywhite, shaking her head, thinking it over, "maybe a sight *too* clever. Maybe that had its part in why she run off."

"What do you mean, Mrs. L?" Is asked with a fluttering heart, for she believed she had some notion.

"Why, love, maybe she saw some faces what she'd ha' done better *not* to see. Let alone draw them down."

"But when would she have seen them?"

"Maybe time she worked for the dentist feller. Denzil Fishskin."

"Fishskin? A *dentist*?"

"He be a cousin of the owd Admiral. But nothing like so grand. A tooth-drawer, he be. And she—yer auntie—used to work for him as his nurse, helping folk rinse their mouths an' all. A notable tooth-puller, he were, that Denzil Fishskin—took three o' mine, an' offered to make me a new set from mammoth ivory, but 'No, thank you,' sez I, 'I'll just mumble along on what I got left.' "

"Mammoth ivory?" said Is, very interested indeed. "But that—"

"*And,*" went on Mrs. Lillywhite, "this is where I reckon yer auntie might ha' put herself in trouble—folk do say the Merry Gentry has tattoo marks on their tongueses."

"In the name of Mystery, why?" demanded Is in astonishment.

"Why, so they can't ever slip off and leave the band. They're marked for good an' all."

"Oh, I see. I reckon that's so. But, croopus . . ."

Is fell silent, considering. Plainly anybody in a position to have seen those tattoo marks—while helping a dental patient rinse his mouth—would also be in a position of danger.

"And if Aunt Ruth drew the faces she had seen—"

"That's it, dearie. If she put 'em down on her bits of paper—"

"Paper? Not board?"

"No, she done her picters of flowers on board. But the faces were on paper. The owd Admiral, he give her a liddle copybook, one time, to make face picters in. 'You have a ree-markable talent, Miz Twite,' he tells her."

He never told us that, thought Is. "Mrs. Lillywhite, do you know anything else about the Merry Gentry?"

"*Hush*, lovey!" The old lady looked very much alarmed. "I dunno as I oughter told ye what I did. And not another thing do I know, not a blessed thing. And wouldn't tell ye if I did. Now run along, I can't talk to ye no more, I begin to feel my apilepsick sweats a-coming over me."

Indeed she shivered violently, and almost pushed Is out of the room, calling after her in a loud voice, "I can't tell ee nothing. Nothing at all! And that's my final word!"

Is made her way down the steps, pondering deeply. As she did so, a man loitering on the other side of the street moved off and vanished down an alleyway.

Although Is had been absent from Cold Shoulder Road for a couple of hours, when she got back she found Arun still gazing at the sea, hunched up in the same despondent position; it seemed as if he had not moved a toe or a finger since she had left him.

"Listen, Arun!" said Is, plumping down beside him. She glanced up and down the beach. Nobody seemed to be within earshot. There were a few fishermen doing things to their boats a long way off. Still, it seemed best to talk to Arun in thought-language. And he might pay better attention.

"I believe it was Aunt Ruth who drew pictures of the

59

Merry Gentry," Is told Arun. "You remember the Admiral's story about Mrs. Boles's husband? How the Gentry left him out in the forest for the wolves, because he said he'd seen pictures of the band, and knew who they were?"

"But there aren't any pictures of people in the house. They are all flowers."

"Aunt Ruth did her likenesses on paper. In a book the Admiral gave her."

"Why would he do that?"

"Wanted to find out who they were."

"But why would my mum do such a thing?" Arun complained. "Why *did* she paint pictures and draw people's faces? She never used to do so."

"Ah, but in those days your dad was alive," pointed out Is.

"Well, I wish she hadn't," Arun grumbled. "It just makes things worse."

Is thought Arun was being amazingly unfair to his mum.

"What d'you expect her to do? You walk your chalks from home, never come back for years, never write her a letter, you expect to find her still a-waiting, a-knitting away at a new pair of socks for you?"

"Well, what else could she do?"

"She *did* summat else, didn't she? My notion is, she's gone off with my sis Penny."

"But they didn't even know each other."

"Ah," said Is, "but I writ Penny from up north, telling her that I'd found you, and that you were alive and well. Penny used to travel the roads, now and again, selling her

60

dolls; she knew your mum was in Folkestone, she might think it was neighborly to drop in and say you was pert and bobbish. And that feller in the lane said summat about a lady with a cat. When we've stowed away your mum's pictures, I votes we go off to my sister Penny's place. Maybe your mum is there. And shan't I be pleased to see my old Figgin."

A faint interest came into Arun's face. "Can't do any harm, I suppose . . . ," he agreed.

It seemed a terribly long time until dusk. Both Is and Arun were hungry again long before the light was dim enough for them to dare start moving the pictures. But there was not a scrap of food in the house. Doubtless anything edible had long ago been taken by Mrs. Boles.

The job was slow and laborious. If they loaded the trolley too heavily they found they were unable to haul it up the steep slope to the East Cliff. In the end they had to divide the pictures into four loads, and were worn out, panting, and hollow with hunger by the time they had piled all the pictures around the wall in the garden room. On none of their trips had they seen a single soul, but when they arrived with the final load, they discovered that a lighted lantern had been left near the top of the ladder in the well, and a note leaning against the lantern said:

KINDLY PLACE PICTURES IN SMALL CAVE AT REAR

"Oh, thanks! And likewise, don't mention it!" tartly commented Is, who had been hoping that another pair of hands would undertake this part of the job. For the last hour she had been thinking longingly of the Admiral's hot supper.

"Oh well," sighed Arun. "Better make a start on it, I suppose. I'll climb halfway down the ladder, and you pass the pictures to me."

"The old gager might ha' left one of all his gardeners to give us a hand," grumbled Is, impatiently handing down the pictures. "My back aches fit to snap in half."

This part of the operation took them nearly three quarters of an hour. By now it must be well after midnight. Then Is, too, climbed down the ladder and stared curiously about her. They were in a round, dome-shaped room, hollowed out of the chalk. The walls were white and glistened faintly in the lantern light. The floor had a sandy surface, covered by a thick carpet of dead leaves. There was a sharp, dry, chill, chalky smell.

"Different from the coal mine," said Is, sniffing. "Croopus, how that place did stink."

"Well, it was under the sea, and all wet."

"Which d'you reckon is the small cave where he wants the pictures stowed? There seems to be a whole passel of 'em."

There were about a dozen door-holes all the way round, leading apparently to farther caves.

"The one opposite the ladder, d'you reckon?" Arun said, pointing. He picked up the lantern and went into the next cave. "Seems dry and clean," he called.

He left the lantern in the second cave, and they started

carrying armfuls of pictures through and stacking them tidily on edge against the rock wall. After a while the floor was covered, so, leaving a gangway across the middle, they began filling a farther cave that lay beyond.

"Last load," panted Is, carrying four pictures together into yet another cave, on beyond the third one. "Odds Fishikins! There's as many caves down here as daisies in a meadow. Lucky that's the lot; I reckon our glim is ready to die on us."

Indeed the lantern was flickering smokily as if running out of oil.

"Hey for the old codger's hot supper. I'm clemmed," said Is.

But on returning to the first cave, now cleared of paintings, they were greatly disconcerted to find that the ladder had been withdrawn. Or at least they were just in time to see its feet and bottom rung being pulled up over the top of the well-hole.

"Oy!" shouted Is. "Don't forget about us! We're still down here! Hi! Hollo! Let down the ladder, ye dumfoozle squareheads. Don't leave us down here!"

There was no reply.

But a moment later, a loud bang overhead caused Is and Arun to jump. Looking up, they saw that a heavy, round wooden cover had been lowered into place over the hole. And a metallic clang suggested that it had been bolted down. At the same moment their lantern went out.

Three

"What the plague do you make of that?" said Is to Arun. "Some knothead's gone and shut us in.

"Let us out of here!" she shouted again, at the top of her lungs.

But her shout came echoing back from the high, chalky dome overhead. It did not seem as if the sound would pass through the heavy wooden trap cover. Or as if anybody intended to take the slightest notice.

Thoughts began whizzing back and forth between Is and Arun like bees darting among clover blossoms.

"D'you reckon it was the Admiral that had us shut in down here?"

"But why? Why would he do that?"

"Cos he wanted to get hold of those pictures?"

"But they are down here in the cave with us."

"Could it have been someone else shut us in? Not the Admiral?"

"But who?"

"One of the gardeners? One of the neighbors from Frog-Hole Lane?"

"Why?"

"Something to do with the Merry Gentry? And Mum's pictures of them?"

"But those ones aren't here."

"The person might not know that."

"What d'you reckon they plan to happen to us?"

"Starve to death? I daresay you could, down here."

"It would take quite a while, though. And they won't be able to get hold of the pictures, all the while we're live lumber down here . . ."

"Maybe they plan to finish us off somehow."

The thought was a disagreeable one.

"Well, let's see if we can't get outa this place. Maybe there's another entrance."

"Not much use to us if it's high overhead, like the way we came in."

Arun, now that he had a real problem to tackle, became much more sensible and alert than he had been while brooding over his mum's mysterious actions. And usefully, left over from those days when he had believed he was a cat, he had eyes that could see in the dark much better than most people's. They even glowed a little when the pupils were expanded, as cats' eyes do, so that Is could see where he was standing. She, too, from months spent working in the northern coal mines, was not much scared at being shut into this underground place, though very annoyed about it.

"They took us for right gull-finches."

"Well, and so we were," said Arun. "One of us shoulda stayed up top. Come on then; no sense in hanging about. You follow after me. Somewhere along that way I think I can hear water running. But don't make a row. For all we know, we ain't the only ones in this place."

"No—that's so. Ain't it a maze, though," said Is, quietly following behind him. And to herself she thought, I just hope there ain't any spider-kin of the Admiral's Rosamund down here.

The notion of outsize spiders scuttling along the chalky passages was a very disagreeable one.

But Arun picked up her thought and said comfortingly, "Don't worry about that. Spiders wouldn't thrive down here."

"Why not?"

"No flies."

"Reckon you're right," agreed Is, much relieved. "Can you still hear water?"

"A long way off. Anyway, so long as we go downhill, we ought to find it."

They walked and walked.

Is had the depressing thought that, if they went on going down, they might end up under the seabed. But Arun, catching this, said, "No, but we are heading north, not towards the sea."

Is knew that his sense of direction, like his hearing, was better than her own.

"It ain't half a plaguey long way, though," she sighed, after an hour or so. "We must have walked two-three miles by now—much farther than from Cold Shoulder to the Admiral's place. I wish we didn't keep going down. We must be deep underground by now."

"But remember," said Arun, "where the Admiral lives is high up, on top of a chalky hill. By now, think on, we've just about got down to ground level."

"Arun, you can be a right sensible chap when you try. But where's this water of yours?"

"Not far ahead. I can still hear it."

His ears were as keen as a bat's. And, sure enough, in a few minutes, they came out into a larger tunnel. Is could feel a faint freshness in the air. Quite soon Arun, with a grunt of satisfaction, stooped and said, "We're lucky. Here's the stream."

It ran out of the wall on their left and trickled along, in a little stony channel, just an inch or two lower than the floor of the cave.

"Good water," said Is, tasting it in cupped hands. "I wasn't *half* thirsty."

The water, filtered by a whole hill of chalk above, was pure and tasteless and very cold.

"It ain't so dark now," said Arun, peering forward.

But soon they were brought to a halt by a mysterious obstruction in the passage.

It was quite high—higher than either of them—and smooth. And curved.

"Feels for all the world like a thundering great earthenware crock," said Arun, tapping it first with a knuckle, then with a fingernail. "Smooth and round."

Is, rubbing it with her palms, agreed. "Feels like one o' them big pots the Admiral has in his garden with rose-bushes and daffydowndillies in. But this is a whole lot bigger. And who in Mussy's name 'ud want to stick a big flowerpot down in a cave?"

Arun had a try at squeezing between the great obstacle and the cave wall, but nearly got himself jammed, and had to wriggle back again.

"No good," he gasped.

"Maybe I could get through," Is suggested. "I'm smaller."

"Don't try. If you got stuck, we'd be done for. We've gotta go over the top, I reckon."

"But how?"

"I'll hoist you up; you take a look and see if there's a way."

"All ruggy; give us a boost."

Is was small and light; Arun had no trouble in raising her up so that she could grab the rim of the mysterious tun, vat, firkin, or whatever it might be, and pull herself up.

There was a squeak and a clank as she balanced on the edge and then tumbled forward on top of whatever was contained inside.

"Good strange! It's crammed full—all piled up with clobber! Right to the top."

More metallic sounds, thumps and clanks and clinks.

"What's in there, then?" he called.

"Blamed if I know! It's hard, whatever it is."

"Can you crawl over it?"

"The roof's mighty close. Just a minute."

Her voice came from farther off. "Oh, blimey, Arun, there's another of 'em, on beyond; another big crock full of stuff. But, yes, I reckon there's jist enough space to wriggle over. Anyway, you come up too—wait'll I give you a hoist."

She swiveled round on her stomach, lying on the hard, lumpy, and mixed contents of the great round cistern, leaned down, and grabbed Arun's wrists. She yanked hard, and he came up with a jerk and a scrabble, rolling in beside her.

"Ouch! Yike! I got stuck on a spike. What the plague is all this gubbage?"

"Blest if I know. *Somebody* musta set store by it. They musta stashed it away here . . ."

Is was now squirming her way over the second of the great pots.

"There's *three* on 'em—all cram-full of loot—boxes and bags and jars. Mint sauce in some, I reckon, they clink. Plates—cups—dangly things—*Hey, Arun!* D'you reckon all this stuff is *swag* that's been stowed in here by the Merry Gentry?"

By now they were resting their chins against the rim of the third and last vat, and peering down into the darkness beyond it.

"No," decided Arun, feeling around with cautious exploratory fingers. "The stuff in here has been lying in this place a lot longer than that—a *real* long time. Feel how thick the dust is on it. These things have been here for years and years. I got a fistful of pennies—or shillings, all coated in dust and lime. These things were here before ever the Gentry started up."

Is groped likewise.

"Forks—candlesticks—I found something feels like a string o' beads . . ."

Arun rolled over, grasped the rim with both hands, wriggled, and dropped. Is, following, landed on soft, crumbling earth and stones. There was a little more light on this side of the vats. She peered at the chain of beads or stones that she had taken.

"Looks like sparklers. Hah! *Jist* what I need, I *don't* think." She was about to toss the necklace scornfully back where it came from; then, on second thoughts, tucked it into her pocket. Maybe it might come in handy. And she had taken a few coins as well . . .

"Confound it. This is not good," said Arun, groping ahead. "I reckon we found the reason why the fellers never came back to pick up the loot they stowed away. Or," he added after a moment, "maybe they did come, and ran into trouble—"

"What's amiss?"

"There's been a cave-in ahead of us, can't you feel? Blocked the passageway."

There was a gravelly rustle as a small landslide of earth and stones came cascading toward them down the steep slope ahead. Is coughed and choked on the dust it brought.

"Still—there is a bit of light along there, over the top; maybe we can scrape away enough of the piled-up grit so as to wriggle over the heap—"

So they lay side by side on their stomachs, carefully scooping and scraping and digging with their hands, and then pushing the soil that they had loosened back behind them. It was a most unpleasant exercise, for dust from the slope below and from the roof above nearly stifled them, and their hands soon became very sore indeed.

"Fingers like ribbons," croaked Is. "And my mouth's full o' sand."

"*Don't* raise your head—the roof comes down at a touch."

Indeed there was one dreadful moment when a whole loose section of roof came thundering down on Arun and buried him under a pile of heavy, crumbly earth and stones.

"Arun!" implored Is in terrified thought. "Arun, where *are* you?"

She began to wriggle toward him and started another landfall.

"Don't fret, I'm here!" his thought came back, and in a moment he pushed his head out of the rubble. "Thought I'd pegged it, did you? Sure was a near thing." He spat out grit and powder. "Just keep on creeping along. But real cautious and slow."

"This place is a right queer-den. Blame that old Admiral."

Arun chuckled. "I'll lay *he*'d like to know about what's stashed down here!"

"That's so," Is agreed thoughtfully. "He'd go numb-jumbous. And he *can't* know, or he'd have had it up in his house long ago."

They crept and scraped, and scraped and crept, for what seemed like two or three hours, and might have been at least one, until finally the whole mass of loose rubble under them began to slope downhill. Then they were able to rise up on hands and knees, and finally, staggering a little, to stand upright.

"Joseph!" said Arun. "That was a rathole! I just hope we don't find we've got to turn round and go back that way."

"Don't!" said Is, shivering and rubbing her scraped hands on her torn breeches. "I wonder where the brook's got to?"

"Buried under the landslip, I guess."

Arun did not add his guess that there might also be human bones buried under that massive pile of earth and rock; bones of the people who had hidden those three huge pots in the cave, years ago, and then, returning to fetch them, had started the collapse of the tunnel roof and never come out again.

"Seems to me there was a tale somebody told me — about a treasure belonging to King Charles and Queen Henrietta that got sunk long, long ago in a ship off the Goodwins . . ."

"I see," said Is. "And then you think somebody came across that wreck — when there was a low tide — ?"

"It happens now and again," agreed Arun. "You can see the Sands, when the tide's extra low; folk go out and race horses or play cricket on them."

"Rummy thing to do. And someone came out one time and found the loot and stashed it away in those great crocks. They'd need ox wagons to shift it all — more than the Admiral's trolley," said Is, chuckling a little despite her sore hands, aching back, and scraped knees. "Hark — there's the brook again."

There it was, bubbling out of a lumpy hummock in the floor. Is and Arun were immensely glad to rinse their hands and their parched throats.

By now the dark of the cave had paled to a gray twilight in which they could follow the windings of the tunnel easily enough.

"I can see a real glim along there," said Is. "Reckon it's coming up to morning time. We put in a whole night in the cave."

"When we come out," said Arun, "we'd better do it real careful and slow."

"You're not just whistling psalms! For all we know, we might pop up in some cove's kitchen garden."

"All the people round here are so unfriendly—"

"Well, you can't hardly blame them," said Is, "with the Merry Gentry putting the squeeze on ordinary decent folk, and your dad's Silent Sect keeping their dubbers mum in that spooky way, no help to anybody, and thinking themselves better than their neighbors—"

"Hush!"

The tunnel had narrowed to a sandy crevice, then to a gully, down the sides of which hung brambles, gorse, and hawthorn bushes. There was sky overhead. The air was wonderfully fresh and pure. The light was misty and gray —plainly it was still very early morning, before sunrise probably. A bird or two twittered; they could hear a lark spiraling away.

Treading as softly as they could, taking the greatest possible care not to shift a pebble or snap a twig, Is and Arun crept along the gully and then, with the utmost caution, where there came a gap in the bramble-thicket, peered forward.

What they saw was so unexpected that both simultaneously sucked in their breath; Is grabbed Arun's wrist and pulled him back.

"All right, keep calm! I can see it too!" he soothed her, in thought-language.

They were looking down a steep slope into what had once been a wide, grassy valley. But now it contained a railway and some brand-new flint-and-stone station buildings. Embankment walls had been cut out of the dazzling white chalk, and shining new rail tracks curved away in both directions, east and west. At the eastern end of the valley, where the sky was now becoming bright with sunrise, the rails ran downhill into the round, black mouth of a tunnel, and across this tunnel mouth a metal gate, composed of a massive red-painted crisscross grid, barred the way.

"Must be the new Channel Tunnel. I wonder how that gate is opened?"

"Done with a counterbalance, maybe. Remember how they got coal out of the mine?"

"Just look at that train!"

"Never mind the train—see what those fellows are doing!"

The train—not meant for passengers, but a series of goods wagons all painted a silvery gray—stood in the sta-

tion, its engine gently steaming. The train's peaceful still-
ness contrasted with the frantic, antlike activity of the men
around it, who were unloading bundles and boxes from the
goods wagons and transferring them to the backs of a train
of baggage ponies that stood alongside the track. The
twenty or so men unloading all wore black hoods with eye
slits. One of them wore a white hat over his hood. He was
somewhat shorter than the rest of the troop, and seemed to
be directing the operation, which was performed with great
skill and speed.

Is and Arun had no need to put into words the thought
that filled both their minds. These must be the Merry Gentry unloading a batch of goods that had never paid customs
duty.

Mammoths' tusks, maybe, thought Is.

The job was nearly done; most of the ponies were loaded
up already and most of the wagons were empty. The first of
the cavalcade started away westward, going at a quiet trot.
Their hoofs were wrapped in sacking. They must be later
than they oughta be, thought Is. Wonder why that is? They
should have done all this while it was still dark, surely?
They are taking a big risk. They'll have to make for the
woods.

Two or three men were busy about the Tunnel gate, setting in motion a great wheel, worked by levers. The wheel
turned; the gate began to rise. Half a dozen wolves darted
out and fled away into a patch of woodland that still remained on the valley's north slope. Nobody paid them any
heed.

I guess they dassn't shoot the wolves, thought Is, because of the noise.

The train let out a faint sigh, like a person waking from sleep, and began to glide downhill toward the Tunnel mouth.

Suddenly there came an interruption. A thin, wild-looking man ran, shouting and waving his arms, slantways down the valley side toward the station, coming from the direction of Folkestone town.

"Where's my boy?" he shouted furiously. "Devils! Devils! What did you do with my son? Where is he? Give him back!"

He made straight for the man in the white hat, who took half a dozen quick steps toward him. There was a lightning-swift flash—a gleam in the rays of the rising sun—and the shouting man was suddenly huddled on the grass, motionless. Two of the black-hooded men picked him up, carelessly, as if he had been a bale of cloth, and tossed him into one of the open goods wagons, now sliding past at gathering speed. The train passed smoothly and completely into the Tunnel.

The red-mesh gate dropped down again, with a slight creak.

All the unloading party were by this time in motion, mounted on their ponies; the man who had worked the gate ran to a pony tethered nearby, bestrode it, and followed the others; in five minutes the whole valley lay deserted and silent, except for the song of larks in the mist overhead. And a small dark patch on the ground.

"Mercy!" breathed Is. *"Arun!* That poor devil of a man! D'you think he was dead?"

"Yes I do," said Arun. "That fellow in the white hat ran him through with a shiv as long as a poker."

"We'd best get away from here," said Is with a shiver, "while there's no one about. This ain't no healthy spot to loiter. You'd think, though, there'd be a stationmaster, or a Tunnel warden, some cove who oughta be in charge down there."

"Probably paid good money to keep away. Yes, let's scarper."

They crawled back through the bramble-brake (getting more scratches in the process) and emerged from it over the ridge and out of view of the valley. On the right, now, they had a glimpse of the sea, a silver gleam in the early light; then a thick white fog came down, blotting everything from view.

"Lucky for us," Arun remarked.

They walked east, then north, Arun going confidently, Is sticking close to him. She guessed that they must now be passing right over the railway, after it had plunged into its tunnel. The sun on their right was like a silver penny, faint in the mist.

Neither of them had anything to say. The scene with the train, and the masked men, and the murder, had been too sudden, too silent, and too shocking, after all their struggles and hardships in the cave. They had come out believing that the worst was over and that things would get better — and instead they had got much worse.

It's like a nightmare, thought Is, trudging silently over short downland turf, through cold wet mist. It's like a bad dream that goes on and on.

At last they struck into a well-worn white chalk track, which presently led them to a carriage road, running east and west.

"Which way?" from Is.

Without answering, Arun turned right. And Is followed without argument. This road would lead them away from Folkestone, which she had thought a glum and unfriendly town. And if it was the Admiral's notion of a joke to shut them in the cave, he was a cove to leave strictly alone. And even more so, if it was not a joke.

After a while they came to a signpost that said DOVER 4 MILES.

"But we don't want to go to Dover, do we?" said Is, rousing herself from a daze of hunger and weariness. Her fingers stung and throbbed from all that digging and scraping; her arms and legs ached and bled from bramble scratches.

"No. I thought we'd go to Seagate. That's not far, on beyond Dover. Just to make sure that my mum's not there with the Sect."

"All rug to me," agreed Is, tiredly setting down one aching foot after another. She was very sorry to delay her return to Blackheath Edge, but felt that she could not desert Arun just now. The poor boy's head is full of bees, she thought; he's haunted by his mum. He'll not rest till he gets some news of her; well, maybe one or another of those

Silent Folk will be able to tell him summat useful. If they can't, though, it'll be bad for him.

Oh well, no sense climbing stiles till you come to 'em.

She was so tired that the mere idea of climbing a stile made her knees buckle.

Then she grabbed Arun's arm. "Hark. I can hear a horse and cart acoming along behind us. You don't think it could be one of *them*?"

"No," he answered decisively. "They'd no carts, remember? It was all pack ponies. Anyway, they were heading westwards; to London, likely."

"Aye, that's so."

Despite this, they both glanced uneasily about them. Around here there was no cover whatsoever; the road ran unfenced across bare Downland.

But the cart coming slowly up behind them seemed to offer no threat; it was a battered farm wagon drawn by a solid, plodding cob; its load was a pile of brown stuff that gave off a pungent smell.

"Hop manure," said Arun. "That smell always tells you you're in Kent."

As the cart drew alongside, Is noticed that the driver was studying Arun. He was a tall, skinny, weatherbeaten man, with a long, sad face (not unlike that of his horse). He wore black trousers, a faded blue shirt, and a battered black straw hat.

"This feller seems to know you," said Is as the cart came to a slow stop.

"He's one of the Sect, he was a friend of my dad. Name's

Micah Swannett. He's offering us a ride. Shall we go with him? He's a decent cove."

The driver was silently jerking his head and gesturing with his thumb at the cart behind him.

"Why not?" agreed Is, yawning. "I'll be right glad to get off my plates. Thank you kindly, mister." The driver nodded silently. "Maybe he can tell you summat about your mum, Arun?"

"He can't talk," Arun pointed out. "And we've nothing to write on."

They clambered onto the cart. The hop litter stank ferociously—the smell wrapped itself round them like rotten porridge—but they were in no mood to grumble; they sank into its dusty comfort and were asleep even before the cob was in motion again.

By the time they woke, they could see that the day was well advanced, for the sun hung directly overhead. It must be nearly noon. The distance from Folkestone to Seagate, Arun told Is, was not above fifteen miles, so plainly the cob had not hurried.

The chalk hills had dropped away behind, and the land they were crossing now was flat; on their left, marshy fields stretched inland, studded with sea lavender and gorse; to the right the sea rolled and murmured against a long shingle-bank.

Ahead of them lay a small huddle of houses.

Seagate was a much humbler place than Folkestone, hardly more than a hamlet. It consisted of two rows of houses facing each other across a sandy lane that ran parallel to the beach.

The houses were humble too. Mostly built of weatherboard, with tiled roofs, they squatted close to the ground. Narrow alleyways threaded between them; the shingle-bank that protected them from the sea was strewn with a clutter of upturned dinghies, spars, oars, piles of nets and tackle, anchors, and pieces of rusty iron. At either end of the village were boat sheds and shacks and tall sail lofts, mostly painted black. A few larger ships appeared to be still seaworthy, but others were merely rotten hulks. Small, pebbly gardens contained coils of rope and lobster pots instead of plants.

Many of the houses, Is noticed as the cob clopped its slow way along, were empty and derelict. Windows were broken, doors hung ajar, piles of sand could be seen within. Seagate had suffered badly from the flood. The place was very quiet indeed, and very few people were about in the street. Most of them were dressed like Micah Swannett, the men wearing blue shirts and flat black straw hats, the women in white shirts and blue pinafore dresses, with blue scarves bound tightly round their heads. Small girls wore dark blue bonnets and blue pinafores like their mothers; the boys had blue shirts. They were all extremely neat, silent, and sober, walking along with their eyes on the ground, never speaking a word to each other, never looking, smiling at, or greeting one another; except that when two people met, they greeted one another by each laying a finger on their own lips.

A right rum, dismal place, Is decided. Even worse than Folkestone.

Only three or four people were not dressed in the blue-and-black costume. And these seemed, if anything, more downcast than the others. They trudged gloomily about their affairs, taking no notice of Micah Swannett and his load.

Well, it must be a rare rum go for the folk who lived in this town before the flood, Is thought, to have so many of their neighbors drownded, and then to have all these Silent Fellers turn up and quarter themselves here. If *I'd* lived in Seagate afore, I shouldn't fancy it above half. I reckon I'd be pretty down in the mouth.

Micah Swannett pulled his cob to a halt halfway along the main street. Here a large inn, the King's Head, stood on the edge of the beach. It seemed to be a very old building, timbered, with all manner of odd gables; tall, twisted chimneys; and extra bits built on, of many different materials, flint, stone, weatherboard, and brick. Upper storeys overhung the street, and a hanging sign showed a sad, dark-haired, bearded king in a gold crown. LICENSEE TOM BRABURN, said the sign underneath.

Micah Swannett was beginning a complicated series of gestures relating to himself and his passengers and the inn, when a bearded man walked out of its door. The newcomer bore such a strong likeness to the portrait on his sign that Is was quite startled; then she realized that he must have sat as the model for the picture, which looked newly painted.

He greeted Swannett in friendly enough fashion. "Good

day to ye, neighbor! Fetched along Sandy Smeeden's load of hop dung, did ye? He'll be right glad to have it. And who are these little hop-o'-my-thumbs?"—as Arun and Is jumped down from the cart.

By his gestures, Micah seemed to be offering to pay for a meal at the inn for his two passengers. But Arun, quickly catching on, said, "Thank you, sir, that is very kind of you to have brought us so far. But we can pay for ourselves—"

Can we? wondered Is. First I knew that Arun had any mint sauce left.

But he thrust a hand into his pocket and fetched out a few coins. The wink of silver was visible through dust and sand.

Micah nodded, satisfied, raised a hand in farewell, and drove silently on his way. Getting news out of these Silent Coves is going to be hard work, thought Is.

"Mind you," remarked the landlord, eyeing his customers, "I never did see such a pair of filthy little corner-creepers in my entire. What happened to ye? And how do I know that rhino is honestly come by?"

"Certainly it is!" said Arun haughtily. "I found it buried in a cave. Only then the roof fell on us, which is why we're so dusty."

"Oh? In a *cave*, eh?" The innkeeper looked extremely alert. "True it is, there's caves in this country that holds more cargo than you'd reckon—but, myself, I'd be *mighty* wary about helping myself to any of what's there—you tread on some folks' toes round here, you end up with a split gizzard. Where was that-ere cave?"

"Ever such a long way from here," Is put in hastily. "A long ride to the south."

"Well, if I was in your shoes," said the landlord earnestly —he looked at their scuffed and filthy footwear as if to emphasize his point—"if I was ye, I'd not go back to that place no more. Or there might be someone a-waiting for ye."

He glanced round him warily.

"In the meantime I'll take sixpence of what ye've got to pay for your brekfasses. Only ye won't object to eating outside on the step, sooner than mux up my clean taproom floor, what Susan just scrubbed?"

He gestured to a broad brick terrace that ran between the inn and the beach, adding, "And you're a mite pongy, if ye don't mind my saying so, along of Micah Swannett's load. Hot rolls and eggs and chocolate suit ye?"

They agreed that these things would suit very well. When the landlord came back with a loaded tray, Arun paid with one of his handful of silver coins.

Is then recollected that, as well as some coins of her own, she had pocketed a chain of beads. She pulled out the chain and studied the beads: pale, clear, brownish stones, the size of acorns, the color of milkless tea. "That's not much use!" she said disgustedly. "I wish I'd taken more chinkers instead." Still, she stuffed the necklace back in her pocket.

When Arun handed one of his coins to the innkeeper, the man stared at it with astonishment.

"Bless me soul, young feller! Is this what you picked up in the cave? *Rex Carolus*, it says—this is from King

Charles's day—him as had his head cut off up yonder." He nodded at the sign that swung above. "And ye say ye found it?"

"Won't it do to pay for the rolls?" said Is.

"Oh, it'll *do* right enough, dearie; being as I'm an honest feller I'll tell ye it's worth thribble as much, maybe more; I'll give ye some change. Well, I never did! Reckon— reckon I'll keep it in the bar as a curiosity. *Where* did ye say that cave was? Dover way?"

Luckily a woman's voice from inside shouted, "Tom? Are you there?" and they were not obliged to give him an answer just then.

"And I don't know that we should," said Arun. "It might lead to trouble. Considering where the cave came out, and what we saw."

Is agreed. But she wanted to ask a question of her own.

"Mister," she said, when the landlord appeared with a handful of change, "who painted that sign of yours up there? It's new—and it's a picture of you—ain't it?"

"Ay, 'tis that," he agreed. "Clever, beant it? Everybody's allus said I had a likeness to owd King Charley the First, and when my sign got blowed off and smashed in the gale, a lady what came to spend a night in the town, she said she'd paint my likeness, if I wanted, for a new signboard."

"A *lady* painted it?" Is was very excited. "Arun! It must have been your mum! When was this, mister?"

"Well—" He gave it some thought. "It were after the gale —but it were a piece afore the Silent Beggars came to town. A two-three months back."

"Is the lady still here?"

"No, she only stayed a night. Then she went her ways."

"Did she have a child with her? Or another lady?"

The innkeeper looked at them very attentively.

"No," he said at length. "She didn't. But she went to my cousin Rena Sloop's shop and bought a passel of child's clothes. Ye say that lady was your mum?"

"My cousin's mum," said Is. "He's a-seeking for her. It sounds mighty like her."

The landlord thought for some minutes. Then he said, "I'll get my Susan," went indoors, and fetched his wife—a lanky woman with a lot of large teeth and shiny gray false curls poking out from under her frilly cap.

"Ye are looking for a lady and a kid?"

"Maybe two ladies," said Is cautiously.

"What size kid?"

"Quite a small one. About four or five, maybe."

The woman shook her head, pressing her lips together.

"A lot of kids goes missing around here." She glanced warily up and down the terrace. Seeing nobody, she said, "The Merry Gentry put up signs outside of inns and post offices and churches. The signs said as how their Handsel Kid had been took, and if it weren't sent back, other kids'd be took, by *them*. And sure enough, two weeks later, our Fenny was took, and we've never seen her since."

Is and Arun looked at one another.

"How dreadful!" said Is. "It's the same here as at Folkestone."

"Folkestone? That where you come from?" said the landlord. "That's where all these perishing Silent Gagers come from. Well, I just wish they'd go back there. Honest, I will say they are—that Micah what fetched ye along, he's a right decent chap—but they're like a blight on the town. Fingers on their lips all day long. Them and their Holy Silence. And never a dram at the pub. *I* say, if they want to keep quiet, let 'em go and do it somewhere else, in the New World, if that's what suits 'em. Not here in our town. That Elder of theirs—de la Twite—he's a rare rum 'un. I'd not trust *him* with my winnings. He's the only one who's allowed to speak, by their rules, and my view is, he'd do best to keep his gob shut."

"Why?" asked Is.

"He keeps on and on about how we oughta stand up to the Merry Gentry. And that's just *asking* to have your toes used for live bait. Fetches the Gentry around like wasps."

Susan nodded sadly. "They're just too strong to be stood up to, the Gentry. We just havta put up with 'em—like bad weather, like floods. We lose our Fenny. Only seven, she was. What can we do? Nowt. But, about your mother, dearie—"

A chaise was rolling along the sandy road toward the inn. It held two men. One of them raised his whip commandingly.

"Talk o' the devil," muttered the landlord under his breath. His wife said, "Tell you another time, love," and vanished indoors.

The chaise came to a halt by the inn's main entrance. A tall, gray-haired man got down from it.

Is said to Arun, "Why don't we walk about and take a look at the place, Arun? If your mum was here—and it do seem so—we might hear news of her. We can come back later and ask Mrs. Curly-locks what she was going to say."

Arun nodded, and slowly followed as Is jumped down from the terrace and crossed the road. Poor thing, she thought, he thought his mum would be here.

Well, maybe somebody here can give us news of her.

The town was so extremely quiet that it was a comfort to hear the sea thrash and tumble on the far side of the shingle-ridge. A few blue-shirted men walked about, their eyes on the ground. When questioned, each of them would shake his head and lay a finger on his lips.

Here and there a door stood open. Is peered through one, inside which a voice could be heard, apparently talking to itself, and found that she was looking into a schoolroom, where twenty blue-shirted boys and one girl in a red dress sat listening to a teacher, who was telling them about Julius Caesar. Once in a while the girl would put up her hand and ask a question. The teacher seemed relieved when she did so. The boys diligently made notes and kept quiet.

I bet the teacher would rather they yelled rude words and threw ink balls, thought Is. Wonder why there's only one girl? *She* ain't a Silent Secter. They'd never let her wear that red dress, I'll lay.

"Come here!" called Arun softly, beckoning from farther along the street. He had found a largish, slightly ruined building, which might once have been a small church or a large chapel. Its door, also, stood open, and Is looked inside, wondering what caused a soft, shuffling, scraping noise that came from within. It was like ears of corn blowing, or feet walking through dead leaves.

The hall, quite roomy inside, was packed with people, gravely and silently dancing. There must have been forty at least, and they were all elderly. All wore the blue-and-black clothes of the Silent Sect. Two lines of them faced each other, soundlessly clapping their hands and stamping their feet. Couples took it in turn to perform figures in the middle, passing, gliding, turning, bowing. A master of ceremonies, who stood on a chair, silently conducted the proceedings by waving his arms.

Nobody smiled. Everybody was serious.

To Is, the sight seemed extremely sad.

They sure need some music, she thought. One o' my dad's tunes—"The Day Afore May-Day"—that'd put a bit of zip into their doings. Ain't it half queer, though, to see 'em figuring away like that, footing it up and down, without even the squeak of a fiddle.

Arun evidently felt so too, for he suddenly—and most unexpectedly—burst into song:

> "Heel and toe,
> High and low
> Hold her tightly,
> Swing her lightly,
> And *sing*, everybody, *sing!*
> Speech is the queen, and music is the king!"

Forty elderly astonished and scandalized faces were turned toward him.

The man who had been conducting the dance hopped down from his chair and came to the door, making indignant gestures as of one who shoos away intrusive pigeons.

"*Hush*, boy! *Go away!*" he whispered when he was close to them. "You disturb our Holy Quiet. Suppose the Elder heard you!"

"What if he had?" said Arun defiantly. "He's not *my* leader."

But already, the spirit that had so suddenly taken hold of him seemed to be ebbing out as fast as it had come; he shrugged, kicked a pebble, and turned away from the door, which was shut quickly but softly behind him.

Then Is noticed that the girl in the red dress was running toward them. All the blue-shirted boys from the class had begun dispersing in different directions, walking very quietly, looking at the ground, clasping their piles of schoolbooks. Lessons were done for the morning, it seemed. Only the girl skipped along cheerfully, kicking up her heels, staring curiously at Is and Arun.

"Hey, was that you singin', you boy?" she asked Arun. "It was a real spanger, that tune! Sing it again! Who are you? Are you staying here? What's your names? Why are you so dirty? I'm Jen Braburn. I'm the worst girl in the town. Everybody'll tell you that!"

"Why are you the only girl in the school?" Is asked.

"Cos the Silent girls ain't allowed to go to school. They gotta stay home and do the dishes. But my dad runs the

King's Head, he ain't Silent, and he won't have me about the pub in opening hours. So I goes to school. My little sister Fenny, she useta go too, but she got took by the Gentry for a Handsel. It's a precious shame. I'm the only one that—"

Somebody tapped Is on the shoulder.

She turned to see a small, brown-faced woman regarding her searchingly.

The woman wore the regular clothes of the Silent Sect—blue pinafore, white shirt—but her soft, curly white hair escaped here and there from under the tight blue headscarf. Her face was weathered, and very much lined, with deep grooves from nose to mouth, but its expression was friendly. Her eyes were a dark brown.

She tapped herself on the breast, then gestured along the street, then beckoned to Is and Arun to follow.

"That's Mrs. Swannett," said Jen Braburn helpfully. "Reckon she wants you to go along to hers. I'll see you later. On the beach, maybe? Or—I'll tell you what." She suddenly leaned close and whispered, "I'll see you at the Talkfest! At Birketland! We has rare times there! We play word games! It's prime! You come along to Birketland—then you can sing that song again." She put her finger to her lips with a mocking grin, whispered, "Lomak!", then scudded away toward the King's Head.

They followed Mrs. Swannett, who led them along the main street, still beckoning to them to follow. Her house was the last, at the northern end of the town. Beyond lay the beach, littered with driftwood. The house was white-painted, trim, and had a small yard in front that contained nothing but cobblestones.

Mrs. Swannett opened the front door and stepped inside, beckoning to them to follow.

The front room, neat and clean, was furnished as plainly as possible. There were four chairs, a table, shelves with some china, and a few pots. No pictures, no ornaments. Their hostess beckoned them through this room into a back kitchen, which had in it a curved copper washtub perched on brick pillars above a fire of driftwood and sea coal. The water in the tub steamed enticingly.

"Reckon the lady thinks we'd like a wash-up," suggested Is.

Mrs. Swannett nodded. Her eyes rested calmly on their bruises and scrapes and general state of filth.

"Well—I reckon we *are* a bit mucky," Arun conceded.

But, wondered Is, if we take our duds off, how'll we ever get them back on again? Mine are just about in shreds. If we had anything else to put on—

To her surprise, Mrs. Swannett seemed to catch her thought; she pointed at the ceiling, then again, decisively, at the hot water. She appeared to measure Is with her eye, then left the room and could be heard going upstairs.

"I'll wash first, Arun, you go after," suggested Is. "Why don't you pick up a bit o' driftwood for the lady while I'm a-splashing; shan't be long."

Arun nodded and walked out of the back door onto the shingle-bank, which lay just beyond.

Is helped herself to a bowlful of hot water and a jugful of

cold from a pail that stood on the floor, and had an enjoyable wash. Her cuts and grazes stung but felt better for being cleaned up. And as she was finishing, Mrs. Swannett reappeared with a pot of ointment, which smelt strongly of feverfew, and a bundle of clothes. The ointment, applied to Is's wounds, greatly eased their soreness. The clothes — black trousers and wool jacket, blue shirt — Mrs. Swannett held against Is, then nodded. She tapped her chest, then made gestures of two different heights from the ground.

"Two children?" guessed Is. "Boys? Yours?" She pulled on the trousers.

A nod. Then the woman covered her face with her hands. Is suddenly received a strong picture of the sea: great black and green waves, white-crested, tossing and curving.

"Drownded?" guessed Is. "In the flood?"

Another nod. But then she shook her head. No . . . not in the flood.

Is picked up the necklace of pale brown, clear stones, which she had taken from her pocket as she undressed, and, on an impulse, offered them to Mrs. Swannett. But the woman, as if horrified, made pushing-away gestures and shook her head violently. Quick, put them away, put them in your pocket, her signs indicated. No, no, they are no use to me. None at all. None.

Now Is was dressed and Arun came back with a large bundle of firewood. Mrs. Swannett beamed at him gratefully and showed him where to put it. Then she and Is went into the front room, where Is was given a bowlful of peppermint tea and offered a hunk of fresh brown bread, which she politely declined, explaining that they had eaten breakfast at the King's Head.

As she drank the tea, Is asked Mrs. Swannett, "How long have you lived here?"

Mrs. Swannett fetched a slate and wrote on it: "6 months."

"Did you know Arun's mother? Ruth Twite?"

A nod. Of course.

"But she's not here?"

No.

Now Arun came in. (He had been much more speedy over his wash than Is.) He, too, had been kitted out with black trousers and blue shirt. He looked neat, clean, and subdued.

"Can you tell me where my mum might have gone to?" he asked Mrs. Swannett, sipping his peppermint tea.

But she shook her head.

"Have you any notion *why* she went?" asked Is.

Mrs. Swannett looked troubled. She frowned, clasping her hands together, twisting them.

Now Is had an inspiration. She broke into thought-speech.

"Mrs. Swannett? Can you hear what I'm saying? Can you hear this? Arun and I can talk to each other this way. It is ever so much faster than using tongue and voice and words and language. Can you hear me? Can you hear my thoughts? Do you think that you could learn to do it too?"

She stared intently across the kitchen table into the

woman's dark brown eyes. Mrs. Swannett frowned, as if a midge or a mosquito were insistently buzzing round and round her head; she rubbed her brows, ran her fingers through her hair, shook her head in a puzzled way as if to clear it.

"Mrs. Swannett!" repeated Is in thought-language. "Listen! Can you hear me? Arun, you say something to her too."

Arun came in, quiet and steady. "Mrs. Swannett? Can you hear us? Can you hear what we are saying to you? If you can, try to answer in the same way. Tell us your name. Your own, your first name."

The woman stared at them, first one, then the other. Her brown, lined face was creased with concentration, then distressed. She looked as if she might burst out crying.

Oh drabbit it, thought Is, maybe all we've done is upset her, poor thing. And I reckon she's got trouble enough already. But it did seem, before, as if she caught what I was thinking. And *I* caught what *she* was thinking. But it's a shame if she's upset for nothing—and when she was so kind, giving us her boys' things—

But gradually Mrs. Swannett's face was clearing. She gave them a small, tense, frowning smile. "Again? Say something more." Her thought came to them slow and hesitant, but plain.

"Tell us your name. That you were given when you were born."

"My first name is Window. Window Wyatt, before I married. Now Window Swannett."

"Window! What a grand name!"

Suddenly Mrs. Swannett was swept by a gust of overwhelming joy and excitement. She laughed and trembled and gripped her hands together. "But this is so wonderful! *So wonderful!*" A pair of tears ran easily down her cheeks. She did not bother to wipe them away. "That people can talk to each other like this! I never dreamed of such a thing. How did you ever learn, ever find out that you had such a marvelous gift?"

"Up north we learned it, in the coal mines," Is told her. "You see, there we were all working in the dark, and cut off from each other, so thought-speech was the only way we could keep in touch."

"And now—now—I can talk whenever I like—I can talk to you—"

Mrs. Swannett could hardly believe her good luck. "Nobody can forbid this!"

"Tell us about your children?" Is asked her.

Tears swam in her eyes.

"My boys—Enoch and Hiram. They were such good, good boys. Hardworking. Sweet-tempered. The Elder—Dominic—he gave orders for all the men and boys to go fishing. On a day when the weather was very threatening. Micah told him the wind was too high, that it would strengthen to a gale. But the Leader said No. He said Go. And so they went, and ten never came back. Both my boys. Micah was abed, with a broken arm. He did not go. Our boat floated back, four days later. But the boys did not come back. *Oh!*" She covered her face with her hands.

"They lived a life of silence. And then they died a silent death. After that, Micah—who is a strong man, in his own way, when it is too late—he sold the boat and bought a cart. He told the Elder he will not go fishing again. Instead he drives the cart . . . He makes some money, enough, not much. The Elder was angry. But Micah is a strong man too; in his own way," she repeated. "But he obeys the Law of Silence."

"Mrs. Swannett, what is a Talkfest?" Is asked.

Mrs. Swannett glanced about cautiously; then her face broke into a radiant smile as she realized that she could not be heard.

"Some of the children—are disobedient. They meet secretly, at High Birket, in the forest, and talk together for pleasure. Their sin—they play rhyme games and riddles. They would be punished terribly if the Elder found out. The Leader is very strict—especially strict—about young people talking."

"The Leader—that's this Twite feller?"

"Dominic de la Twite. He came to us from the Low Countries to take the place of Amos Furze, who sailed to Connecticut."

Arun said, "I remember Amos Furze. He wasn't a bad fellow. What sort of person is this Twite?"

Mrs. Swannett thought.

"Do you like him?" asked Is.

Mrs. Swannett thought some more.

"You are not meant to like the Leader. He is the voice of Duty. Duty is seldom pleasant. Duty orders us to save every penny we can until we have enough to sail to Connecticut, where Amos Furze plans to buy a plot of land."

Arun asked, "Did my mum like Dominic de la Twite? She and Dad liked Amos Furze well enough. I was going to work for him. They used to drink tansy tea with him, now and then."

Mrs. Swannett said, "Your mother had strong views about Dominic de la Twite. She said he was the servant of the Demiurge."

"Servant of *what*?"

"The Demiurge," repeated Mrs. Swannett. "The origin of all evil."

"Croopus!"

"Your mother said," went on Mrs. Swannett, who now seemed almost delirious with the pleasure of being able to make contact with other people in this way, and was a remarkably quick learner—Is could not remember any of the workers in the mines catching on so speedily—"your mother said that it was a wicked thing, the way that Twite and that sister of his treated that poor Handsel Child, who lodged with them. That was when we all lived in Folkestone still, when the Elder lived in the house next to your parents in Cold Shoulder Road. She—"

The front gate squeaked. There was a step on the pebble path. Then the house door opened.

Is flashed a rapid question to Mrs. Swannett. "Shall you tell your husband that you are able to talk in this way?"

Mrs. Swannett frowned for a moment, thinking. Then: "No. At least, not just yet. He—I am not sure if he would approve. I think—for him—it might seem that, even talking to one another in this speechless way, we are breaking into the Holy Silence. Which ought to wrap each one of us in a thick, thick quilt of solitary wonder and mystery."

While Arun and Is were slowly pondering this statement, Micah Swannett came into the room and gave them a kindly nod. He did not pause, but strode straight through to the back kitchen and, in his turn, washed off the tang of the hop manure, then returned and sat down to a bowl of lentil stew.

He glanced in a friendly way at Is and Arun, and nodded approval of their changed appearance. His long, gloomy face was not adapted for smiling, but it was plain that he was glad the boys' clothes fitted them. They could feel him deciding, slowly and solidly, that it was better the clothes should be put to use rather than lie upstairs in a chest, filling his wife with sad thoughts. He was a simple, direct man, and the movements of his mind came to them in clear shapes, as if he were talking aloud to himself. Whereas Window's thoughts lay at a much deeper level and, except when aimed at Is and Arun, could not be heard at all.

After he had eaten, Micah wrote on a slate, "The Leader told me to bring you to him," and handed the slate across to Arun.

"What about me?" said Is. "Don't he wish to speak to me?"

Mr. Swannett shook his head. He took back the slate and added the words, "I will take you to him now," then stood up and walked to the door.

Arun stood too, casting a doubtful glance at Is. His cat-look had come back. He said to Is, "What d'you think? Hadn't you better come—see what he wants?"

Is considered. "I dunno. Maybe not. We don't want to start by putting him in bad skin. Let's wait and see what he has to say to you. He might cut up rusty if I barge in."

Just the same, she thought, I'm not going to be far away from that palaver, not if I can help it.

Arun went out with Micah, and Is followed to see which way they turned.

To her surprise, Micah did not go back into the town, but walked along the crest of the shingle-bank, going north toward a group of sheds and sail lofts that stood inland on a thistly patch of sand.

Window Swannett's thought came to Is. She, too, had come into the little pebbly garden. "The Elder has made himself a room for study and hearkening, in one of the sail lofts. He lives there with his sister Merlwyn. He chooses not to be close to other members of the Sect. Look, there he is now."

A massive man, dressed all in black, stood somberly, with arms folded, on the shingle-ridge, staring out to sea. The wind lifted his thick gray hair off his brow. He was a little taller than Micah Swannett, who now approached him, and much more solidly built, with a huge head like that of a lion. At this distance Is could not see his face clearly, but from the way he stood and held himself she caught a feeling of great power and strong will.

He sure looks like a Leader. I hope he don't come the old

bag over Arun, she thought uneasily. Arun—specially just now, when he's worried about his mum—can be uncommonly easy to overset. And I guess that feller—*de la Twite,* as he calls hisself, though I bet he's as much *de la* as my cat Figgin—I guess he's real sore at Arun's mum, and real keen to get that Handsel Kid back. So he's liable to lay into Arun, one way and another.

I dunno—maybe I should have gone along with Arun.

She watched the meeting intently. She saw the Leader lay what looked like a benevolent, fatherly hand on Arun's head, and she saw Arun flinch; then Micah Swannett, obeying a sharp jerk of the Leader's head, walked away from the pair and left them alone on the shingle-ridge.

"He has very great power, that man," said Window Swannett's voice in Is's mind.

You're not just whistling "Annie Laurie," Is flashed back. What's he a-going to do to my cousin?

"Is your cousin a strong character?"

"I dunno," thought Is doubtfully. "In some ways, yes; some, no."

"Then I think you should go along, get as close as you can, out of sight, and try to help him."

This seemed like excellent advice.

Is ran like a sandpiper along the middle road, out of sight, behind hulls of ships, and sheds, until she was within a short distance of where Arun and Dominic de la Twite were standing.

The pair had now moved down the shingle-bank on to the sandy lower beach. They began walking to and fro. Is squatted down behind an upturned fishing smack and listened keenly.

"I miss your dear, dear mother so *much*!" the Leader was saying. "A truly original soul! A maker! An inventor! How very rare that is! Her pictures are so startling—so brilliant. I hope very much that, wherever she has retired to, she is still creating such beautiful offerings to the Great Spirit. And do you, dear boy, follow in her footsteps? Do you paint pictures?"

"No I don't," said Arun. His voice was low and mumbling compared with de la Twite's loud, confident, ringing tones; he sounded hostile and ill at ease.

"Ah, but now, I do recall—you wrote *songs*, was that not so?" de la Twite said distastefully. "And this was a sad cause of contention between you and your good father. Or so I have heard. For song, of course, is a terrible infringement of the Holy Quiet. But could this activity not be transposed—could you not, like your dear mamma, turn to painting pictures? A delightfully silent occupation."

This de la Twite can't really be such a clodpole, thought Is, as to believe a body could just change over from songs to pictures. He's gotta be after something. But what?

Arun remained silent. He had not replied to de la Twite's suggestion. Is sent him a thought-message: "This cove is a real Captain Sharp. You want to watch his fambles all the time, or your dinner 'ull be in his pudding box."

She received no answer from Arun.

"And your dear mamma's pictures—what has become of them?" de la Twite was inquiring solicitously. "I *do trust*

they are in safe keeping? I do trust they are not still repos-
ing in that sad little empty house, at the mercy of hostile
neighbors?"

"No, sir. The Admiral's got 'em. Admiral Fishskin. He
has them in his cave," Arun said stolidly.

There was a short silence. Is wished very much that she
could see de la Twite's face.

Then de la Twite said reflectively, "Ah, yes. I think I
have heard of him. Admiral Fishskin. A cousin, is he not, of
our own esteemed Denzil Fishskin, the dental practitioner.
And, I believe, a most excellent, worthy old gentleman. No
doubt he will take the best possible care of the pictures. In
his *cave*, you say? Ah—were there any portraits among the
paintings, did you say?"

Is could feel the Leader's thoughts hammering like
knuckles on Arun's mind. "Let me in! Let me in!"

"No, Arun, no! Don't you let him in!" Is silently urged.

After a pause, Arun said, "No, there wasn't." Is sent him
an urgent message, and he added slowly, "Not unless the
portraits was fixed up so as to look like flowers."

"Ah, indeed. Now that is a very interesting notion," said
de la Twite thoughtfully. "But now, my dear lad, we must—
must we not?—go in search of your deeply esteemed
mother. You—most naturally—wish to be reunited with
her. And I—am *intensely* anxious to resume our friendship."

Arun said nothing.

"So, all we have to do, I am sure, is put our heads together. And, without a shadow of doubt, we shall come up
with the answer."

"The answer," repeated Arun flatly.

" 'Wind for music and seagulls for dancers!' " exclaimed de la Twite, suddenly changing his tone to a high and fluting one as he broke into verse. " 'Soon or late, we'll discover the answer!' Ah hah! my boy, you didn't know that I, too, am a poet! As well as being the Leader of the Silent Sect, I, too, in my humble way, have a right to be considered a Creator. Not on the same level as your wonderful mother, but still, an artist." And he recited several more lines of verse. "What do you think of those, my boy?"

"Very nice," said Arun lamely.

"But now, to our task. I understand, from various sources, that your mother has been seen in the company of some female relative. Can you attest to that?"

"Some say so. I dunno," said Arun.

"A female relative called—if I mistake not—Penelope Twite. Such an interesting, varied family, the Twites! I look forward with the liveliest pleasure to meeting another member of it."

Now, how the pize did he hear that? wondered Is.

"Do you think it might be safe to conclude that your dear parent has gone to reside with this Miss Twite?"

"As to that I can't say," said Arun.

"So, all we have to do is discover the whereabouts of Miss Twite's rural abode!" concluded the Leader in a voice of triumph. "And that—most likely—is something that you have at your fingers' ends. Eh?"

All the time, while he talked, Is could feel de la Twite's thoughts, like plucking, prying fingers, teasing, twitching at

104

the network of Arun's mind, as if they meant to push their way to its extreme innermost core.

"No, Arun, no! Don't let them in!" Is sent her own thoughts whizzing like darts across the beach. "He means harm, I'm sure of that! Your mum didn't trust him. She thought he was the Devil's boyo. Don't you tell him *anything*.

"Anyhow you don't know where Penny lives. Which is just as well."

But Arun, plainly, was beginning to give way to this continuous, relentless pressure. His voice became drowsy; his thoughts were slowing down as if he were in a helpless drift toward sleep.

"No . . . ," he said, half yawning. "No, I don't know where Penny lives. But Is knows. Is used to live with Penny. Penny's her sister."

"Is? Ah! Your cousin. Your companion? That shabby girl I saw outside the inn?"

Great Scissors, mister! thought Is huffily. *You*'d look a mite shabby if you'd crawled through a cave on your stummick for seven hours.

But the Leader was saying, "Let us go in search of her directly. We shall need a carriage, I presume, to travel to Miss Twite's abode?" And Arun was answering, "My cousin will be in Mr. Swannett's house, sir." — meek as a perishing choirboy, thought Is, enraged — so there was no time to be lost.

Keeping low to the ground, Is darted away, screened by boats and piles of net, until she had put a safe distance between herself and Dominic de la Twite. Then she took her way back to the Swannett house, gloomily enough, and plumped down on a chair by Window, who was sorting through her and Arun's ruined clothes.

"They're a-coming here," said Is in thought-speech, in answer to Window's look of query. "I wish we'd never come to Seagate. That big feller's properly put the come-hither on Arun—got him hoisted and hog-tied."

"Oh, that is a terrible pity. Yes, I was afraid that would happen. The Leader has great mental power over people."

"What'll we do? They're a-going to ask me where my sister Penny's ken is, in the woods. They believe that's where Arun's mum might be hiding out with the Handsel Kid. And maybe it is! What'll I do? Where can I take them?"

Mrs. Swannett thought for a minute. "You could lead them astray. Does Arun know your sister's house?"

" 'Tis only a barn. No, but he does know that it's on Blackheath Edge. I'd at least have to take 'em that-a-way."

"How far?"

"Matter o' forty mile from here, I reckon. It'd take three or four hours in a chaise."

Window Swannett reflected. "I have a syrup made from poppies and belladonna that I gave to my Hiram when he had the fever; there's a good half of the flask left. If you could get the Leader to drink that on the journey—in a flask of tansy tea, say—then, before you had reached the place, he'd be drowsy, and you and your cousin could perhaps slip away from him and run off into the woods—it is all forest round there, is it not?"

"Yes, for miles and miles." Is felt a spark of hope light in her. "And if he was drowsy-like, maybe he'd loose his grab-hold on poor old Arun's wits."

Mrs. Swannett walked swiftly into the back kitchen. "I will put you up a few oatcakes and dried plums as well, for the journey," her thought came back. "Then the flask of tansy tea will seem natural enough. But mind! Do not you or your cousin touch any of it— It is extremely power-ful."

To their dismay, though, when a chaise drawn by two horses presently drew up outside the front door and Domi-nic de la Twite jumped down from it, they saw there was a driver as well—a big, wooden-faced fellow with ginger hair.

"Oh, mercy! That is Will Fobbing—the Leader's body-guard. I should have thought of that—I doubt there will be enough cordial for two—"

"*Bodyguard?* He has a bodyguard? What for, in Hengist's name?"

"Oh, there have been various threats against him—from the Merry Gentry, we are told—and from people of Sea-gate who resent the Silent Sect—"

The front door burst open and the Leader strode in with-out troubling to knock. Arun, behind him, looked like a sleepwalker.

"Where is Micah?" demanded de la Twite.

Mrs. Swannett made gestures as of wheels turning and

pointed northward. She curtseyed politely as she did so, but Is, catching her thoughts, found them full of mutiny and dislike.

"Oh. A pity. He could have come too and been of use. Never mind. You—girl—shift yourself. We go to look for Ruth Twite. You must ride with us now to show where your sister lives."

His commanding eye rested on the air about a foot over Is's head, as if she were not worth a direct look. Seems he don't think much of females—excepting Arun's mum, thought Is, and had a warning message from Window Swannett:

"Watch out! The Leader is no fool! Keep your thoughts well away from his. And—make no mistake about this—he *hated* Ruth Twite."

Now Mrs. Swannett was handing Is a parcel of food, neatly wrapped in brown paper, and a stone jug with a cork in it. Provisions for your journey, she mimed to de la Twite, and he acknowledged the things with a gracious nod.

"Thank you, that was well thought of."

"And these things were in your pocket—a penknife and some acorns and hazel nuts and the silver coins," Window told Arun, gently touching his arm. He took the things dazedly, not seeming to catch her thought-message. She gave him a look full of worry and concern.

"How far to your sister's?" the Leader asked Is, pushing her impatiently toward the waiting chaise.

"Couldn't reckon to get there afore sundown," she answered shortly, climbing into the carriage. The only vacant seat was facing Arun and de la Twite, with her back to the driver. She sat down. De la Twite kept his hand on Arun's neck in what seemed a friendly, fatherly gesture but, Is guessed, was no such thing; it was to maintain total control over him.

She kept trying, over and over, to make contact with Arun's thought-stream, but could get nowhere near. He was locked away from her.

But as they drove away from the house, she had a sudden picture, painfully clear, of Window Swannett walking wearily back into her empty room, sitting down at the table, and bowing her head onto her folded arms in a terrible seizure of grief and loneliness.

Now she hasn't even got their clothes, thought Is.

The chaise bowled briskly out of town.

Four

Dominic de la Twite was a tall, bulky man, gray-haired, but with a smooth, youthfully rounded, high-colored face. His hair, long, coarse, thick, and wavy, curled and swept about his head; a lock of it kept falling forward, which he constantly swept back. He wore no hat. There were deep dimples in his chin and cheeks, and when he smiled — which happened every time he spoke to Arun — his large, round face sparkled with warmth and interest, two curved grooves flashed out on either side of the big, jutting nose, the eyes crinkled, and the nose itself appeared to tilt eagerly forward.

And it's all as big a sham as a tin sixpence, thought Is, coldly regarding him. Aunt Ruth was dead right in what she said about this cove, he's as bent as they come.

She remembered what the Admiral had said about de la Twite: "Impressive presence. *Godlike*" — pursing up his thin lips. "I would never choose a man with eyes that color to be my first officer."

Though, thought Is fairly, I wouldn't take the Admiral's advice either, if I was buying a pony; not if he stood to gain by the sale. I reckon him and Dominic are a pair.

When he was angry, the Leader did not scowl, but his face went curiously blank, as if a light had been blown out. This happened several times on the way out of Seagate, when the carriage passed a wall or stretch of fencing on which the word LOMAK had been written. Sometimes it was just MAK. Each time he noticed this inscription, de la Twite made Will Fobbing stop the horses, get out, and wipe off the offending letters.

"What's it mean, mister—that word?" Is inquired the third time this happened. "Why does it rile you? Is that somebody's moniker? Who is Lomak?"

The Leader glanced at Is coldly but did not deign to reply, except to say, "Girls should be seen, not heard."

"*I* ain't a member of your sorbent Sect," Is pointed out. "Nobody can't stop me speaking."

"Then why did you put on our raiment?"

"Mrs. Swannett kindly give 'em to me and Arun cos ours was in shreds and her boys drownded."

And it was *your* fault they drownded, Is recalled. She glared at the Leader, who ignored her glare. It was then that Is noticed, under his seat, a gleam of something wrapped up in sacking. Something that looked uncommonly like pistols and pairs of handcuffs.

"Hey! Arun! They've got duke-irons aboard! What kind of a havey-cavey start is this? What do they want famble-snickers for?"

She poured out these messages to Arun, but he was not receiving anything she sent him.

Arun had curled up against the Leader, fast asleep, like a

111

cat; even the whites of his eyes had turned up, as those of cats do when they are stretched out in deep slumber.

Dominic de la Twite gave Is a cold, sharp glance, and she wondered if he could be catching some restless movement, some kind of mental draft, from the thoughts she had been hurling at Arun. Better not chance it any more just now, she decided. Instead she turned and gazed out through the glass, thinking sadly how pleasant it would have been to ride through the country like this, traveling toward her sister Penny—if only she were certain that Penny would be there at the end of the journey and, to be sure, if the carriage held different traveling companions.

On either side, the fields of Kent rolled past. Sometimes there were orchards, coming into bud, sometimes marshy meadows. They struck into a straight Roman road and made better speed. Now the meadows were replaced by hop fields, where men were striding to and fro on stilts, setting up the high, spindly framework of poles and fine cords needed for the summer's hop harvest.

They passed a tiny hamlet, just two or three houses nestling among trees, about a quarter of a mile from the highway.

WOMENSWOLD, said the sign pointing to it.

Where have I heard that name lately? wondered Is as the horses trotted on. Somebody spoke of it in the last day or two—now, who? A place where something right odd happened—now, what?

As they drew away from the village and entered the forest, which lay very close by it, she remembered. It was

Captain Podmore. A thirty-three-gun frigate had been blown inland by the gale and had come to roost in a chestnut tree.

As the memory returned, she had a far-distant glimpse of what might be the ship itself—something bulky and black, lodged in a huge tree, among a clump of other huge trees. She would have liked to rouse Arun and draw his attention to the interesting sight, but they had drawn past it before there was time to do so. And anyway, poor boy, let him sleep, she thought. Maybe it wasn't the ship after all. Maybe somebody just took a fancy to build a house in a tree. Would be a fine way to keep out of wolves' reach. Recalling various battles that she and Penny had fought to prevent wolves from entering their forest dwelling, she drifted into a light sleep.

When she woke she found that the hop fields with their spiky poles had given way to dense forest on both sides— the great oak woods of Kent. Mighty trees crowded close to the road. Mostly they were leafless and bare still, but just the presence of the forest round her made Is feel at home and comfortable.

After all, she thought, I know these parts well; it'd be a rare rum go if I couldn't contrive to give these nikeys the slip. But Arun? How will I ever rouse him? What about Arun?

She looked up from her considerings to see the Leader giving her a cold, assessing stare.

After a few minutes, he asked, "Do you know your aunt Ruth Twite?"

113

"Never met her," Is told him promptly. And she added, "But she sounds a real nice lady. And clever too."

"Your uncle Hosiah? Did you know him?"

"Met him only the once."

Is did not mention that she had given her uncle Hosiah, on his deathbed, a promise to find her runaway cousin Arun and see him safe back to his sorrowing mum; Dominic de la Twite certainly had no right to that piece of family information.

Anyway—*was* Arun's mum still sorrowing?

Arun continued to sleep; she had never known him sink into such a deep slumber. Maybe he was still tired out from their struggle through the cave last night; or maybe it was something to do with the Leader's baneful presence.

De la Twite went on with his catechism. "Did you see Ruth Twite's pictures, girl?"

"Sure did, mister." Since Arun had already told the story, there would be no point in concealment. "Arun and me shifted 'em all into the old Admiral's cave. There he thought they'd be safe from neighbors."

"*All* of them?" said de la Twite. "The portraits as well?"

"There wasn't no portraits, mister. Maybe," Is added consideringly, "the owd Admiral had took those already," and got a very sharp look from the Leader. This feller must certainly be acquainted with the Admiral, Is thought, if he lived right next door to the Twites in Cold Shoulder Road. For they was right matey with the old boy; Uncle Hose used to mend his brogans and play golf, and Aunt Ruth looked after his missus. So—stands to reason this Mr.

114

Dominic musta been acquainted with him, or at least know him by sight.

But the Admiral's a pretty rum customer; a *mighty* rum customer; he's tough and I reckon he's sly. In fact—come to think—he and this Leader cove are two of a kind. . . .

"So—where is this cave?" asked de la Twite carelessly, "this cave of the Admiral's?"

Is decided to be economical with the truth. "Well, mister, that I can't rightly tell you. We was only there in the dark, see, a-stowing the pictures away. But it's somewhere not too far from the Admiral's house."

I reckon the Leader is just dying to get his paws on those pictures, she thought. Let him just try, that's all. He'll come up against Rosamund maybe, that'll surprise him.

Soon after this they passed a signpost pointing to Eltham. All this time the horses had been keeping up a very respectable pace. Sixteen-mile-an-hour prancers they must be, thought Is.

But we're getting mighty close to home, now, she realized. Time I took a hand.

Aloud she said, "How about a bite of prog, mister? Care for an oatcake or a dried plum? Arun! Stir your stumps, boy! How about a bite to eat? Or a sup of tansy tea?"

Arun woke up drowsily and accepted a dried plum. His thoughts were still screened away from Is; she could not tell what was going through his mind. The Leader carelessly accepted an oatcake and a morsel of cheese.

"How about the driver?" suggested Is. "Isn't he peckish? Won't he want summat?"

115

She hoped that they might pull to a stop, for dusk was now beginning to creep through the trees. Once they came to a standstill, surely it would not be hard for her and Arun to give these men the slip and vanish from view. If only she could transmit her plan to Arun! But he was looking dazed and bewildered, hardly seemed to know where he was.

"The driver needs nothing. He is well enough without," said de la Twite shortly.

But at this the driver—who could evidently hear all they were saying—suddenly bawled out, *"No, I bain't!* I've a thirst on me like the go-shop desert; I'd break me neck for a sup o' drink."

"Oh, all right, very well," said de la Twite shortly. "The gal's got some tansy tea; she'll pass you the bottle."

"Tansy tea! What sort of a jossop is *that*?"

But still, he accepted the stone bottle when Is handed it over the box; to her dismay, he then drained it completely.

"Oh!" she exclaimed. "Now there's none for you, mister."

"Wouldn't have touched the stuff anyway; tea is about as welcome as water in my shoes," said the Leader shortly, and drank from a bottle of his own that he produced from his greatcoat pocket.

But oh, drabbit it, thought Is; *now* what'll we do? If only it had been the other way round! For that driver fellow seems as thick as a plank, no sweat getting away from him; but the Leader's quite another basket of eels; now we're really in the suds.

Indeed, the Leader appeared more and more alert as they

approached Blackheath Edge; he kept asking Is for directions at every crossroads, at every path or turning, almost at every tree; his eyes bored into her like drills, and Is found that—entirely against her own will and convictions —she was guiding him, willy-nilly, along the tangled way through the forest to the remote and unvisited region where she and Penny had lived in their peaceful barn.

Supposing Penny's there with Arun's mum, she thought desperately; how'll we manage, what'll we do? How could I have let this happen? How *could* I?

The horses were tired now, plodding along more and more slowly; or perhaps it was because the driver sat nodding, almost asleep, on his seat. The last part of the way followed a woodland ride, grassed over, where the trees crowded close to the track, so that it was just as well the pace of the chaise had dwindled to a weary walk.

Ahead of them in the dusk could now be seen a low one-storey building; and Is hardly knew whether to be glad or sorry that no light showed in the slit windows, no sound came from it, no sign of activity showed around it.

"Is *this* the place?" Dominic de la Twite asked, and his voice was full of scorn—and disappointment as well. "Is *this* your sister's house? This shed?"

"Yes, mister. This is it," croaked Is, from a throat pulled tight with trouble and pain. She scrambled out, looking hopefully around the clearing for her cat Figgin. But no shadowy form came running to plunge against her legs. Nobody answered her knock on the door. No light kindled. She filled her lungs and did her best to shout, "Penny! Ho there!" loudly and cheerfully. "I've come home!" But nobody answered.

An owl hooted somewhere in the forest, that was all.

It was one of the worst moments Is had ever lived through.

All of a sudden she felt a huge sympathy for Arun. Now she had an inkling of how baffled and disappointed he must have felt when they entered the damp, silent little house in Cold Shoulder Road.

Dominic de la Twite descended from the carriage and strode authoritatively to the door. He rapped on it, long and loud. "Is anybody there?" he shouted. "Open up, if you please! Miss Twite! Mrs. Twite!"

But there was no response. He rattled the latch. The door was locked.

"You, girl!" He turned on Is. "Do you have a key to this place?"

Is looked at him consideringly. Then she looked back at the carriage. Arun had climbed slowly down and was standing staring about him, his face a white blur in the dusk. Will Fobbing, slumped on the box, his elbows on his knees, his head on his arms, could be heard snoring loudly.

"Well," said Is after a pause, "I *do* have a key, as it comes about."

Very slowly and deliberately, she drew out a raveled piece of grubby string, which had been round her neck, with a key attached to it, and pulled it over her head. De la Twite stepped forward to snatch it from her, but she neatly sidestepped him, skipped to the door, and unlocked it. The

Leader followed her, almost treading on her heels, as she walked inside.

"Is there a light?" he demanded.

"Hold on a minute, mister. Don't be in such a pelter." Feeling about with the ease of long habit, Is found a shelf by the door, a flint, tinder, and a candle. She struck a light, kindled a flame. Light slowly grew, and showed a big, shadowed room, table and stools carved from bits of tree trunk, shelves against the wooden walls holding pots and cups, two beds, and a few books. There were ashes in the central hearth. But these ashes were stone cold; nobody had lit a fire here for days, weeks, perhaps months.

De la Twite, glaring about him, swore long and softly and savagely. What specially riveted his attention was two pictures hanging from nails on the wall. As he stared at them, Is moved to the table, on which there stood a saucer containing a few coins and a scrap of paper. These things she quietly pocketed. Then she caught hold of Arun's hand —he had followed her in, blinking and confused, moving like a sleepwalker.

"Come quickly, *quickly*," she said to him in thought-speech, and pulled him out of the barn. "You can see they aren't here. Quick—after me."

Once outside she hastily and soundlessly relocked the door and slung the key on its string back round her neck.

While they were out of sight, Will Fobbing had climbed, or tumbled, down from the box of the chaise and now lay stretched out at full length on the mossy turf. He snored loudly.

Let's just hope the wolves don't get him, thought Is, swiftly beginning to unbuckle the harness of one of the horses.

"Quick, Arun, you untie the other."

Automatically he did as she directed. Thanks be, she thought, he's hearing me again.

"Good! Now lep up on his back. He'll not be resty— poor beasts, they're both as tired as can be. But they'll carry us a mile or two farther."

Both horses, in fact, pleased to be free from the shafts, trotted away briskly enough out of the clearing. Is turned for another look at the place that had been her home for so long.

Now a furious banging and shouting broke out inside the barn.

He better not do too much of that, thought Is, it might attract the wolves.

Arun rode along beside Is in silence, in a kind of dream, for some considerable distance. Then he mumbled confusedly, "Where are we, Is? Where did these horses come from? Where are we going?"

"*First* thing we're doing is getting away from that skellum," said Is grimly, kicking the fat sides of her bareback mount. "Do you know what he had in the coach, under his seat? Handcuffs! And a pair of barking irons as well. What'd he want those for? When he was going to see your mum and my sis?"

"For the wolves?" Arun suggested vaguely.

"Well—maybe! But I never heard of putting wolves in

handcuffs! That man means no good. Not to us, anyway. And I believe he meant harm to your mum."

Arun still looked confused and only half awake. But the fresh air and the rhythm of the trotting horses were helping to rouse him. After they had ridden a mile or so farther, Is began to hope that the Leader's grim influence was wearing off.

She took a right turn, southward, down a ride that crossed the one along which they had come.

Behind them, far away in the clearing, a speck of bright, fiery light began to dance among the trees.

"Where are we bound for?" Arun asked again, sleepily, after they had ridden another couple of miles.

"We're going to a Cold Harbor," Is told him. "There used to be one down somewhere here-along. It was south-wards of where Penny and I lived, a matter of nine or ten miles."

"What's a Cold Harbor?" he asked, yawning.

"Oh—*you* know—a place where trampers and travelers can put up. A poor folks' refuge. It'll do for us. We can't go back to Seagate—now we know your mum ain't there any-how." She gave a brief chuckle. "Did you see them pictures up on the wall, back in Penny's place?"

"I didn't notice."

"Two of 'em there—they'd come since my time, Penny and I hadn't no pictures when I was at home. And guess what they were! One was a picture of the Admiral— a real nimble likeness—and t'other was of old Domino Twite his own self. Didn't I notice him take that in! He was fair dumbstruck! That was how I was able to nip out the door and lock it. And it shows your mum *musta* been there with Penny, and not so long ago, neither. She and Pen musta reckoned, for some reason, that they'd best scarper off to another pad. Maybe they figured old Domino 'ud come seeking them there. After all, lots o' folks knows Penny; she sells her dolls all over the countryside."

"But why—I don't understand," Arun said helplessly. "I thought—the Leader said—he liked my mum."

"Hah! So he *said*! The way a fox likes a chicken. You're still a bit dumfoozled, matey," Is told her cousin kindly. "You'll see things clearer when we've got ourselves well away, and had a rest, and maybe a drop o' summat hot."

"Hot? Here? In the middle of this great wood?"

"You'll see. Like I told you. In the Cold Harbor. Not far now—I hope."

They had been climbing, and the forest had changed from oak to beech. By this time it was full dark, and a misty moon was keeping pace with them in the sky above, visible from time to time through the branches. They crossed over a ridge and began to descend again.

Now, ahead, a dim glow could be seen through the trees, and they smelt woodsmoke. The horses pricked up their ears and went on a little faster.

"Hope there's a bit o' fodder for the poor brutes," said Is. "They've come a perishing long way."

The refuge, when they reached it, was a queer building, unlike any other. It stood in a small clearing of the wood and consisted principally of four huge stones, three of them

122

standing up like fingers and the fourth one, which was big as a farm cart, balanced on the tops of the other three, forming a roof. Round this structure more stones had been added later, in a rough wall, to make a kind of shelter.

"The place is called Pook's Pantry," Is told Arun. "It's very, very old."

A fire burned in front of the refuge. Across from it, on the far side of the clearing, grew a huge and venerable yew tree, with a trunk that ten people holding hands could hardly encircle. Its canopy of needles above was so dense and dark that it formed a roof. Another horse was already tethered under it.

"Lucky the branches is so high overhead," said Is. "Yew leaves is downright pizen to nags. Hey, look, some thoughtful soul has left a bit of hay and chaff. Can you draw a pail of water from the well, Arun?"

When the horses were fed and cared for, Is and Arun went over to the fire, where six or seven people were quietly resting, or talking in low voices, or cooking their supper.

"Evening, all," said Is politely, and received a mild rumble of greeting in return.

Branches lay piled against the stone hut. She and Arun added a few to the fire, then heated some water in a metal pot they found by the entrance.

"I've a flask of rose hip syrup, young 'uns," offered a tall Gypsy woman. "Ye can have a spoonful apiece, if ye're so minded."

"Thank ye kindly, missus. We've got dried cherries," said

Is, and offered them in exchange. They drank hot water, flavored with rose hip, out of wooden mugs.

Two men, who said they were sailors, paid off at Dover and walking to the Port of London, where they hoped to pick up another ship, were willing to share their rabbit stew. A bagman on his way north offered a mouthful from his bottle of grog, but this Arun and Is, remembering the Admiral's fearsome brew, politely refused. A tinker gave them a bit of his bread and cheese, which was very good.

Nobody presumed to ask any questions except an old white-haired fellow, apparently a traveling preacher, who studied them attentively in the mixed fire and moonlight, then said, slowly, "How come ye wear the clothes of the Silent Sect, at Seagate, young 'uns? Are ye runaways?"

"No, sir," Is told him. "Our own duds was all in tatters, so a lady at Seagate gave us her boys' things, acos they was drownded." The old fellow seemed sincerely interested, so she went on explaining: "My cousin's mum used to belong to that Sect. We're a-looking for her. Has anybody here heard tell of her, maybe? Her name's Missus Ruth Twite."

A thoughtful silence settled over the group round the fire.

After a while the bagman said, "*Twite*. That's an okkard kind of name. I've heard tell of Twite, afore now."

"There's a rhyme," said the tinker. "Many knows it:

Twite black, Twite white,
One's wrong, one's right
One'll help ye with all his might

One'll rob ye out of spite
One's dark, one's light,
One's day, one's night
One's blessing, one's blight,
Twite black, and Twite white."

After the tinker had said these lines, nobody spoke for some time. Then the tinker asked Is and Arun, "Did ye never hear that rhyme, young 'uns?"

"No," said Arun. "I never heard it before."

"Nor did I," said Is. "But it sounds to me like a true rhyme. There's bad Twites, and there's decent ones. And the ones that's bad, they are bad through and through. My dad was one o' that kind. An out-and-out no-good, he was. Though," she added thoughtfully, "he made up some real choice tunes. But Arun's mum, that we're a-searching for, she sounds like a right nice lady, and paints pictures that you never saw the match of."

"So," said the old preacher after some thought, "you two young 'uns are both Twites, eh? Cousins?"

"That's so," said Is.

"And are ye black Twites, or white?"

"Blest if I know!" said Is. "No one ever asked us before! But that Dominic de la Twite, him as is Leader of the Silent Sect over at Seagate, I reckon he's a black 'un."

"I never heard no harm of the Sect," said the bagman. "Queer pernickety folk, they be, for sure, but they keep themselves to themselves and do no ill. Not like the Merry Gentry. Now *they* do harm, no question."

125

"Ah! that they do," said the tinker. "Any that threatens to split on them to the Preventives, or the Coastguards, he'll never eat another breakfast. Let alone dinner."

"I marvel ye dare speak so free," said the Gypsy woman. "How do ye know there ain't somebody here as belongs to the Gentry?"

There was a short, chill silence. But then one of the sailors said, "Ah, hokum! Any cove what belonged to the Gentry, he wouldn't be sitting here in the dark sucking rabbit bones. He'd be in the Old Maison Dieu, drinking sherry wine."

"That's so," they all agreed, relieved.

A general easement set in; the sailors offered more rabbit stew all round and, when that was declined, began singing sea chanteys.

Then the Gypsy woman sang a sad ballad about a dear lost companion, and the tinker sang a song about three jolly huntsmen.

"Do ye know any songs, lad?" the bagman asked Arun.

"Um," he said. And then, to the complete amazement of Is, he stood up and sang:

"If I had a bird that would bounce
  or a ball that would fly
    no field would be long enough
    net would be strong enough
    song could be sung
    bell could be rung
    to give voice

to our joy
my companions and I
I would toss up my bird on the wind
bounce my ball on the sky.

If I had a rope that would roll
or a wheel that would swing
  no slope would be steep enough
  hole would be deep enough
  space could be found
  on the ground
  no plain to contain
  our wild wayfaring
all winter I'd spin on my rope
whirl my wheel in the spring!"

"Hey! Boy! That's a sparky tune you've got there," said the tinker. "Sing it again."

Arun sang it again. It was indeed, thought Is critically, a *very* sparky tune, intricate and lively, half sad, half playful. And I ought to know, she thought, being Dad's daughter, I've heard a plenty good-enough tunes in my time.

"When did you make that up?" she asked Arun, as the group began singing a song about a saucy sailor boy.

"Oh," he said vaguely, "it was the first tune that ever came into my head. When I was four or five, I reckon. And I sang it to my dad, and he was shocked to death. Told me I was cutting a hole in the Holy Silence. So I never sang him any of the others."

"Are there lots of others?"

"Of course. A fair few."

And indeed, when asked for more, he sang, very simply, without shyness or pride, four or five others, one about tales of whales and snails, one about the hedgehog in his prickly vest, one about a soldier with a hole in his sock who could not go to war, one about the last snowflake of winter.

Is listened and wondered. Those songs are as good as my dad's, she thought; maybe better. Why wouldn't he ever sing them before? Except that one time in Seagate when the old 'uns were dancing? Was it the life in the mines, up north, put a stopper on him? But if so, what started him off again?

Perhaps, she thought, puzzling about it, as the tinker sang "Polly Put the Kettle On," with a lot of rude extra verses, perhaps that sleep, that queer deep sleep in the coach, perhaps that unknotted something that was knotted up in Arun. It was the Leader who sent Arun into that sleep. Maybe, without meaning to, old Domino did Arun a good turn. But, if so, I'll lay a hundred crowns it was the only good turn he ever *did* do to anybody in this land. And not a-purpose.

She remembered the Leader's eyes boring into her own, and how she had almost felt obliged to obey his orders, take him where he wanted to go.

He's a cove to keep well away from, she decided, and if we can find Aunt Ruth we must warn her that he's out a-looking for her and that Handsel Kid.

After the tinker's song, everybody felt sleepy and retired

128

to bed. Since the small stone refuge hut was fairly crammed already, with six people in it, Is and Arun piled themselves beds of bracken under the shelter of the great yew, and slept peacefully.

Sometime in the small hours, Is woke up and, needing to relieve herself, stole away to a private distance. Then, feeling alert and wakeful, she settled on a rock, among giant clumps of heather in a small clearing, and thought about Arun.

I sure do hope we find his mum. If we don't, he's liable to go out of reach. He gets so low. What that tinker said about black Twites and white, that was mighty strange. But it's so, no one can deny. And I'm feared Arun might slip onto the black side, just now, if things don't go well for him. . . .

His singing oughta help.

Best he don't meet that Leader again.

That Leader is poison.

Wrapped in these ponderings, Is had been sitting still as a stone, with her chin on her knees, for about half an hour, when she was petrified to hear two whispering voices that seemed to come from quite close at hand, beyond the clumps of heather.

"What kept you for so long?"

"I was delayed. Obliged to borrow a mount." There was ill temper in the second voice.

"Too much delay. Far too much delay." First Voice was severe. "And last night was inexcusable. Why was the delivery delayed? What happened?"

"Trouble on the French side. A load of tusks held up south of Ostend. And two loads that went astray. Never turned up."

"Deplorable inefficiency! In any case, word should have been sent across by the *Merry Gentian*."

"The *Gentian* had been held up by a Revenue cutter."

"Anything found?" First Voice demanded sharply.

"No, no. The men know their business better than that."

"What about that woman? Any news of her?"

"Only false trails. The boy and girl seemed a likely clue, but it was a balk, and they slipped from my keeping. . . . I shall come up with them again."

"The boy and girl?" First Voice whispered the words, as if utterly confounded. "But I had them penned up tight— clapped under hatches. How *could* they have made their way out? It was impossible! What *can* you mean?"

"They did make their way out," said Second Voice with a touch of contempt. "And furthermore, listen to this, my friend—"

An owl hooted. Is missed the next few words. Then something about "your sister" and "when we are in the Azores."

"Now," said First Voice, "as to the next levy—and the payment—"

"But what about the children? The boy I can hold in the palm of my hand. As to the girl—"

The voices moved farther away, became indistinct. Is sat frozen, hardly breathing, for what seemed an infinitely long time. Then she heard the soft whinny of a horse, perhaps a

130

quarter of a mile distant. That's one of 'em gone off, she thought; but where's t'other? I ain't stirring from this spot till I'm dead sure he's well clear.

First Voice must have been the Admiral—mustn't he? Saying he had us clapped under hatches. That's just what the owd Admiral would say. But in that case, the Admiral must be hand in hand with the Gentry. *That* sticks out like a man-o'-war's mast.

And the other one—Voice Number Two—must have been de la Twite. Saying he could hold the boy in the palm of his hand—humph!

What a pair, Is thought. They're enough to turn your hair to cobwebs. The best thing Arun and I could do is get away from here, up to London maybe.

But then, what about Aunt Ruth? And the Handsel Kid? And all the folk that live in awful fright? She thought of Mrs. Boles's husband, left with his hands clipped in an ash tree for the wolves to find. And the man she and Arun had seen stabbed, by the Tunnel entrance. And the Swannett boys. And Fenny Braburn, taken from her family.

Something oughta be done about it all, Is thought slowly and sleepily.

Then she toppled into a deep well of sleep, with her head pillowed on a tussock of heather. In her sleep she dreamed she saw the Admiral, riding on his Dupli-Gyro, flying a kite in the sky on a long string. Only the kite was not a kite but a ship, the *Merry Gentian,* and it pulled the Admiral into the air, and he lost hold of the string and crashed into the sea. . . .

In the morning, when Is woke, she found that it was already late. The other wayfaring inhabitants of the Cold Harbor had all gone their ways, except for the Gypsy woman, who was thoughtfully and silently rubbing her feet with goose grease out of a little stone pot.

The first thing Is did was to pull out of her pocket the few coins and the scrap of paper that she had taken from the saucer in Penny's barn. Now, in daylight, she could read words written on the paper in Penny's clear script:

Dere Is—This is for you if you cum home

Is gulped. So Penny didn't forget me, she thought. She left a message for me when she moved out.

Like Arun's mum did.

For the first time in many hours, Is remembered that other scrap of paper that had been tucked behind all the pictures in Arun's little sleeping closet in Cold Shoulder Road. On the front had been a verse by Arun, on the other side, in his mum's writing, the words *Somewhere in the woods.*

Well—we're in the woods now.

But there's an awful lot of woods.

Arun, who had still been fast asleep in his bracken nest when she returned to the clearing, woke up slowly and easily, yawning and smiling at Is. He looks more like a boy today, she thought, relieved; not near so much like a cat.

"Arun! You remember that bit o' paper we found in your mum's house, with a song by you and a message from her? Have you still got it?"

"No, I lost it. Probably got scraped out of my pocket

when we were crawling through the cave. Or I left it at Mrs. Swannett's house. Why?"

"I found this one from Penny. In our place back there."

She passed him the slip of paper. "And there was a few pennies with it." She chuckled. "I left one o' them silver King Charles ones behind instead. That musta given old Domino Demiurge summat to puzzle over, if he found it."

"Dunno as that was such a bright thing to do," Arun remarked thoughtfully. "He'll think that Penny or my mum found it, that they know where King Charles's treasure is. That'll give him all the more reason for going after them."

"Yes—that's so," admitted Is. "But then—he don't know where they are."

Should she tell Arun about the voices in the night?

The boy I can hold in the palm of my hand.

I'll wait awhile, she decided. He gives me the cold habdabs, that feller.

Arun turned over the slip of paper.

"Hey! Here's one of my mum's little drawings."

The picture was tiny, no bigger than a rose petal. Drawn in sharp black lines, it showed a ship with wings.

My dream! thought Is.

"A flying ship!" said Arun. He gazed at the sky as if seeing a vision there. "Wouldn't that be just prime. Maybe they'll have them one day, in a hundred years or so. Just think! You could fly from London to Blastburn in a couple of hours. And there'd be no need for a Channel Tunnel— you could just fly over from Dover to France. On a thing like the Admiral's Dupli-Gyro but with wings."

The drawing had given other ideas to Is.

"Arun," she said slowly. "I believe I've a notion where your ma and Penny might be. . . ."

"Where, then?"

"I'd rather not say aloud; it's only a guess."

But then she looked across the clearing at the only possible listener, and said, "Oh!" rather blankly. For the Gypsy woman, who had been leisurely rubbing her toes with goose grease, had apparently finished the operation while they were feeding and watering the horses, and had wrapped her shawl about her and silently slipped away among the trees.

"Romany are unsociable folk," said Arun.

"She seemed sociable enough last night."

"So did the rest. But they all went off without saying goodbye."

"Well—let's get away from here. I wouldn't above half fancy sleeping in that ken," said Is, staring at the enormous piece of rock that formed the roof of the Cold Harbor. "Suppose it got loose and come down in the night and flattened ye?"

"Well, you'd never know, would you? I wonder how many tons it weighs?"

As was the custom, they gathered up a bit of firewood and fodder for the next wayfarers who might make use of the Cold Harbor, and then set off northeasterly. It was a mild, foggy spring day; the woods smelt fresh and sharp, of earth and primroses; the birds were twittering quietly, waiting for the sun to break through the gauzy vapor.

"So where are you taking us?" Arun asked Is, as they ambled at an easy pace among the trees.

"Womenswold. It ain't above six or seven miles from Seagate, so we gotta go carefully. Then the horses oughta be able to find their own way home to Seagate from there."

"Womenswold?"

"You were asleep when we passed it yesterday. It's only a guess."

"And if the guess is wrong?"

"Oh, well," she said sighing, "then us'll have to think again. Arun, whyever don't you earn your living singing at fairs? You could do right well."

"But I can't always sing."

"Why?"

"I don't know. Sometimes nothing comes out. As if I'm plugged up."

Maybe you're unplugged now, thought Is, but she kept the hope to herself.

They took a roundabout course, keeping away from large tracks. Is wished to avoid any possible chance of coming across Dominic de la Twite.

"For he's sure to have battered his way outa the barn in the end," said Is, without mentioning what she had heard in the night. "I daresay Penny'll be sore when she comes back to find her door broke, but what else could I do? It was the only way to get you clear of that cove. He'd put a regular spell on ye."

"I can't remember a single thing that happened yesterday," said Arun. "After Micah Swannett took me to see that man on the shingle-bank. It was like being hit on the head by a loaded sock. The rest of the day is just a blur."

They stopped for a drink and a midday rest in a little clearing among birch trees where a spring bubbled out of a steep rock face and a tiny thatched cottage huddled against the side of the bank. Chickens pecked about the grass, ducks swam on the brook, and an old woman, coming out of the cottage, offered them a boiled egg apiece if they would chop some logs for her.

"And I wish ye'd wipe those letters off for me," she said, pointing up to a smooth part of the rock where the letters MAK had been scrawled in charcoal. "Sometimes the Merry Gentry come through the forest this way, on their night rides, and it'd be as much as the thatch on my roof was worth to have them see that, if the moon shone that way. They're mighty touchy, the Gentry, with anyone as slights or crosses 'em. And 'tis too high for me to reach."

Is climbed on Arun's shoulders and removed the offending letters with a birch broom.

"Who put it there, missus?" she asked. "And what does it mean?"

"How should I know who writ it? There *was* a party o' girls and chillun in the 'oods one day, it might ha' been them. Girls gets up to foolish tricks, times. What's it mean? 'Mothers and kids,' I heard one of 'em say. 'Mothers and kids.' But what have *I* got to do with mothers and kids? 'Tis long since mine went off in the world. Here's your eggs, now eat 'em up quick, for 'tis time I called in my chicken;

136

there's worse things than wolves and foxes in the forest at night."

"What's this place called, missus?" Is asked, as they left the old lady shooing her ducks inside a wooden coop.

"Why, Birketland. . . ."

Dusk was falling as they approached Womenswold. They made a circuitous approach, crossing the Roman road farther south and then working back from a northeasterly direction. The little village—no more than two farms, some outbuildings, and a bridge over a brook—was three-quarters surrounded by forest. The grove Is remembered lay a mile or so west of the houses. There were about a dozen trees, oaks and chestnuts, all equally huge, grouped together on a knoll.

The mist had begun to thicken again as dusk fell, so that the bulky shape that was lodged in the middle of the central tree could hardly be distinguished until they were right underneath it.

They had taken the precaution of leaving their horses tethered a quarter of a mile off and going the last part of the way on foot, very quietly, hand in hand, Is with a finger at her lips.

"Well, I am blest!" observed Arun in thought-speech, looking up through the boughs. "A whole genuine naval frigate, guns and all, lodged up there, snug as a hen in a nesting box. I reckon even the First Lord of the Admiralty couldn't fetch it out of there."

"No, he surely couldn't," agreed Is. "But what d'you bet

there's somebody a-lodging up in there? And who d'you bet it is?"

He had no need to answer. And she herself had no further possible doubt, for a furious *"Morow!"* snapped the silence, a small form, hard as a bullet, butted against her leg, and a frightfully sharp set of teeth gouged into her calf.

"Figgin! My cat Figgin! My cat!"

But Figgin was extremely angry, and had no intention of stopping for a friendly exchange with his long-lost mistress. He growled and spat at her, and scurried up the trunk of the chestnut tree into the obscurity above.

Five

First of all they had an argument about the horses.

"Why don't we just set 'em free," argued Is. "They'll wander their own way home. Everybody round here will know they come from the King's Head at Seagate. They'll take no harm. After all, *we* didn't hire 'em."

But Arun said that the Merry Gentry might steal the horses, and why should poor Tom the landlord be the loser. "I'll take them back tomorrow," he said. "For tonight they can bide where they are, tethered under the oaks; there's plenty of pasturage."

From above, a voice hailed them. It was high and weary, rather sarcastic; it was a voice that, at many desponding moments in the past year, Is had been afraid that she would never hear again.

"Well, you two! Are you coming up? Or are you going to stand parleying there all night?"

Now they noticed that a rope ladder had been let down. For the lowest branches of the huge chestnut tree were well out of reach.

"I'll go first," said Is. She had spent a great part of her life in trees, and felt comfortably at home in them. She shot up the ladder as nimbly as a squirrel, until she arrived at where the boughs began. Here it was necessary to push her way through a kind of thicket, for the ship, when hurled by the gale into the midst of the tree, had smashed and torn a great many branches. These had not fallen to the ground but jammed crisscross among the framework of the tree, so that the frigate was gripped in a regular cage of branches, some alive, some dead, pointing in every possible direction. They helped very much to screen the hull from view, besides making it most unlikely that it could ever be removed from the tree.

Is found that the last part of the climb entailed pushing through a mass of twigs and dead leaves that still clung doggedly on to the parent branches.

"Well, stranger!" said Penny, receiving her sister over the ship's rail with a tight, cross hug. "It took you long enough to come up with me!"

"Blame it, Pen! Hold hard! I only *found* your message last night! We come as quick as we was able. Before that we'd took a wrong cast—went to Seagate, looking for Arun's mum there. This here's Arun, Penny," she added as he came over the rail.

Penelope gave Arun a scrutinizing, cousinly nod. "Y'mum's been worrying herself threadbare about you," was all she tartly said. He gave her an equally cool stare, and saw a skinny, freckled, fair-haired woman who looked as if she'd stand no nonsense from anybody. But "Welcome aboard the *Throstle*," she added in a friendlier tone. "She makes a right handy nest for us fly-by-nights, don't she?

And I reckon we can use a feller like you aboard; you make up songs, don't you?"

"Is my mum really here?" asked Arun, looking about him.

Penelope had brought a horn lantern. She picked it up and threw a dim light over their surroundings.

The quarterdeck of the frigate Throstle was about twenty-one feet long, very narrow, and the space along it even more reduced by some guns on one side and various ringbolts on the other. The ship's masts and rigging had been smashed and battered by its arrival in the chestnut tree, and hung in a tangle overhead, still further obstructing passage along the deck. But somebody had painstakingly sawed through branches and spars and had coiled up ropes, clearing paths through the jungle. Along one of these paths two people now made their way.

Two people.

"Who's *that*?" growled Arun to Is in thought-speech, and she answered, also without making a sound, "Had you forgotten? Why, it's the Handsel Child."

Ruth Twite was not so tall as Penny, but was very thin, so that she seemed tall. Her straight iron-gray hair was drawn back into a big loose knot at the nape of her neck. Her pale face seemed to be all made up out of triangles, thought Is—deep three-cornered eye sockets, a pointed chin that stuck out, deep lines from her nose to the corners of her mouth. Is could see why people in Folkestone had taken her for a witch. She did look like one. The child who clung on to her hand was vaguely familiar. After a moment or two Is remembered why. It was the same child—boy or girl?—who had loitered around the street market in Folkestone, who had exchanged broom-twigs for fish.

Arun and his mother stood looking at one another without speaking.

That's rum, thought Is. But then she remembered that, of course, they never *had* been allowed to talk to one another.

Mrs. Twite spoke first, awkwardly, as if she hardly knew how to begin. "Here you are, then, my son. At last! How many times had I given you up for lost. I hardly expected to see you again. This is Pye."

Pye scowled horribly at Arun, squinting, sucking a thumb.

Pye is a right queer little goblin, thought Is. He—or she?—was a thickset, solid child, aged perhaps four or five, with a round face, a blob of a pink nose, and round, staring, squinting pale eyes.

"Wotcher, Pye!" said Is kindly. "My name's Is."

Pye made no answer, only sucked and stared and squinted the harder.

"Pye can't speak," Penny explained.

And Ruth added, "She screamed so much, while she lived with Dominic de la Twite, that we believe she screamed herself dumb. But we are hoping that time will mend this."

"She ain't deaf?" asked Is, wondering if it was kind to talk about the kid like this, to her face.

"Oh, no. She hears us very well."

Pye put out a long pink tongue.

"Are you hungry, you two?" Penny asked quickly. "Why don't you come below and see our quarters? There's plenty of room for you on this craft. She used to carry a crew of fifty, I believe."

She led the way down a companion-ladder, along a passage past cabin doors and into quite a fair-sized paneled room, shaped to the curve of the ship, containing a mahogany table and chairs.

Why the *pest*, thought Is, following, don't Aunt Ruth have a hug or a kiss for Arun? If she'd given him up for lost, if she'd worried about him so? What kind of a welcome is *that*? She talked to him as if he was the rent collector. These Silent Sect folk sure are a cussed lot.

As they sat down to a meal, everybody—except Pye, perhaps—felt a good deal of awkwardness and constraint, the kind of curb on natural chat that falls when people have not seen each other for a long time, people to whom a whole lot of strange and drastic things have happened in the meantime.

Moreover, Is had never met her aunt Ruth before, and Arun had never met his cousin Penelope. And besides, Is noticed, Arun had taken a strong instant dislike to Pye, which she returned with interest; she often stuck out her tongue at him and scowled horribly; then he would give her an angry look, at which she clung even more tightly to Ruth's hand.

"We use the officers' mess for eating," Penny was explaining matter-of-factly. "And the galley next door we cleared out too. Chock-full of chestnut burrs, we found it.

There's a plenty cabins with hammocks in 'em. But the hold down below is a real mess. Everything under this deck got pretty well mashed."

"What was in the hold?" asked Arun.

"Gunpowder, mainly," said Penny dryly. "So don't go poking around down there with a candle."

While Penny spoke, she was ladling out a stew of rabbit, parsnips, chestnuts, and mushrooms—much tastier, Is thought, than what the sailors had provided last night in the Cold Harbor. Pen always had been a right handy cook.

Ruth Twite fed little Pye with a spoon.

"Can't she feed herself yet?" demanded Is, surprised and shocked.

"Not always." Ruth raised her brows. "Some times better than other times."

Pye clung to Ruth's wrist all through the meal and insisted on being fed.

Afterward, while Ruth put Pye to bed in the second officer's cabin, Penny showed Is and Arun the rest of the ship.

"Pen—how long d'you reckon to *stay* here?" Is asked her sister.

She had told Penny about leaving de la Twite locked up in the barn, and her fear that he might have done the place some mischief when breaking his way out.

"He musta been as mad as a hornet by the time he got loose. I'm right sorry, Pen."

"And he's a nasty chap to tangle with at best, by all accounts." Penny shrugged and sighed. "No, I've not met

144

him, but I've heard plenty about him, and that sister of his, from Ruth. Well—it's too bad about the barn, but it can't be helped. So long as Pye's with us, I reckon we'll have to keep on the run."

"But Penny—does Aunt Ruth mean to keep Pye *forever*?"

Arun had wandered off to investigate the rigging; he had climbed up the shrouds and now was high in the chestnut tree's upper branches, looking out over the forest into the night sky.

Is went on, "Pye's such a spooky little chavey! And there's such a *lot* of trouble rising from her; the Merry Gentry taking other folks' kids—two, at least we've heard on—and everybody scared to put a foot out of doors. Is it *worth* it, Pen, just for that little hobgoblin?"

Penny said in a dry voice, "You mean it'd be better worth it if Pye had long gold hair and taking ways, then she'd be more value for people's trouble?"

"Well, no—perhaps not that—"

Penny said, "Ruth ain't one to turn back off a job once she's begun it. And she reckons it'd be a big step forward if the kid can get back her voice and learn to talk. Or write. Then, d'ye see, she could tell what she's seen. The Gentry had her as a hostage, you know, before she were handed back into Twite's keeping; only, it seems, the Gentry found her own folks didn't want her, so then, as no one cared what became of her, the Gentry passed her back to Twite, when Uncle Hose said there should be a Gentry hostage. Of course Twite was sore as a bear when he found out she'd no folks to care, for that lowered her value. But the

Gentry said she'd *the knowledge,* and could lay information about many of them. Only, of course, she can't talk. That's why Ruth is trying to teach her to write. Then, maybe, there'd be enough evidence to cop the Gentry."

"On the word of a little dumb kid? Teach her to *write?*" said Is dubiously. "Ain't she a bit young for that?"

"Young she may be," said Penny, "but she's sharp as a needle. Make no error about that! De la Twite, though, he gave her a real hard time. Hung up in a basket, so they say, all day, every day, over the rail track where it goes into the Channel Tunnel. Of course I've never seen it—"

"Croopus," said Is, who had, *"why?"*

"As a warning to the Gentry. She could be dropped down anytime. Under the train, you see."

Is remembered the round, black entrance, the red gate with its crisscross bars. She shivered.

"And at night he shut her in a box."

"A *box?*"

"So's she couldn't escape. She'd tried, ever so many times. That was when Ruth used to hear her screaming every night—when they lived next door in Cold Shoulder Road, you know. So, well, Ruth couldn't stand it. Happened I come down that way from Blackheath Edge, selling dolls to the fancy shops in Folkestone Parade, and I called in on Ruth, which I'd took the habit of doing, to ask if she'd news of you or Arun, and she said to me, 'What shall I do? I can't a-bear it any longer.' She'd asked the neighbors, she'd asked the parson, everybody said it wasn't their business, and it wouldn't do to rile the Gentry, and what did it matter about one half-witted kid? Dead scared, everyone was. Didn't want to meddle. So I said to Ruth, 'It's none of my affair either, but if you want to snatch her, you and she could hole up in my barn, and no one the wiser. No one visits there, not above twice a year. And I'm just off westwards, to buy wool in Dorset and china clay in Cornwall.' I give her a key to the barn. So that's what she done."

"You weren't there when she flitted?"

"Me? I was away in St. Ives. Didn't I just say? Then, as ill luck would have it, along came that pesky gale, and done a lot of damage, and all the Silent Blokes took and moved up the coast to Seagate. Ruth might ha' stayed where she was, and wouldn't have had Twite next door no more."

"But she'd still have thought of Pye screaming every night," said Is, half to herself. She asked, "What made you leave the barn, then?"

"We found one day a stranger had been, while we was out. Footprints. And your cat Figgin was real gnarled in his temper. It worried Ruth. She didn't want to take no chances. Little Pye had just begun to act a bit more human. And we heard about this-here ship, lodged in the tree, reckoned it might make a good place to perch. So we come and give it the once-over. And moved in."

"Aren't there neighbors who'd tell on ye?"

"In Womenswold? Nary a soul. It's only two farms. All the men were snatched by the Gentry when they were short of hands. And they got killed in some fray. The wives aren't agoing to tell on us. And one of the daughters is only ninepence in the shilling. We get milk and eggs and they help

when we need provisions. Take Pye for an outing sometimes."

"Ain't that risky? Someone might see her."

"Not round here. But once Henzie—that's the simple gal
—she did take Pye to Folkestone market. Ruth was wild
about that, when she heard. So now we don't take Pye to
the farm no more."

Is remembered her glimpse of Pye at the Folkestone market.

"I saw her at Folkestone. She didn't seem so babyish
there; she acted right sensible. Buying fish."

"I know," said Penny, sighing. "She acts babyish when
she's with Ruth. To get notice took of her. Makes me wild,
sometimes. But Ruth says we havta let her. She'll get over
it by and by."

Pye's babyish ways at breakfast next morning made Is
very impatient too, but she supposed Aunt Ruth knew what
she was about. One certain thing in Pye's favor was that
the cat Figgin seemed decidedly fond of her. He followed
her about, and jumped on her lap when she sat down—a
thing he had not yet deigned to do with Is, who was still in
disgrace. And Figgin was no fool at all when it came to
people.

People and cats is full of cussed ways, thought Is.

Indeed at breakfast Arun and his mother fell into a pain-
ful, sharp-edged quarrel.

It began when Ruth said that she saw no need for him to
take the horses back to Seagate.

"It is only putting yourself at risk. Quite needlessly."

"The man at the King's Head ought to have his horses back," said Arun doggedly. "Why should he be the loser, poor fellow?"

"Twite is a dangerous man. We'll be worried all day about you. Oh, when I think of how your poor father walked up to London, searching for you, *seventeen* times, and never found you—inconsiderate—just like a boy—never think of putting yourself in someone else's position—"

"Dad walked to London seventeen times because he *liked* rambling about the country—I'll lay he wasn't only looking for me," argued Arun. "He was always going off on those roaming walks. You can't deny that. Long before I ran off he'd be away for days on end, hunting for Ladies' Tresses orchids or Birds' Nest orchids. Ma! You know that's so."

"Oh! I believe you are just like him. A real Twite!"

"You're a Twite yourself!" retorted Arun. Mother and son glared at one another. Pye began to snuffle and tears poured down her cheeks. She stuck out her tongue at Arun as far as it would go.

"Keep on doing that! Maybe you'll learn to talk that way!" he snapped at her.

"Oh!" exclaimed Ruth. "How can you be so heartless to the poor afflicted child?"

"Maybe she needs more of that and not so much cosseting!"

Arun removed himself huffily and went off to Seagate, riding one horse, leading the other.

Is took him on one side before he went. "Arun! You will

149

be really, really careful, won't you? Y'mum ain't wrong about the risk."

And what Ruth don't know, thought Is, is the awful, baleful power that Dominic de la Twite has—over Arun, anyway. She thought of Arun's spellbound sleep, the gap in his memory covering all the time he was with the Leader. Yet she did not dare offer to go with Arun; that would seem as if she did not trust him to carry out a simple errand.

"But do make haste back!" she urged him. "We'll be right anxious till we see you."

"Never fear, never fear," he answered impatiently, and went off to where the hobbled horses were grazing. She watched him leave, kicking his mount into a trot. Bless him, she thought, I daresay he needs to get clear of all us females. Could be he's ashamed of being led off like a pig to market, yesterday, by old Domino. Let's hope this ride sets him up a bit in his own mind.

Sighing, Is went off in search of Penny.

Penny, never one to let the grass grow under her feet, had set herself up a doll-making workshop in the cook's galley of the *Throstle*. The fire in a brick box provided her with a means of melting wax and glue, singeing feathers, heating a flatiron; and she was busy, in the way Is remembered seeing her for years past, stuffing cotton bodies with sheeps' wool gathered from hedges, and fastening them onto china or porcelain or wax heads. Automatically Is sat down and began to help.

Penny nodded thanks, but said, "Better maybe ye should go and see if ye can be any use to Ruth, help learn little Pye to read. Or tell her stories, you used to be a rare hand at that."

"*You* used to tell *me* stories, Pen."

"Other way round as well." Pen threaded a needle, knotted the thread. "And it'd be a good turn to Ruth. She's mortal upset that Arun hardly more than handed her the time of day when they met."

"What?" cried Is, greatly astonished. "When *she* was so standoffish with him, and gave him no more than a little bit of a snippety nod? She must be moonstruck!"

"You gotta remember," said Pen, "she belonged to that plaguey Sect for most of her life. She ain't in the way of showing what she feels. She *never* used even to talk to Arun. Let alone hug or pet him. You gotta keep that in mind."

"Was Aunt Ruth always in the Sect?"

"No. She met Uncle Hose when she was fifteen, she told me—they were cousins, she's a Twite too—and they fancied each other and fixed to get wed. So she was obliged to join the Sect, for he was in it already."

"What a shame!" said Is. "I bet she was sorry. Fancy having to stop talking! I bet she hated it."

"Very like. Soon as he died, she began painting those pictures. As if someone had taken a lid off. Talking too. First time I met her, she hardly talked. Then, after I'd been to Folkestone a couple of times, we got friendly."

"That Sect are a rum lot," sighed Is. "I dunno what to make of 'em. Some of 'em ain't so bad. The only way the old 'uns seem to let loose is by dancing—have you seen 'em do that?"

Penny shook her head, biting her thread. Is described the solemn dance session she and Arun had watched in Seagate. "And I've heard the young 'uns gets together secretly at nighttime just to *talk*. That's a prime treat for them."

"They could do worse," said Penny briefly. "And I think the folk in the Sect are decent enough. It's only that Leader who's a wrong 'un. There's nowt wrong with silence. Most folk gab too much."

"I reckon the Leader's got pals in the Gentry," said Is.

She was about to tell Penny what she had heard at night in the forest, when a series of ear-splitting shrieks broke out in the officers' mess. Is leapt up from her stool, but Penny remained unperturbed.

"Pay no heed. That's Pye. The only sound she ever makes. She does that when summat riles her, or she can't have what she wants. Or tries to do one o' the things Ruth shows her, and can't."

"Croopus! How you *stand* it!" said Is, as the row went on. "I don't wonder Aunt Ruth snatched her, if she did that next door every night. "I only wonder nobody drownded her."

"Well," suggested Penny, "why don't you go and see if you can pacify her?"

"Me?"

"Why not?"

Is went into the officers' mess and found Ruth sitting at the mahogany table opposite Pye. Between them on the table lay a piece of paper and a slice of bread.

On the paper were written the letters B R E A D.

Pye was shrieking with terrific intensity and beating her fists on the table until they must have been bruised black and blue.

Is asked, "What's amiss with the chavey?"

Ruth was perfectly calm.

"I'm trying to make her see that *that*" — she pointed to the piece of bread — "and *these*" — she pointed to the letters on the paper — "and the spoken word *bread* all mean the same thing."

"Can't she take it in? Maybe she's too little — or too thickheaded — to understand?"

"Oh, no, she understands very well. But she wants to eat the bread."

Indeed Pye made a snatch for the slice while Ruth was speaking, and Ruth neatly whipped it out of reach. Pye stood up on her stool and jumped up and down in a passion of fury. Her round face was purple, her eyes were invisible, screwed into slits; she reminded Is of somebody. Who?

"She can't be that hungry?" Is said. "She had a big breakfast. I watched her. An egg, an apple, and four slices of bread and honey."

"No. She is not usually so demanding," Ruth answered quietly. "But, you see, she is jealous of Arun. Because he is my son. She is very quick at picking up other people's feelings. She knows well that I have been worried about Arun for so long, before he came here. Now that he has come, she is afraid that I will love him the better of the two. Is she not a foolish child?"

There was a smile in Ruth's voice. Is wondered if Pye

heard it. Pye still continued to shriek, but Is felt quite sure she was listening to what was said.

"Arun is afraid of the same thing," Is said. "He thinks you love Pye best."

"People wear themselves out with such needless worries," Ruth said.

And you do it too, Is thought.

"Aunt Ruth?"

"Well?"

"Can I try something with Pye?"

"By all means," said Ruth.

Is said to Pye in thought-language, "Pye? Can you hear me? Can you understand what I am saying to you? I am thinking about a fox and a big black bird. Both of them want that piece of bread. The fox is running, the bird is flying through the air. Which do you think will get to it first?"

Pye looked up, astonished. Her pale eyes had become round again, round as marbles. I wonder if she needs glasses? thought Is. I suddenly have a picture of her with glasses on her face. Rimless ones. Now, why should I think that?

She said to Pye, "Do you know the word for bread? Those letters on the paper make that word. These are their sounds. B-R-E-A-D. Press your lips together, then open them as if you were going to take a bite. Then bring your tongue forward and press it just behind your teeth. *Bread*. That is what those sounds mean, written down on the paper."

Pye said, in thought-language, "The big black bird is going to get the bread first."

Then she jumped down from her stool and, with tears streaming down her face, rushed to Ruth Twite and grabbed her round the waist, burying her face in Ruth's lap. In thought-language she shouted at Is, "Go away! Go away! I hate you! I don't want you here! Not at all. This is *my* home, not yours!"

Is looked doubtfully at Ruth, who laid a calming hand on Pye's head.

"Perhaps you had better leave her with me, just for the time. But I do not think that you have done her any harm. No, not at all."

By dusk three people in the ship *Throstle* were not even trying to conceal their worry about Arun.

"It *couldn't* take him more than a couple of hours to walk here from Seagate," Ruth said, half to herself, over and over.

"Maybe he had to wait till dark to start out, so folks wouldn't see him," Penny suggested.

"Or take a roundabout way in case he was followed," said Is.

"Oh, why, why did I ever let him go with those horses?" Ruth demanded. "One of the girls from the farm could have gone. Why didn't I think of that?"

Arun would never have agreed to that, thought Is. For it would have connected the farm to the horses and the trip to Penny's barn.

But there was no sense in arguing.

Little Pye clung like a limpet to Ruth's hand. The cat Figgin marched restlessly about, jumped on the table, finally consented to come and push his face into that of Is, but with a growl that said, Don't you dare to leave me for so long, not ever again!

It's the first time that Arun and I have been apart for so long since we came south together, Is thought; I do wish I could catch some echo from his mind, just to give me a notion where he is.

Just as she thought this she *did* catch the echo—perhaps it had prompted the wish. She knew that he was trudging wearily through the forest, but that, for some reason, he was coming from an unexpected direction, from due west.

Could he have got lost? Or did he have to muddle his trail? Was somebody after him?

Not wishing to raise premature hopes, Is slipped away from where the others were sitting.

Pye had already gone off on some errand of her own.

"It's nearly your bedtime, Pye," Ruth called after her.

Very handy for Pye she can't speak, Is thought; she need never trouble to answer.

Going to the quarterdeck to let down the rope ladder—for, with a huge rush of relief, she now knew that Arun was only a bowshot's length away—Is found Pye, at the top of the ladder, busily engaged in sawing through the strands of the rope with a sharp kitchen knife.

Is could hardly believe her eyes.

"Why—you—little—*monster*! Just you pass over that schliver! Right away!"

Pye gave her a stony look. But Is was much larger and stronger. The knife was sullenly passed over. Pye would then have made off along the deck, but Is grabbed her stubby wrist and held her fast.

"Do you want I should tell Ruth that you were fixing to break Arun's neck? Do you?" Is asked Pye in thought-language.

"Let me go! Let me go!"

"Pye? Where are you? It's past your bedtime!" came Ruth's voice.

Pye wriggled free from Is and ran off nimbly through the tangle of spars, ropes, and branches.

Is, hard at work retying the rope ladder with the slashed length of rope safely above the top shackle bolt, called out reassuringly, "Pye's along here, Aunt Ruth. And I can hear Arun a-coming!"

"Oh, thank goodness," said Ruth in deep relief.

And Is sent a message along the deck after Pye: "You and I will have some business to settle tomorrow, young 'un!"

When Arun climbed back on board he looked deathly tired, very much more like a cat than a boy. "What happened to you?" Is flashed to him in thought-speak, and he flashed back, "I'll tell you when I've sat down and had something to eat."

In the officers' mess he flopped down with his head on his arms until Penny put a bowl of soup in front of him.

And even then, he was able to eat only half of it; Figgin kindly finished it off.

"What happened?" Is asked again, aloud this time.

"I took the nags back to the King's Head," Arun said. "It was early still. Tom Braburn was sweeping his chimney before breakfast. He was pleased as Punch to get his horses back—he'd been puzzled as he'd looked to have them home the same day and got no word on the matter from Twite. I said Will Fobbing had been taken queer in the woods and Twite had gone for help so we fetched back the horses —it sounded pretty scaly and he gave me a queer look and said he hoped to get paid for the hire of them soon. I said would he like help with the chimney, because I used to do that with Dad and knew how; and he said yes, which was lucky, for not long after, in comes the Leader himself. *'Don't tell him I'm here,'* I whispered to Tom, and I rubbed handfuls of soot all over my face and stuck my head up the chimney.

"Twite was in very bad skin. He'd had to walk miles to find a farm and another pair of horses that he could borrow to bring back the chaise. And Fobbing had wandered off into the woods in a dozy state and not come back for hours. And the two kids had run off and left Twite in the basket, he said, and he got stuck inside a barn and had to burn it down to get free."

"Burn down a barn?" said Is, horrified. But Penny just shrugged.

"What d'you expect?" she said. "If he's a wrong 'un, barns is just tiddlywinks to him."

"What happened then?" asked Ruth, who had returned from putting Pye to bed.

"Twite was paying Tom for the hire of the horses—I was still hid behind the bar with my face blacked, out of sight—when Twite chanced to see that Charles the First coin that we gave Tom for our breakfast the other day, and he got very excited, looked and looked at it, and said, Where did it come from? Lucky Tom said he wasn't sure, he found it at the end of the day's takings. And de la Twite said he'd got one too, and that must mean somebody had come on Charles the First's treasure from the Goodwin Sands."

"Where did the coins come from?" asked Ruth.

Is had left it to Arun to tell his mother about the transfer of her pictures to the Admiral's cave. So far he had not done so.

"We found some crocks of stuff underground," he said vaguely. "Near Folkestone."

"Did you so? Good heavens! The cache that your father was always hoping to find!"

"*Was* he?" said Arun indignantly.

"Always. Amos Furze had heard this tale of all the money and precious objects which had been lost. To him it seemed that treasure must have been laid up to help the Silent Sect travel to America, and buy land and settle there."

Is thought of the three huge earthenware containers filled with heaven only knew what—coins and forks and cups and necklaces, doubtless all made of silver and gold.

More than enough, surely, to fix up the Silent Folk in comfort in the New World.

But Arun's thoughts were traveling in a different direction. "So—all the time that Dad gave out he was hunting for Bee Orchids and Green Man Orchids—he was *really* just after King Charles's treasure? And that tale he told of traveling to London seventeen times a-hunting for me—walking back and forth—that was just a load of gullyfluff?"

"No, it was *not*," said Ruth sternly. "He *was* looking for you too."

Is agreed. "When I saw him—that last time—it was you he was a-seeking, Arun. No question."

Ruth sent her a grateful look.

"But go on with the story," Penny demanded. "What happened with Twite? When he saw the coin?"

"Oh, he told Tom a long tale about two thieving children who were supposed to take him where the Handsel Kid was hid, and how they had robbed him in a wood, and locked him in a barn, and poisoned Will Fobbing, and how he was going to tell the constables and have us hunted down and taken up, for he guessed we had summat to do with the Gentry. And I could see Tom didn't quite know which of us to believe, so I crawled on my stomach through the coal hole while Tom was drawing a pint of cider for Twite. I was feared to death he'd spot me. But he didn't. And then, on the beach, who should I see but that Romany woman who was at the Cold Harbor. She walked into the inn. I dassn't loiter, so I ran like a hare to the Swannetts'

160

house—they were both there, and I asked if I could hide till Twite was out of the way. Micah wasn't best pleased, but Window allowed me. I told what had happened in the woods and she said we did right. But then, chase me if Twite himself didn't come a-knocking, to ask if they knew aught of my whereabouts. Window began writing slowly on a slate, so I slipped out the back way, onto the beach. I thought I was done for . . . But that girl—do you remember?" he said to Is. "That teasing black-haired girl we saw after the old folks dancing—"

"I remember," said Is. "Her name's Jen Braburn. The landlord's daughter. She had a red dress."

"She was on the beach, a-dragging along a big basket on wheels, piled high with crabs." Arun shuddered. "She said, 'What's up with you, boy, you running off from your teacher?' I said no, it was that cove Twite who was after me, so she said, 'Dive in among the crabs and I'll wheel you off the shore.' So I did. I dived in under a whole lot of live crabs"—he shuddered again at the memory—"and Jen wheeled me away from the beach. She was laughing fit to split her stays, and she started to sing as she walked along —at the top of her voice. She sang that song I made up when we saw the old ladies and gents dancing. Remember?" Is nodded. "By and by she said, 'Well, boy? Didn't I learn your song good? Can you guess why I was singing it?' I said no. She said, 'Cos Twite hisself was walking by and he purely *hates* singing. I knew that'd make him hurry by, and it did.'"

"So where did Jen take you?"

"Took me to her grandma's house. The grandma has a donkey cart and was just going to drive off to Each End with the crabs. So they loaded the crabs into the cart on top of me, and the grandma drove me all the way to Each End —not the way I wanted to go, but it got me out of Seagate. Jen came along part of the way and she told me about LOMAK."

"What *is* LOMAK?"

"Like the old girl in the woods told us, it means something about Mums and Kids."

"What do they do?"

"Meet together, I suppose. Talk."

"What's the good of that?"

"Better than nothing, I reckon."

"What was the song?" Ruth wanted to know. "What was the song you sang, Arun, when you saw the old people dancing?"

"Oh, just an old bit of a song," said Arun hastily. "I can't sing it now."

He scowled and added, "I'm all tuckered out, I'm off to bed."

Ruth looked mightily disappointed, Is observed, as Arun limped off to his hammock.

Figgin went after him, attracted by the strong smell of crab.

"Aunt Ruth?" asked Is. "Have you painted any more pictures since you came here?"

Ruth sighed.

"No, I have not," she said. "Partly for lack of materials.

162

There is no lack of canvas—I could cut squares from all these dangling sails, and stretch them on frames made from spars—but I have no paints. I left them behind."

Is was shocked. "We could get you paints!" she said. "Easy! Pen and I could go off to Canterbury—or Maidstone—couldn't we, Pen?—where folk don't know us. Why not?"

Ruth said, "I'm afraid that painting pictures is a form of self-indulgence. My most important task is to teach Pye to talk. And to write. When she can put her thoughts into words, she will not have so much choked-up anger inside her. And also," Ruth added practically, "she will be able to give useful information about the Merry Gentry."

"But *you* can do that—can't you, Aunt Ruth? You've seen all their faces and made drawings of 'em—when you worked for the dentist, Fishskin? That was what old Mrs. Lillywhite told me. They all have tattoo marks on their tongues, so you know which of 'em were in the gang."

Ruth burst out laughing. "Is that what people believe? Oh, good heavens, the nonsensical tales that fly around—especially when crimes are committed, or people are afraid . . . It is quite true that I used to make drawings of Denzil Fishskin's patients, at night, after I had gone home—but as for tattoo marks on tongues, no such thing! That is pure invention. I do remember one man who had a burn mark on his tongue—he told a most unlikely story about a toasting fork—I thought at the time it could hardly be true—but as for tattoo marks, fiddlesticks! That is the way false rumors start to circulate."

Is was very disappointed. "What happened to the man with the burnt tongue?"

"I believe he died not long after—gored by a bull—"

"But what about your drawings of the dentist's patients?" Is asked, wondering if her aunt had heard of the fate of Mr. Boles, who boasted that he had seen pictures of the Gentry, and came to his horrible end in Shadoxhurst Wood.

Ruth laughed again. "Oh, Pye scribbled all over them when she was in one of her tantrums. Nobody could recognize his own mother from *those* pictures. No, I fear the Merry Gentry run no risk from me. But if only Pye could learn to speak . . . She has seen them all, many times. It makes me angry that this evil group should keep the country round here in such a grip of terror. Everybody should work against them."

"Well," said Is, "I'm with you there, Aunt Ruth, buckle and thong. And if teaching that little flip-flap to talk is the way to make a start, let's get right to work."

Ruth said, "I could see that, earlier, you were able to meet her mind in a way that I cannot."

"Why, you see, Aunt Ruth—Arun and I have learned to talk to each other in thoughts. We learned how when we was up north. *It's like this,*" she went on in thought-speech to Ruth. *"Can you hear me? When I talk like this?"*

Ruth looked at her blankly.

"Can you hear what I am saying?" Is repeated. Then, in words, "You didn't hear?"

Sadly, Ruth shook her head.

"Some people can, some can't," Is said. "It's like being able to sing in tune."

"Arun's songs," said his mother. "How I wish he would start to sing them again. I loved them so much."

"You heard them?" Is was astonished. "I thought he never dared sing them at home."

"Nor he did, poor boy. He used to slip out and climb the brambly hill at the end of Cold Shoulder Road." Is nodded. She remembered that hill. "He used to sing them there, very softly, to himself. He didn't know that I used to slip out too, and listen, hiding in a hawthorn bush. Oh, his father would have been so angry with us! Breaking the Holy Silence! Oh, why do men make these stupid rules for themselves?"

Ruth wiped an indignant tear from her eye.

"I think he'd like to start singing again now, and make up more," said Is. "It's as if the songs are all jammed up inside and can't come out. But he's getting better. The other night, in the Cold Harbor, he was singing away like a throstle."

"Well—let us hope that it will happen again."

"But Aunt Ruth, about your flower pictures—I'm afeered you won't be best pleased when you hear. Mrs. Boles your neighbor was right desperate to get 'em away, and old Admiral Fishskin was right anxious to lodge 'em in his cave—so that's what we done. We shifted the whole load up to the Admiral's place."

"Humph," said Ruth thoughtfully. "I—once, when I was in the woods, looking for one of Hosiah's orchids, after he

165

died—for he did truly love orchids, he wasn't *only* a treasure hunter—I saw something strange—"

"What, Aunt Ruth?"

"No," said Ruth, "I will not talk about that yet. It would be wrong to pass on what is only a suspicion. We should not encourage others to think evil thoughts of people, for suspicion breeds faster than sickness."

Not a word more would she say. She asked Is, instead, to tell the story of how the cousins had met in the ruined city of Blastburn, and how they managed to save the coal miners before the mines were flooded.

Is went off to sleep in a hammock in the third lieutenant's cabin, thinking how much she liked her aunt Ruth. Wisht *I'd* had a ma like her. Too bad Arun can't act more kindly to her.

But then, of course, when he was small, she never talked to *him*.

If you ask me, thought Is, swinging impatiently in her hammock, which took some getting used to, those Silent Coves have a lot to answer for. Holy Silence my great-aunt Abigail!

Next day Is said to Arun, "Listen, boy, we gotta teach that little half-jigger to talk and scribe. And that right fast."

He was sitting morosely up in the crosstrees, which were tangled into a complicated mare's nest among the seven or eight main boughs of the chestnut tree.

Is scrambled up and sat beside him. The view over the

top of the forest was magnificent. Most of the neighboring trees were oaks, just coming into rose-colored bud; north-ward, the spires of Canterbury could be seen, and west-ward the dark, furry heights of the North Downs.

"Why?" Arun demanded. "Why should I put myself out to teach that little goblin anything? Every time she sees me she spits or puts out her tongue."

"Maybe if she put out her tongue a hundred times an hour, it would start her talking."

"Who wants to hear her talk? She's a pain even when she keeps quiet."

"Arun! You gotta remember she was hung in a basket over the rail track for months on end. And at night, shut up in a box. You can't expect her to be a holy angel."

"Holy terror, more like. Well," he said reluctantly, "what are *we* supposed to do?"

"She catches on to thought-speak pretty well . . ."

"You two!" called Penny from below. "Can you go to the farm and get some eggs and milk? Ruth's teaching Pye—or trying to—and I'm making dolls' slippers. A person usually comes from the farm about now, and they haven't—I hope nothing's wrong. Go carefully—keep to the bushes. It's all woods till you get to within a stone's throw of the haybarn."

As they climbed down the ladder they could hear Pye's indignant shrieks and Ruth's patient, instructing voice. It's a bit hard on Arun, Is thought, that when he does find his mum again, she's so taken up with teaching that little mon-key.

As they neared the farm buildings—a big brick half-timbered house, and a group of thatched barns—Arun halted warily.

"I feel," he said in thought-language, "there's trouble—do you get it too?"

"Yes I do. Someone's in awful pain or grief—someone we know. Wait: I know who it is. Oh, mercy, Arun, it's poor Window Swannett! She's there, in the house. And she's in bad trouble."

Arun nodded. He had got the message too.

They crept forward warily, skirted the haybarn, and went, without waiting to be invited, through the back door of the farmhouse, which stood open. A passage led to the spacious farm kitchen, which they found filled with people, and also with a feeling of wretchedness, so thick that it was like smoke.

Later Is came to know the people well, and had them sorted out. There were two Mrs. Lees, two Mrs. Warrens, three Lee daughters, and two Warren daughters. There was also Window Swannett, with a black shawl over her head, sitting on a footstool, racked with sobs, drowned in tears. Jen Braburn was there too, in her red dress.

But the person who took all the attention of Is and Arun, when they first entered the room, was the woman in the armchair beside the glowing range, at whose knee Window Swannett was sitting.

She was by far the biggest human being Is had ever seen. She must weigh as much as an ox—no, more, Is thought. I wonder they could find a chair to hold her! And how old she looks! She could be a hundred—easy.

This monumental woman wore loose black clothing, a black headscarf wound tight, and gold hoops in her ears.

Her hand was on Window Swannett's shoulder, comforting her.

She was blind.

But, for all that, highly alert.

She turned her head as Arun and Is came into the room, and her thoughts picked them up in a flash. "There you are, then! And not before time!"

Other heads now turned to look at Is and Arun.

"We're from—from the tree," Arun began explaining, in halting words. "My mum's Mrs. Ruth Twite—"

"Tell us something we don't know," said the massive woman. Now she, too, spoke aloud. "Trouble's coming up to a head, here. And it's you two who have to untie the tangle."

"Why us?" demanded Arun. But Is cried, "What's *happened*?"

A middle-aged woman, who bore a strong resemblance to the huge old lady, said, "I'm Mrs. Hannah Lee. That's my mother there, Mrs. Nefertiti Lee. Mrs. Swannett, here, she's come to us, because they took off her husband—"

"*Micah?* Who took him?"

"Men in black. First they dragged the poor devil behind a cart, with his hands tied, all along the road through Seagate. Then they dumped him in a boat, hoisted the sail, and sent it out to sea."

"The Gentry did this?"

"Who else?"

"But why? Why should they take Micah? What harm had he done them?"

"It was to make an example," whispered Window. "To frighten the rest."

But Is had a miserable feeling that it was because of her and Arun; that Micah was punished for taking them into his house and befriending them. It's our fault he was taken, she thought.

Dominic de la Twite is connected in some way to the Gentry. I thought it when I heard those whispering voices in the wood. Maybe the Silent Sect don't realize that their Leader is mixed up with the skellums. But I'm certain of it.

But what to do about him?

"You must work on his weaknesses," the voice of Mrs. Nefertiti Lee broke in on her thoughts. "All men have weaknesses, and wicked men have many more than others."

"But what *are* his weaknesses, missus?"

Is looked at the pale, massive old face, which was like a mask cut from rock.

"He loves pretty things. Colors. The Silent People don't approve of such things. So he must keep that failing of his a secret."

Is thought of the Admiral, hiding away Ruth's pictures in his cave. What kind of thing would Dominic de la Twite choose to hide away? And where would he hide it?

Arun spoke suddenly, surprising everybody.

"I think . . . that Micah is not dead," he said. "Just then I had a faint, faint touch from him—like a nod, over miles of emptiness—"

170

"You are strong for receiving such messages," said old Mrs. Nefertiti Lee with approval. "Go back to your tree and throw yourselves wide open—try to find out where Micah has gone. Then it may be your task to go in search of him."

Is could almost have laughed, Arun looked so appalled.

He mumbled, "But my mum wants us to teach that brat to talk—"

"Do that first, then! But lose no time about it. Now go—hurry."

Her thoughts almost pushed them out of the farm kitchen.

"Missus," said Is. "Just a moment. Feel these."

She pulled the string of brown beads from her pocket. Window had wrapped them in a scrap of oilskin. Is unwrapped them, wiped off some of the dust, and handed them to Mrs. Nefertiti. The old hands, gnarled as tree roots, held the baubles for a moment, pouring them to and fro like sand.

"Tangerines!" said the aged voice unexpectedly.

"*Tangerines*, missus?"

"They will do especially well. They must have been sent. I think this is a sign that the current has turned, and is now running in our favor."

"But—but what am I to *do* with 'em, missus?"

"That is for you to discover, child," said the old voice with impatience. "But now leave me to comfort this poor one."

Already, though, Window Swannett was beginning to

show a look of faint hope. She was not quite so drenched in misery.

"You'll stay here with us, now, dearie," Mrs. Warren was saying comfortably. "Till matters mend, as they surely will, you stay here."

Croopus, what have Arun and me got laid on us? thought Is, trudging back to the chestnut tree with her share of a load of eggs and milk.

They soon discovered that teaching Pye was harder work than any job they had done before in the whole of their lives.

"Chopping out coal in the mines was easy as daisy chains compared to this," growled Arun after the first day.

Pye would not sit still for more than about three minutes at a stretch; she was off chasing Figgin—always happy to be chased—or hanging upside down from the yardarm, pulling faces at her would-be teachers; or weaving strange little basketwork mats out of twigs, or drawing crisscross patterns with charcoal twigs on bits of canvas, apparently taking not the slightest notice of the thoughts they kept launching at her. But just the same, every now and then, they knew that a streak of thought had slipped past her guard.

"Leave me alone!" she would hurl back. "I'm not going to talk your stupid words. I'm *never* going to talk. What good has talking ever done *you?*"

"It's done us a whole lot of good," asserted Arun.

And Is said, "Arun wasn't *allowed* to talk when he was

your age. And that made him wholly miserable. He's ever so much better now."

"If he's better now," rudely retorted Pye, "he must have been rotten-awful before!"

And she scurried into the rigging, with Figgin in enthusiastic pursuit.

Is picked up their lunch of rolls and cheese and went after the pair.

"You want a bit of bread and cheese, Pye?"

Pye nodded, and made a grab. Is dodged it.

"Say *bread*, then! Say *cheese*!"

Pye glared at her, and made another unsuccessful grab. Thoughts came hissing out of her like red-hot arrows.

"You tyrant! You beast. You big bully! Why should I say words because *you* tell me to?"

"Because you might get to like it, once you start. You never know! You like drawing pictures, don't you? You like weaving those mats. Using words is like weaving mats. You can make poems with them. You can make songs. You can make patterns."

Pye furiously stuck out her tongue.

"Keep doing that," teased Arun, who had climbed up beside Is. "Your tongue might learn to speak all by itself."

Pye hastily snatched her tongue in again.

"Give me a bit of that bread and cheese," she ordered in thought-language.

"All right. But first you must say *bread*. Say *cheese*. Say *bread and cheese*."

Arun suddenly began to sing:

"High up in the trees
we're singing bread and cheese
as tuneful as the finches
under leafy canopies . . .

High up in the trees
easy as we please
we're munching as we gaze across
unbounded distances . . ."

He took a bite and chewed it with a look of tremendous relish, then sang, with his mouth full:

"High up in the trees
we picnic at our ease
we wouldn't change a banquet for
our lunch of bread and cheese . . ."

All Arun's tunes were as simple as "Baa, Baa, Black Sheep." This one was too, and yet Is was sure that she had never heard it before, that it had never *existed* before. Is joined in:

"High up in the trees,
and rocking in the breeze
we wouldn't change our crust of bread
for duckling and green peas —

"Come on, Pye! You sing too!"
And Is tossed her a roll with cheese in it.
Pye opened her mouth. Apparently without her permission, words poured out of it:

"High up in the trees,
   Arun's just a tease!
   Why should I be made to sing
   for measly bread and cheese?"

And then she furiously flung the roll down onto the deck, where Ruth was standing, and jumped after it.

They had been a good height up among the branches, and she might have hurt herself badly had not Arun hurled himself downward, grabbing at the shrouds as he went, and managing also to grab Pye in midfall.

She was not a bit grateful, but struggled with him as fiercely as a wildcat, pulled herself away, and grabbed a metal-ringed grommet from the deck. She flung it at Arun, hitting him in the face. Then she ran to Ruth and clung around her waist as if she would never allow herself to be prized loose again.

"I *won't* talk! I *won't!*" she was shouting at the top of her lungs. "Pye won't sing your silly song. Not ever! Bread-andcheese! I won't say it! I won't!"

"All right, my honey," said Ruth, half laughing and half crying. "No one shall make you, I promise. No one *can* make you. You can talk or not, just absolutely as you choose."

"And that won't be *ever!*" roared Pye, picking up her roll and taking a tremendous bite out of it.

Arun was spitting teeth and blood onto the planking.

"Little demon!" he gasped indignantly. "Look what she's done to me!"

"Oh dear me! You'll have to pay a visit to the dentist now, my son. Aren't you sorry, Pye, for what you did?"

"Not a bit!" said Pye. "It's his own fault."

And she took another bite of bread and cheese.

Six

Ruth was terribly distressed when she heard the story of what had happened to Micah Swannett.

"But he was a *good* man! That poor, poor woman! And she had lost her sons—what can she do?"

"She's going to stay on at the farm," Is said.

"Yes, Mrs. Nefertiti will be able to help her if anyone can. Advise her."

"Aunt Ruth—who in the world *is* Mrs. Nefertiti?"

Ruth said, "She is Mrs. Hannah Lee's grandmother. She came to the farm a few months ago. Where she had been before, nobody quite knows; it seems she had walked the roads with her husband, Pharaoh, but *what* roads, and where, she has not said. . . ."

"Her husband Pharaoh? What happened to him?"

"I think he died. She told me, 'He went on ahead,' and she said something about setting fire to his ship and sending it out to sea."

Is shivered, thinking of Micah Swannett. "How can we stop these Gentry, Aunt Ruth?"

Ruth pressed her hands to her forehead. "One day," she said to herself, "men will learn to split the atom."

"What's an atom?"

"It's the smallest grain of the basic stuff from which we are all made. As cakes are made from flour." Ruth held up her slender, worn hand. Her fingers were transparent against the spring sunshine. "Pull that grain apart, you release a torrent of energy. Like—like an egg hatching. Crash! Out comes an eagle! In the same way—I think—out of each person, each simple, plain person, can come such power that, if properly used, it could shoot an arrow to the sun. Or sow a thousand oak trees and make them grow overnight to the height of a tower. All you need is to harness that force."

"Yes, but how d'you reckon to do that, Aunt Ruth?" Privately, Is thought that her aunt Ruth's ideas were all a bit too faraway, not much use for the practical present.

"That is the hard question! First we have to unlock the frightful cage of fear in which greedy, wicked men, for their own gain, have so many good, simple people imprisoned."

Is remembered what Mrs. Nefertiti had said. "Look for their weaknesses, the old gal told me."

"Yes. Like splitting a rock—you study the grain, strike where a crack shows—"

"But what's the weak spot of the Gentry?"

Ruth sighed. "The weaknesses of their leader. Whatever those are."

Penny and Arun came out on deck. Penny had already started to work over Arun, to change his appearance so that he could go to the dentist in Seagate without being recognized by anybody. She had stained his skin light brown with walnut juice (which she used for dying dolls' tippets). Now, out on deck, she cut his hair a good deal shorter, and darkened it with tar and grease until it was almost black. He had also been fitted out, from the ship's stores, with a sailor's canvas trousers, white drill vest, reefer jacket, black kerchief, and round black hat.

He looked thin and changed and foreign.

"You'd best tell the dentist that you are a midship-lad who had his teeth knocked out in a gale by the swinging boom."

"Or somebody bashed me with a marlinspike. And I'm on my way to London port to pick up another ship," mumbled Arun, recalling the sailors at the Cold Harbor. His tongue was swollen and sore; he found it hard to speak, and quite impossible to sing.

"Best not be too free with your tales of ships," Is suggested. "If that Fishskin dentist is a rib-chum of his cousin the Admiral, he likely knows all the craft that puts in to Dover and Folkestone."

"I wish I needn't go to *him*," croaked Arun. "If only there were another—"

"Phoo, phoo, boy, you can't walk around for the rest of your days with two teeth busted and one missing," said Penny. "You can't talk, you can't sing, and that broken dogtooth is wearing a hole in your tongue. Sooner that's set right, the better."

Nobody had scolded Pye for the damage she had done to Arun, since it was plain that she had not intended to hurt him so badly and was startled by what had happened. And it was clear, too, that she felt some guilt and dismay; instead of stumping noisily about the deck on her own concerns, as was her usual habit, she had retired into a corner of the galley and stayed there, curled up defensively, sucking her thumb, with Figgin huddled beside her.

When Arun's disguise was complete and he was pronounced fit to set off to Seagate, Pye sidled up to him and pushed a dirty scrap of paper into his hand.

"What's this, then, cully?" he said in some surprise, peering at it.

On the paper Pye had written with a stick of charcoal: PLES FOR GIV.

"But Pye!" mumbled Arun, coughing out a little more blood in his astonishment. "When did you ever learn to write?"

"I been learning this while," whispered Pye, with downcast eyes.

"Well, you are a proper little caution!"

Everybody exclaimed over Pye, and Arun rumpled her spiky hair and gave her a bloodstained, gap-toothed grin.

"You and me 'ull have some parleys, I reckon, when I get back with my new teeth, young 'un."

"*Try* not to get into trouble, Arun," Ruth said anxiously. "Penny has certainly done a notable job on changing your looks, but I shall worry—"

Just so's he don't meet Old Domino in the street, thought Is. I'd back Old Domino to see through that window dressing. After all he really *studied* Arun. But she kept that fear to herself.

180

"Pye," she said suddenly, struck by an idea, "what are tangerines?"

Pye scowled and shrank away. Was she going to slip back into her old hostile habits?"

"Tangerines?" said Ruth. "Why should you ask Pye that?"

"Something the old gal said about the things Twite is keen on."

Again Is unrolled the dusty brown beads from their waterproof cover, and rubbed away a little of the dust with one finger. A brilliant golden gleam flashed out. The stones were like little suns.

"Bless my soul!" said Ruth. "They must be worth a pretty penny!"

And Penny, looking over Ruth's shoulder, exclaimed, "Well, I'll be dragged! Brown diamonds!"

"*Brown* diamonds? What in tarnation are they? And how d'you know that, Pen?"

"Remember Mr. Van Doon, the Dutchman what used to lodge with us?" said Penny. "He knew a deal about gemstones. And he told me about brown diamonds. Showed me a tiny one once. In the trade they are called tangerines. They come from High Brazil. They must be just about the rarest, most uncommon stones there be."

"That's what these are?" Is cast her mind back to the old lady at the farm. "Yes, Mrs. Nefertiti said the same . . ."

Pye was now eager to speak. "Tangerine *rubies*, too," she said. "Twite has. In a spark-pin, like a twig with fruit."

"A brooch? You've seen this, Pye? When?"

Pye nodded vigorously. "One night. In Twite's house. Pye wide awake. Sleep not. Get out of bed. Go down stair. Twite has tray with stones. Shine. Pretty! Brown. Gold. Orange. Ginger color. Red. Burnt yellow. All shining. Twite sees Pye. Oh, terrible angry. After that, shut in box. Every night. Tells Pye, you speak these things, I drop under train. So Pye don't speak. Not ever."

"And I don't blame you," said Ruth, giving her a hug. "Pye did very sensibly."

"Now, steady the buffs," said Penny. "This-here Twite is crazy-keen on collecting sparklers. Extra-specially, tangerine-colored ones. That right, young 'un?"

Pye nodded again, big-eyed.

"So all we gotta do is show him one of these mibbies— and say we have more of 'em salted away—and then we'll have him on toast?"

"Ye-e-es," said Ruth doubtfully. "But—even supposing we could persuade him to come somewhere, by means of such a temptation—*then* what would we do?"

"True," said Penny. "He's not going to mend his ways just for one necklace, even of brown sparklers."

The cat Figgin came back from a bird's-nesting foray in the upper shrouds and jumped up onto the captain's card table, which, as the day was fine, Ruth had brought up on deck so that Pye could do her reading and writing lessons in the fresh air.

The dusty necklace of brown diamonds still lay in a tangle on the green baize.

When Figgin saw the beads he behaved strangely. Hissing and growling, with his ears back and all his fur on end, he retreated at speed from the table and made off to a far corner of the deck, where he washed himself furiously all over several times.

"Saints save us!" said Penny. "What's got into the cat? He sure don't like those stones."

"Perhaps he mistook the necklace for a snake?" suggested Ruth.

"Figgin's not such a dummy."

"Perhaps something bad happened to it once?"

"He's never acted so before." Is was puzzled. She slid the beads into her pocket. "Here, Figs, Figs, Figwiggin!"

But so long as she had the stones on her, the cat would not come near.

"Maybe that's why he was so unfriendly when I first came aboard."

"Well," said Penny, "if the stones are that valuable, it's best, anyway, you shouldn't carry them loose in your britches pocket all the time—you might lose 'em or drop 'em. Why don't you put them in one o' those little rowan-wood boxes I bought from a peddler for keeping dolls' eyes in."

"Rowan wood should be good," agreed Is, "if there's owt spooky about the stones."

She rewrapped and packed the beads neatly into the little wooden casket.

Arun unexpectedly said, "Can I have a single stone? Just one? To take along with me?"

Ruth gave him a doubtful look.

"What for?"

"In case—in case—oh, I dunno. To be on the safe side. Maybe to pay for my new teeth!"

"Are you mad, boy? You offer the dentist a brown diamond, he'd have you clapped in the pokey before you could sneeze. I can give you *plenty* of dibs for your teeth," said Penny firmly.

But Arun still persisted. "If Twite has such a craving for stones, perhaps I could contrive to drop one in his way—with a clue as to where it came from."

"Sounds a mite dicey," said Penny, giving him a sharp look.

Is caught a picture in Arun's mind: the cave by the three great tubs of treasure—the loose, terribly dangerous sandy roof. If Twite could be lured into that cave, Arun was thinking, he might never come out alive.

"But, Arun," she said, speaking aloud, "that cave's a death-hole. You mustn't go near it yourself! Promise!"

"How can I promise?" he said impatiently. "How can I tell what will happen? I just think it would be a useful thing to have one of the beads along with me."

"Oh—very well." She took the beads from their rowan-wood box and passed them over to Penny, who, with skilled fingers, unknotted the silken plait on which they were threaded, unfastened the clasp, slid off the end bead, reknotted the silk, and put the clasp back on.

Arun nodded his thanks, tied the bead in the corner of his regulation calico midshipman's neckerchief (which had the words PROPERTY OF H.M. NAVY embroidered by the hem

184

in red chain stitch) and mumbled, in an effort to sound carefree, "I'll be off, then. See you by cock-shut," and climbed over the rail.

They heard him go off through the wood, trying to whistle but not succeeding very well.

Then, when he must have been about a mile away, long since out of earshot, Is, to her astonishment, began to catch, in thought-form, the sound of his voice singing. It was like a tickle in her mind, and she cried out involuntarily. "Oh, how queer! How very queer! That's never happened before!"

"What is it?" asked Ruth.

"You got hiccups?" said Penny.

"No, but I suddenly heard Arun singing—inside of my head!"

"You think there's something amiss with him?" Ruth at once asked anxiously.

"No—no—he sounded quite happy—just walking along, singing inside of his mind."

"What song?"

Ruth sounded a little wistful—not envious of Is, but just as if she would give anything in the world for a chance to hear her son sing inside his head.

"A song he sang the other night in the Cold Harbor." Is sang it herself: " 'If I had a bird that would bounce or a ball that could fly—' "

"Oh yes, I remember it." Ruth smiled a little in recollection. "That's one he made up when he was quite small—no bigger than Pye." Pye scowled horribly. "He used to steal out and sing it on the hill above Cold Shoulder Road where he thought he'd not be heard, and I used to steal out and listen to him."

Ruth sang it herself softly:

"No field would be long enough
net would be strong enough
song could be sung
bell could be rung
to give voice
to our joy
my companions and I . . ."

Oh, Aunt Ruth, Is thought, not for the first time. Why in the world didn't you tell Arun *then* how much you liked his songs? What a deal of trouble would have been saved.

Pye had climbed to the crosstrees, a spot where Arun liked to sit when he was on board, and squatted there, hunched and frowning.

"What's come to Pye?" said Penny. "Dodging lessons, is she?"

"Oh, she's jealous," sighed Ruth.

"Jealous, what of?"

"Jealous of Is being able to hear Arun sing inside her head," Ruth said with sad certainty. "Now she has spoken to Arun, Pye wants him for herself."

"Oh, for the land's sake!" Penny was impatient. "That young 'un's got more tangles in her than this ship's rigging! How you put up with all her whim-whams has me in a puzzle! I'd give her rats' rations!"

Ruth shook her head.

"When a person—specially a child as young as Pye—has had nothing but bad usage, you have to go slowly with them. A step at a time. Just now, I am the only person in the world that Pye has learnt to trust, a very little. A very frail trust! If she lost that—then we'd have to start all over. And the second time round would be harder."

Penny looked as if she doubted whether this would be worth the bother.

But after a while Pye came down, sidled along the deck, and edged her way up to Ruth, giving Is a sulky, defiant glare.

"Right: time to start our lessons," said Ruth. "Hallo—what's this?"—for Pye was handing her a folded square of paper. "A *note*? Where had you this, Pye? The ladder is drawn up—nobody could have got onto the ship."

Pye shook her head and, from the other hand, which she had been holding behind her back, produced an arrow.

"Stuck in deck," she explained. "Paper on point."

Sure enough, there were four neat holes in the folded paper where the arrow point had pierced it.

"Well, I never! Lucky one of us didn't get spitted. Why in the world couldn't whatever fool it was just give us a call?"

Ruth opened the paper and read it. " 'Please Ruth come to farm. Missis Lee took poorly.' Oh gracious me. I wonder which Mrs. Lee that is? I hope it isn't the old lady."

Ruth hurried down to the cabin, where she kept a bag of medicines and bandages and herbal remedies.

Returning on deck, she said to Is, "I've a queer feeling—kind of a premonition—that those brown beads are going to be needed."

"Like a medicine, Aunt Ruth?"

"I don't know. I just feel—very strongly—that I ought to have them with me. Would you mind, Is, if I took them with me?"

"No, that's all rug," said Is, passing over the little rowan-wood box. "Maybe the old lady can work a cure with them."

"Pye come too!" announced Pye, when Ruth walked to the rail.

"No, Pye. Not this time. I'll be busy, looking after the sick lady. You must stay on board and learn your lesson with Is."

Pye went black in the face. She began, obstinately, to follow Ruth, who turned and gave her a long, clear look, then let herself nimbly down the rope ladder. Pye opened her mouth wide, ready for a scream, and drew in a huge breath, but before she could let the scream out, Is whipped a thought into her mind.

"*Pye, listen!* Arun will hear, if you scream. He'll hear you inside his head—all across the wood, he'll hear you—the way you are hearing me now. And he'll think you have gone back to being a baby again. *What a pity!* he'll think."

Pye let her breath out very slowly, staring at Is. "How can you tell that?" she asked in thought-language. "Where is Arun now?"

Is shut her eyes and frowned, concentrating. "I can see

188

him in the main street in Seagate. He's talking to a girl in a red dress—her name is Jen. He's asking her the way to the dentist's house. . . . Now he is walking to the edge of the town. . . . Now he is knocking at the door."

"Can you see Ruth too?" Pye demanded.

Is opened her eyes. "It's no use, I can't find Ruth that way. She doesn't talk in thought-pictures as you and I and Arun can. And I can't always do it with Arun. It's very hard work. Like trying to remember something that happened a long, long time ago."

"*Nothing* happened to Pye a long time ago!" shouted Pye in a passion. She sat down suddenly on the deck. Tears poured from her eyes like water over a weir. "Pye wants Ruth," she sobbed. "Pye wants Arun. It's bad without them."

Penny shrugged. Is looked at Pye rather helplessly.

To her surprise, she suddenly felt sorry for the poor little being.

"Pye," she said after a moment. "Ruth and Arun aren't gone for good. You know that. They'll come back."

But will they? she wondered to herself. How can I promise that for sure? There's nothing but danger in these parts.

Still, she forced her voice to be calm and reassuring. "Why don't you pass the time till they come back making something nice for them? A present? Then you'll be working for them, and it'll be as if they were here, because you are thinking about them. See what I mean?"

Pye stared at Is for a long time out of large, round, pale, tear-filled eyes.

"Make bread," she said finally. "Pye can do that."

Is looked inquiringly at Penny, who nodded. "Yes, she can. Ruth taught her."

"All right, then, Pye. Let's go to the galley. You show me."

At least mixing flour and water and yeast and thumping it will keep the kid out of mischief for a while, Is thought.

I wonder how Arun is getting on at the dentist?

"Yes, yes, indeed, my young sir, I can most readily furnish you with highly superior new teeth, there will be no difficulty whatsoever. They can be screwed to the stumps of those broken ones," Mr. Fishskin the dentist was telling Arun. His own wide smile revealed two shining rows of big, well-shaped white teeth that looked as if they had been designed as an advertisement for his work.

"How much will they cost?" Arun asked doubtfully, hoping that the money his cousin Penny had lent him ("Pay me back when you are rich," she had said) would be sufficient.

"A trifle, a mere trifle," the dentist replied airily. He looked remarkably like his cousin the Admiral, Arun thought; the same round, flat face and pale, intent eyes, screened by thick spectacles. I don't like him, not one bit, Arun decided. I wish he weren't the only dentist for miles. But it's true, if I don't have those teeth mended, I shan't be able to sing.

And at least Denzil Fishskin seemed to have accepted the story of the midshipman and the marlinspike readily enough.

"Now, just sit in this armchair, my lad, make yourself comfortable, lean back; so; and now, we must clap this mask, which is soaked in ether and nitrous oxide, over your face," went on the dentist, producing from a large basin a soft, thick, round, white pad about the size of a soup plate. "Lie well back—so. Just imagine that you are lolling in your hammock in the midshipman's quarters and that your ship is becalmed in the balmy Bahamas . . ."

I don't care for this *at all,* thought Arun, and that was the last thought that came into his head for some considerable time.

Is lined up a number of Penny's dolls' heads and painted red mouths and black eyes on them while, rather inattentively, she supervised Pye, who was thumping and pummeling a large, gray, loaf-sized mass of elastic dough, which was steadily growing grimier and grimier.

"Don't you have to leave it to rise now?" Is suggested after a while.

"Soon," panted Pye, bashing away as if she had the Leader of the Silent Sect laid out on her pastry board. "Bread wants banging real hard, Ruth says."

She pounded on.

When Arun's thoughts next began to reassemble themselves inside his head, he realized, first, that he was desperately thirsty, and, second, that his mouth felt horribly sore and uncomfortable. He was dizzy too, and his surroundings seemed to be whirling round him so rapidly that it was safer—just for the moment, anyway—to keep his eyes shut.

But the worry that had gripped him from the moment when Pye broke his teeth was still with him, and now worse than ever. Would he be able to sing properly with these great bulky fangs stuck in his jaw? He explored the new teeth nervously with his tongue. They took up a huge amount of room in his mouth. They seemed as large as tombstones.

Not far away, he could hear quiet voices talking. Absorbed in his worry, he paid them no heed.

"I shall need some more mammoth tusks next time the troop come this way. I am now down to my last. . . . And a jug or two of Barbados rum would not come amiss. . . . I can use it on the rougher type of customer. . . ."

"It was ill advised and thoughtless of the men to dispatch that group. It may lead to undesirable attention from the authorities in London. An individual here or there, yes; a whole group, decidedly no."

"London is a long way from here. And a new reign has begun. Government will be in disorder. Meanwhile the local people were becoming restive . . . murmurs . . . this will bring them to heel."

Never mind about the murmurs and the mammoth tusks, thought Arun muzzily.

Mammoth tusks, though—who was talking about mammoth tusks not so long ago? But never mind, never mind, never mind about *that*—the important, the terribly important question is, will I be able to sing?

There seemed only one way to find out.

Arun opened his mouth wide and sang out, suddenly, at the full pitch of his lungs:

"Heel and toe,
  high and low
  hold her tightly
  swing her lightly
  and sing, everybody, sing!"

That's all right then, he thought in deep satisfaction. The new teeth haven't spoiled my singing. Improved it, if anything.

A stunned silence had fallen.

Then a voice said, "But—good god—that was the boy—that's the boy—that's the *Twite* boy, the one who gave me the slip in the wood. Here, let's have a look at him."

Oh, croopus, thought Arun. I know that voice.

With an effort, he hoisted up his eyelids and found that he was staring straight into the large gray-blue eyes of Dominic de la Twite.

"Denzil, I must trouble you for another helping of ether and nitrous oxide," announced the voice of the Leader, after a moment. "Pass me that swab, will you, my dear fellow?"

Arun sank down again, into a white and whirling fog.

Seven

"Can you see Arun now? Or hear him?" Pye asked, still vigorously pounding away at her dough.

"No. Not just now."

Is most certainly was not going to tell Pye that she had, in fact, received a very queer, worrying impression, which had slipped into her mind following a few jerky notes of a song. The song was sung loudly, almost bawled, not quite in tune, as if Arun was trying to prove something to himself. But then had followed a quick confused vision of Arun tipping headfirst into a deep well smoking with white, foggy vapors.

"Arun! Where are you? What's happening?" She poured out the thought-call, with all her energy, over and over. But not a sound, not a sign came back.

And it was becoming a long time since Ruth had gone off to the farm. Two hours? Three? A *worryingly* long time.

"*Now* put bread on top of stove to rise. Now we wait," Pye said importantly.

How quick she learns, Is thought. This morning she'd have said, "Pye wait." She's crammed half her growing into one day.

"What I do while bread rises?" Pye demanded.

"Umn. Could you make up a song?"

"A song?" Pye looked utterly taken aback.

"Why not? A song for Arun to sing when he comes back with his mended teeth. Old Dominic de la Twite hates songs, somebody said. A song to annoy Twite."

"What about?"

Is remembered how Twite had stopped the chaise and made Will Fobbing wipe the chalked letters LOMAK off walls and fences, how angry he had been.

"About mothers and kids."

Pye frowned. Is could not tell whether the frown came from perplexity, or meant she disliked the subject. However, Pye went off to a corner and curled up, apparently deep in thought. Figgin came down from the crosstrees and curled up beside her.

Is walked along the deck to where Penny was washing a bundle of sheeps' wool gathered from briars, in a pail of water laboriously hauled up on a rope.

"Pen," said Is quietly, "ain't it a longish time for Ruth to be gone? You think there's summat real bad wrong with Mrs. Lee? Does Ruth often put in such a long spell at the farm?"

"No," Pen answered in the same low tone. "It's not like her to stay away from Pye so long. Tell you the truth, I'm bothered."

"Best one of us go down to the farm, then? See what's up?"

"Humph," said Penny. "Which of us?"

"You've known Pye longer. She's used to you. Maybe you should stay here? We don't want her kicking up one of her tantrums."

"Ay," said Penny, "but you managed her pretty well just now. You can get through to her in that creepy thought-talk that you and Arun are so fly with. I think you'd better stay with her, Is. And you've been overseeing the bread, after all."

She gave her dry sniff of laughter. "Hope it don't give us all the galleygripes."

I just hope we're all here to *eat* it, thought Is. She said, "All ruggy, then. You go to the farm, Pen. But hurry back! It's like 'Fly away Peter, fly away Paul.' I know Arun can't be looked for yet awhile, but I wish—"

"Wish what?"

"Never mind. Reckon I just got the habdabs for some reason."

"I got 'em too. I'll go to the farm. But pull up the ladder when I'm down."

"You can lay your sweet life I will!"

"Where Penny going?" At the sound of the ladder being dropped among the branches, Pye came bundling up on deck.

"To the farm, to find why Ruth's so long."

"Pye go too!"

But Is countered this instant response by a firm argument. "You got to put your bread in the oven and be there to take it out."

Luckily the dough, though still very gray, had risen in

the most encouraging manner; it was laid on a large broken shovel and slid into the oven to bake.

"Have you made up a song yet?" Is asked.

Pye nodded. But she said, "You write down," and fetched Is a bit of chalk and a slate that Ruth had salvaged from the ship's schoolmaster's supplies.

"Go on then, I'm ready."

Pye then astonished Is. She recited in a loud, clear drone, all on one note:

"Mums, kids, hold together,
    hen to chick, cub to bear
    learn, pay heed, each to other
    sow to piglet, foal to mare."

"My word, Pye, why, that's *prime!* You're as good as Arun!"

Pye looked proud. Her pale eyes could not change, but a faint hint of a smile rumpled her pale cheek. "Arun make tune," she said. "When he come."

"Yes. He'll put a tune to it, easy as fall off a brick," said Is, and clenched her hands, because for some reason they were shaking. She added, "Why don't you think of some more words to add on? There's *fin* and *feather—paw* and *claw—*"

"Think some more," agreed Pye, and retired to her corner.

It seemed, however, that she was having trouble with the next verse of her song, for she sank into a long silence, from which Is roused her eventually by saying, "Bread smells good, Pye. Don't you reckon it's time it came out?"

Pye nodded, and stumped off to the oven.

They had just wrapped a piece of sail canvas around the hot shovel handle and withdrawn a large, well-shaped loaf (only slightly too brown but smelling most delicious) when Is heard Penny's whistle and hurried off to let down the ladder.

To her dismay, Penny was alone.

"Where's Ruth?" Is whispered, the moment that Penny was on the ladder.

Penny finished the climb without replying, pulled up the ladder behind her, and made it fast. Her face was paper-white and the freckles stood out like currants in dough.

"She never *went* to the farm."

"Pen! What happened to her?"

"They never sent us any message. There was naught wrong with Mrs. Lee. That note was a fake."

"Somebody musta grabbed her. I knew it," said Is. "I had a feeling—"

"And there's worse." Penny's voice was low and hoarse. She went on in a mutter, "There's a place in the wood called Birketland."

"I know it. I've been there."

"An old gal lived there in a cottage, Mrs. Dryhurst. The kids from Seagate used to go there sometimes of a night, for what they called their Talkfestesses—"

"So?" Is asked with a dry throat as Penny came to a halt.

"Where's Pye all this while?"

198

"Gloating over her bread. Pye's all right. What happened at Birketland?"

"All burned up. House, trees, the copse—and . . . and *people* too." Penny stared at Is in horror. "Liza from the farm went there with milk at daybreak and she said there's naught but a big burned patch . . . and . . . and some feet and hands."

"No!" whispered Is in horror. "Not—not Ruth?"

"No. This musta been last night, Liza said. It was the old woman, Mrs. Dryhurst, and some young 'uns from Seagate. And a paper was stuck on a tree. It said, 'Take warning. These were unfriends of the Merry Gentry.' What do you think of that?"

"But they had nothing to *do* with the Merry Gentry."

"Maybe not," said Penny. "But something like that sure puts a fear in anybody else who might think of crying rope on the Gentry. And Is, I'll tell you a thing that puts *me* in a quake—as I came back here from the farm—and I can tell you, I came mighty mousey, not on any path, but keeping in the thick bushes—"

"Well?"

"Well, I was waiting to cross the turnpike road, hid in a clump of holly, and who should ride by but the Admiral Fishskin, his own self, on that two-wheeled scooter-shay of his; he had a big red kite slung over his shoulder and he was smiling away to himself like the cat that's swallowed a cock robin."

Is shivered at the picture Penny had called up. "What's *he* doing in these parts? Folkestone's where he lives. He's got to be part of it all, that old Admiral, no question. I don't like his being so close."

"No," said Penny gloomily, "we gotta shift from here."

"From the ship?"

Penny nodded.

"But what about R-Ruth? What about Arun? When they —when he comes back?"

"We better leave a message. Like we done for you. Mrs. Nefertiti said the same. Said we'd best flit. Somebody— whoever shot that arrow—knows we're here. Sides, having us here makes a risk for them at the farm."

Is signed. She could see this was true. "Maybe we should go *right* away—go up to London? See somebody—the King, like? Tell one of those high-up fellers about the horrible goings-on here."

"The King? I don't reckon much to kings," said Penny with a curl of her lip.

"No, but Pen, he's a cove we know—that Simon feller, used to be Duke of Battersea. Not a bad cove."

"Oh, *him.*" Penny's tone expressed even more doubt. "I got to know *him* when he lodged with Mum and Dad in Rose Alley—I doubt he'd be much use. Didn't have two fardens to rub together in those days. Anyhow we couldn't go off to London now, not without any notion of what's come to Ruth. Or Arun—we gotta wait for him."

"No. That's true. We couldn't go. What did Mrs. Nefertiti say?"

"She said a queer thing. Two queer things. She said,

200

'Rest your head on a cold pillow.' And then she said, 'Remember the tortoise.' "

"Tortoise?"

"Well, I did have a tortoise once—when I was Pye's age. Aunt Tinty—you'd not remember her, she used to have a vegetable stall at Covent Garden. And she found a tortoise amongst the greenstuff and she gave it to me. Diggory, I called him. But he wandered off . . ."

"What's that got to do with anything?"

"Blest if I know," said Penny crossly.

"But 'Rest your head on a cold pillow'—now, that does make sense," went on Is, considering. "I reckon the old gal must mean the Cold Harbor. How about we up-sticks, do a moonlight, and hike off there tonight? The Cold Harbor ain't so far. Matter o' four hours' walking."

"Ah," Penny agreed thoughtfully. "That ain't a bad notion. Arun or Ruth'd surely think of that place. If they come back and find us gone."

Neither Is nor Penny could bear to suggest that Ruth might never come back.

How can we find her, *how?* wondered Is, and, my eye, Pye's liable to cut up rough.

"How come Pye's so quiet all this time?" Penny said, as if catching her thought. "It ain't like her not to come bustling."

The reason for this, they soon found, was that Pye had not been able to resist sampling the new loaf of hot bread. About one third of it had been nibbled away, and Pye was lolling against a pile of sail canvas in a sleepy stupor.

201

"She'll never walk to the Cold Harbor in that state," said Is. "We'll have to carry her in a sling."

"And she'll be a fair old weight with all that pannam inside her."

They rigged up a carrying-sling with ropes and canvas, and each packed a small sack as well, of food and needments.

"Shame Ruth took the beads."

But Is privately hoped that if, as seemed probable, Ruth had been snatched by an enemy, she might use the necklace as a bargaining counter. It was a faint hope.

"Where's Figgin? Figs, Figs, Puss, Puss?"

But he was not to be found.

"He's got sense enough," signed Penny. "He'll follow in his own time. Pity about all those dolls of mine." She looked at her orderly shelves. "Still—I can always make more. Come on—I've a powerful feeling it don't do to dawdle about."

"Me too." Is wriggled her neck as if at any moment an arrow might hurtle through the branches and lodge between her shoulders.

But she took time to find a piece of paper and make a drawing of three big stones and a fourth lying across their tops. This she folded and poked right into the middle of Pye's nibbled loaf, and left it on the galley table.

"Right. Let's be off."

Neither of them had the heart to eat any of the loaf. Food just then would have choked them.

They had to let Pye down in her hammock; she was fast

asleep, sucking her thumb, bloated with bread. Then, slinging her between them—and Penny was right, Pye was no featherweight—they set off, as quietly as possible, between the trees, not following any path, but going southwest, keeping the setting sun on their right-hand quarter.

They passed through close-set patches of dense wood, climbed over ridges, crossed valleys, waded through brooks. When they came to an open patch of heathland, they circled carefully round it, keeping under cover.

Pye woke up as the light began to dim, and grumbled. "Where we going? Where Ruth? Where Arun?"

She wriggled about until they had to put her down; then she wept and whined. "Want Ruth! Want Figgin!"

"So do we!" said Penny crossly. "And Arun too. Wanting's not the same as having."

"Why we here?" whined Pye. "Pye don't like this place."

It was a bad sign, thought Is, that she had gone back to saying "Pye" instead of "I." In a minute she might begin to scream, and that would be very bad indeed. The spot where they had set her down to rest was in a grove of yew trees, old and dark and close-set. But they grew on the edge of a broad expanse of bare moorland, with grassy patches, low-growing stretches of heather, and a wide bridleway that ran across the center, past a smooth, bare rock. The trackway was well used; three or four times, while Is, Pen, and Pye had been cautiously skirting round the open area, they had seen horsemen or carriages or light farm vehicles pass along the track. It ran only a bowshot from where they were hiding; if Pye screamed she would certainly be heard. Is flogged her mind to remember one of Arun's songs, about whales and snails, which he had sung at the Cold Harbor, and poured it hastily into Pye's mind. She had the tune more or less right, but some of the words arrived back to front.

"That's *silly*," said Pye peevishly. But she calmed down and seemed less likely to start screaming.

"You make a better one yourself, then," said Is.

Penny whispered, "Quiet, both of you!" and grabbed Is by the arm. Her fingers dug in like iron pegs. With her other hand she pointed back along the track.

They shrank deeper into the shelter of the yew grove.

Far away down the grassy ride the Admiral could be seen, briskly spinning along on his two-wheeled runabout. And behind him was another man, wearing a black hood, riding a bay horse; the horse seemed extremely nervous of the Admiral's riding machine and kept its distance. But the two men were clearly together; when the Admiral reached the flat rock in the middle of the heath, he slowed down, alighted, and laid his machine on the ground. His companion also dismounted and tossed the reins over the horse's head.

"They're going to fly a kite?" breathed Is. "Why the plague do that, in the middle of nowhere? What a rare rum business!"

But this was certainly what the two men had come to do. They walked at first, then ran, back and forth along the bridleway, tossing up the kite, which was scarlet, five-sided. At last a strong southeasterly breeze, which had risen as the sun declined, snatched and carried the kite up into the pale twilight sky.

As it sailed higher, the kite caught and shimmered in the last rays of the descending sun. Something had been attached to its tail, a small packet, and there seemed to be a hook on the tail also.

"Oooooo!" breathed Pye, full of wonder, watching as it climbed.

"Hush! Don't make a *sound!"*

"Mysterious set-out, though—ain't it?" whispered Is. "D'you reckon the old boy's sending messages to the moon?"

"I'd not trust him to do anything so sensible. More likely dropping lighted matches on a neighbor's hop field."

The kite had now caught a layer of high-level wind and was hurrying northward, far away, no larger than a scarlet speck in the sky, over the black outline of the forest beyond the heath. The Admiral paid out more and more line.

"He musta had a ball of twine the size of a millstone!"

At last the kite began to descend. The two men made no attempt to haul it in; seemingly their plan was to let it drop into the wood.

"Blest if I understand," muttered Penny. "Wouldn't you think they'd want to reel it in? Not lose it?"

But plainly the men's intention was quite otherwise. Calmly abandoning the line, the Admiral climbed back onto his runabout and pedaled away southward at a rapid pace; his companion gave him a short start and then followed at a canter. They had been in motion only a few minutes when a dull boom was heard, massively loud, a long way off to the north, at the point where the kite had last been seen. A brilliant V-shaped flash suddenly split the black outline of the forest. Flights of rooks and starlings shot up into the air, clattering and chattering. Then there was silence again.

"What did I say?" muttered Penny. "He *did* drop a lit match on someone's hop garden. Let's just hope it wasn't on Womenswold."

"Oh, Pen!" Is clapped a hand over her mouth in horror.

A few minutes later it seemed as if something—some very large thing—went hurtling past overhead. They felt the wind of its passage. And, shortly afterward, they heard a tremendous thumping crash to the south of them.

Again, flocks of birds flew upward in loud-voiced dismay.

"Now what?" Penny and Is stared at one another in the dusk.

Pye began to whimper.

"Don't like. Pye scared!"

"Hold your hush," Penny said dourly. "We ain't so sparkish ourselves. But let's hope it was just a thunderbolt. They don't often come in pairs."

"We can't be so very far from the Cold Harbor now," said Is, when they judged it safe to go on. They had watched the Admiral and his companion turn eastward and disappear over the curve of the moor. Bearing steadily southwest, Is and Penny soon came to a spot that Is recognized, where—how many days ago now?—she had overheard that cryptic small-hours conversation about the *Gentian.*

"Now it is just down this slope—"

But Is stopped short in total consternation.

The whole neighborhood around the Cold Harbor had been completely transformed. Shredded timber, snapped wood, crushed branches, scraps of rope, of metal, of canvas —glass, tools, weapons, chains, broken china, guns, even cannonballs, were strewn as thickly as autumn leaves over the ground.

And—even more unbelievable—the three huge sarsen stones of the Cold Harbor refuge had been hurled outward, knocked flat—hurled by the battered, almost unrecognizable object that had come to rest on top of them.

It was the frigate. It was the *Throstle.*

Eight

When Arun next thought of singing and had a try, he found it much more difficult: his tongue had swelled up, all his teeth ached, and his head did too; also he was miserably thirsty, and yet his throat felt much too sore to make swallowing possible.

He found, after thinking about it for a while, that he was lying on his back. With a strong effort, he rolled over onto his side, and looked ahead. He could see very little. He seemed to be lying in a large, high, dimly lit place with nothing in it. In the distance he could hear faint, shrill cries, which after a minute or two he identified as the voices of gulls; also, not far off, the sound of waves washing on the shore.

Am I in a ship? he wondered.

His hands, he now realized, were tied together behind his back; and because he had been lying on them, they had grown completely numb; but now that he was off them, the circulation began creeping back into them, and the result was five minutes of excruciating agony. He lay sweating and gasping, and wished that he had never woken up, never moved; wished that all this was nothing but a dream.

The trouble was that it all seemed only too disagreeably real. I couldn't possibly imagine all this, he thought, I am lying on what feels like a pile of fishing nets, the floor under them feels sandy and gritty, and I could never have invented the sound of the sea or the voices of the gulls.

Somebody had once told him that if you are thirsty and have nothing to drink you should think about lemons: imagine their shape, their pale color, the shiny, firm texture of the lemon peel, and, last of all, the sharp, pale yellow juice; that will very soon quench your thirst.

He tried it. The fierce taste of lemon juice was almost more than his sore throat could bear; but it did, he found, help a little. Then, having imagined lemons, he went on to other scents and flavors: the strong, aromatic whiff of fever-few with its green, delicate leaves; oranges, gentle and winy; mint, dark green and pungent; the dewy fragrance of primroses, and the mysterious fresh scent of violets, inter-changeable with that of cucumber. Thinking about cucumber helped him to swallow a little more; in fact he found the cucumber more helpful than the lemons had been.

After ten minutes or so he felt able to try singing.

For why shouldn't I sing? he thought. If there are people, and they can hear me, they'll come to help—if they are friends. And if they are not friends they'll know that I'm not scared.

But I am scared. Will they drag me behind a cart? Put me in a boat and push it out to sea?

Well, never mind that.

He sang:

"Whales and snails aren't troubled by thunder
Snails and whales make merry in gales
Snails glide over and whales swim under
Weather's a pleasure to snails and whales. . . ."

His voice was somewhat hoarse and cracked, but the tune was a good, rolling, rousing one, and just the sound of it in his own ears helped to cheer him. Also it produced an almost immediate effect. He heard a step on a wooden stair, close at hand. It was a firm, sharp, decided step, somebody coming downstairs. Then a bolt rattled.

A door opened. A voice said, "Stop that disgusting row, boy. At *once!*"

"I'm thirsty," Arun said. "I need a drink."

"You can't have one. It's not convenient."

"But I'm parched. I might die of thirst if I don't get a drink."

"You'll just have to wait."

"Then I'll sing." He started off again: " 'Whales and snails . . .' "

"Oh!" exclaimed the voice furiously. "You exigent boy! Why should *I* have been left with this nuisance on my hands?" And it muttered something under its breath about "pillar to post . . . obliged to leave a good, comfortable home in Nijmegen and end up in this rat's nest . . ."

"I need a drink badly!" shouted Arun.

Shoving downward with his hands, he managed to lever himself to a sitting position, and looked about him. He saw that he was in some kind of lofty warehouse, built from black, tarred timbers. The floor was merely rough sand and shingle, with nothing on it except the pile of tarry nets against which he had been lying. There was a cold, dank, salty smell, not unlike the smell of the house in Cold Shoulder Road.

Standing by the half-open door was a tall woman, staring at him. She held a heavy blackthorn club in her hand.

"Well, you don't look as if you'd be much trouble," she said coldly. "And you had better not be, or I will knock out all those nice new teeth with this." And she shook the club.

"All I want is a drink of water," Arun said.

She thought about that. Then she said, "After all, you may as well come upstairs. If you try to make any commotion, you won't be heard so easily up there. And it saves me bringing water down to you. So get up on your feet and walk, slowly, to the door."

She spoke carefully, one word at a time, as if, although she knew English very well, it was not her native language. She had a slightly guttural accent.

Arun climbed onto his feet with caution and difficulty, and stood swaying. His head still felt muzzy and his legs weak.

"No, you are not very big, are you," said the woman in a tone of mild contempt. "To me, you seem of little value. Now then: Walk that way, but slowly."

Arun could not in any case have walked fast. He made his shaky way toward the woman, and she backed carefully out of the door.

"You need not think you can run anywhere," she told

him when he was through the door, and found himself in yet another large empty granary or boat shed. "For the outer door is locked, and the key's upstairs. Now, you walk up that stair, and if you try anything stupid, I shall break your ankle with this stick. So just climb up quietly."

Arun had no wish to try anything stupid. The stairs were a flight of unbalustraded wooden steps, set into the timber wall. Feeling weak and sick, he took them slowly, one step at a time, staying as close to the wall as possible. The flight was long and steep; he counted twenty-four steps. By the time he reached the top, which was a large trap opening, he was close to fainting; he took half a dozen paces away from the top and sank down onto the floor. This, he felt vaguely surprised to find, was thickly carpeted.

Now the woman's face rose up over the stair top and he had time for a proper look at her. It was a long, flat, expressionless face, with no-color hair, which was done very tidily in some kind of bun. She had a slight furry mustache and looked as if she might be about fifty years old. Her eyes and nose resembled those of Dominic de la Twite, but (thank goodness, thought Arun) the eyes did not have that queer, luminous, predatory look of Dominic's, they did not bore into one like drills, they were just yellowish gray, opaque eyes, which turned to slits when she was angry.

Still, she was a large, tall, strong-looking woman, with thick arms and legs, and behaved as if she was used to having her own way.

"Good," she said, seeing Arun on the floor. "Stay like that." And she crossed the room, went through a door, and

212

came back in a moment carrying a pewter beaker with water in it. "Here—"

As Arun's hands were fastened behind him, she held the cup for him, tilting it farther and farther forward as he drank. She did this without particular care, and the last couple of mouthfuls cascaded over his chin. He would have liked at least one more cupful, but something about her face told him there would be no point in asking for it. She put the cup away and sat down in an upright chair with padded arms, watching him as if he were a rabbit or a lizard that had been brought into the house.

To escape her scrutiny, Arun looked round the room, and found it most unexpected. Though it was only the upper floor of a grain store or sail loft, it was furnished quite handsomely. On the walls hung woven tapestries with pictures of hunting scenes. A deer flashed through a thicket; men pulled fish from a tank of water. The floor was covered thickly with rugs and carpets in gorgeous colors. The chairs and sofas were of polished and gilded wood, their backs and seats upholstered in satin and brocade.

"You are surprised?" the woman said coldly, observing his look. "My brother . . . likes to be comfortable."

"Your brother, ma'am?"

"My brother Dominic. My name is Merlwyn Tvijt. You may call me Mevrouw Tvijt." She pronounced the last word with a click. "So you are, perhaps, my young cousin —many times removed? Your name also is Twite?"

"Yes . . . but I daresay we ain't related, Mevrouw," Arun said hastily.

"Why should you think not?"

I just *hope* we aren't, was what Arun would have liked to say.

Instead he asked, "Why are my hands tied?"

"To stop you from running away," she said with raised brows. "As you did once before. To my brother's great inconvenience. He wishes to ask you questions. He will be back later. Just now, he was called off in a hurry. Would you like to know why?"

From her tone of voice, Arun felt that he would *not* like to know, but nonetheless, with a dry mouth, he could not help asking, "Why, then?"

"He has gone to see your mother. To interrogate her. We had one of our people set to watch outside the farm at Womenswold."

Arun felt a sickening jolt of fright. Mechanically he repeated, "My mother?"

"Dominic has been wishing to talk to your mother ever since she abducted the little child who was left in our charge—the Handsel Child."

Miss Twite took a pinch of snuff from a small ivory box, laid it carefully in a line along the back of her big, muscular, bony wrist, then sniffed it up. She did this twice more, and sneezed a couple of times, in a controlled manner, with a stiff, bristly noise. Then she said, "That was a remarkably foolish act of your mother's. It has led to a great deal of trouble. My brother has been at great pains to find her—to find out why she did it."

"She did it because the kid was unhappy," said Arun.

214

Miss Twite said in a measured way, "Sometimes children *need* to suffer, for their own good. It is to be hoped that the child will soon be back with us, her proper guardians."

No it isn't, thought Arun. This is a crazy conversation. Pye is an awkward little cuss, but she sure don't deserve to be lodged with such a pair.

"Now that Dominic has come up with your mother," went on Dominic's sister, "no doubt we shall soon have the child under our charge again. It is best so. The people are more quiet."

So at least you haven't got Pye yet, thought Arun. But where did Dominic catch Ma? At the ship? If so, where are the others?

He felt dreadfully anxious. If only I could talk to Ma in thought-language . . . But it was no use. He probed and probed, called and called, but nothing came back. Then he tried to find Is—and got a queer, faint flash, which came from a long way off.

"Arun—where are you? The ship's gone—smashed—we're out in the cold—cold—cold . . ."

"Where is my mother? Where is Mr. Twite?" Arun asked the woman.

"They are going to Folkestone. Mr. Twite now has another very important question to ask your mother. For it seems that she knows the whereabouts of King Charles's gold."

"Of Ki—?" Arun felt his mouth dry up again; his eyes almost shot from their sockets.

"King Charles's gold," the woman repeated impatiently.

"You know all about it—the treasure that Queen Henrietta brought in the ship *Victory*, that came from the Low Countries, that was lost, that was never recovered. The first founder of the Silent Sect, Brother Manoah Enticknap, he had the gift of prophecy. And he prophesied, thirty years ago, that the Sect, at this time, would be supplied with a great treasure from under the ground, which they would use to pay for their establishment in the New World. And of course it is quite obvious that your mother has found it and knows where it is."

"B-B-But she *doesn't* know," spluttered Arun.

"Do not tell me stupid lies, boy. It is evident that your mother has access to the treasure. In the place where she was staying, in the wood, Dominic found a Charles I sixpence. And, tied up in your handkerchief, a brown diamond of the very finest quality. Ah!"—as Arun's hand flew to his neckerchief and found the knot untied—"You see! It is not the slightest use trying to pretend ignorance now."

"*I* found the necklace. My mother didn't."

"*The necklace?*" She pounced. "Not just one stone? A whole necklace?"

"My mother has no idea in the world where it came from. Why didn't your brother ask me about it?"

"All in good time. People are best interrogated singly, he says."

"But my mother doesn't know."

"Stupid!" Mevrouw Twite irritably pulled her large fingers, with a sharp cracking noise. "Of course she must

216

know—if you know. And of course Dominic will find out from her. He is very good at that. He opens minds like oysters. And she must immediately return the Handsel Child."

"And if she doesn't?"

"That would be a pity," said Miss Twite. She spoke in a cold, measured, angry voice that caused chilly shivers to run down Arun's spine. He thought of Micah Swannett, put out to sea in an open boat, with his hands tied. Where was Micah now?

"And my brother's plan for *you,*" Miss Twite went on, without going into particulars as to his plan for Ruth, "his plan for you, if necessary, is to send you over to France, where, from Calais, a ship will shortly be setting sail for the slave plantations of the Tornado Islands. They take hundreds of boys your age. So you see, you had certainly better tell my brother all that he wants to know. Otherwise your future life will not be a very happy one, though it will be very hardworking. Now you had better go on up those stairs to the top floor. You may pass the rest of the night there."

A second flight of stairs, even steeper, even narrower, rose to an open trapdoor.

"Can't I have my hands untied?"

"Certainly not. Go along. And no singing. My brother detests singing. And so do I."

Arun climbed the stairs. The room above was an empty loft, lit by an unglazed square hole in one wall, and a few panes of glass set into the roof in place of tiles. As soon as

Arun was through it, Miss Twite slammed and bolted the trapdoor.

Arun sank down onto the floor—there was no furniture of any kind—filled with miserable forebodings.

Where can Ma be? What is happening to her? he wondered, over and over.

After a while he curled up, like a cat.

At that moment, as Miss Twite had said, Ruth and Dominic de la Twite were traveling together in a chaise along the road from Seagate to Folkestone.

Ruth sat quietly. Her hands and feet were fastened with iron handcuffs, but she was not struggling. It was never her way to make a fuss, particularly when it would be quite useless to do so. She remained watchful and silent, studying the man who sat opposite her.

He was in a high state of excitement, but the only signs of this were the extreme brilliance of his eyes and a slight dew of sweat on his forehead.

At the moment he was busily engaged in re-joining the single brown diamond, which he had taken from Arun's knotted kerchief, to its nineteen companions on the plaited silk string. The empty wooden box lay on the seat beside him. He did this with remarkable care and skill, despite the motion of the carriage. His large fingers had great dexterity. When the task was completed he gave a sigh of satisfaction, and sat for a moment or two in almost spellbound contemplation of the glittering pool of gemstones that he held in his hands.

They flashed, even in the dim light of the horn carriage lantern.

"Twenty brown diamonds the size of olives! They are like a moorland river—a crystallized river," he said fondly. "I could hardly have imagined such a masterpiece. Such *absolute* beauty. I am really very beholden to you, Mrs. Twite, for having led me to this treasure."

Ruth shrugged. She said, "Different people have different values. I wouldn't give a plate of porridge for those stones—if I was hungry."

Dominic de la Twite laughed and laughed. "Dear lady! Such a sense of humor." He tossed the chain from hand to hand, then, with a huge indrawn breath of triumph, fastened it round his neck. He was wearing a white ruffled shirt and high white stock; the brown, glittering stones seemed to flow in and out among the snowy linen like a snake gliding among white rocks. Twite glanced down complacently; he could just catch a glimpse, a sparkle, from the corner of his eye.

"I wonder why I have come across no history of this necklace? It must be one of the most perfect pieces of jewelry ever made."

"I recall my husband referring to it once," Ruth remarked coldly. "He occasionally took an interest in such things. He had read about it in a history of King Charles's lost treasure. It had a name: 'The Living River.' "

She seemed about to say more, but checked herself, and instead gazed out at the dark landscape flowing past outside.

"The Living River—a perfect name for it! The stones do seem alive—as if they held a power of their own. But there —I sound positively fanciful!" Twite laughed again.

Once more Ruth made as if to speak, then decided for silence.

De la Twite fell into a long reverie, evidently an agreeable one, for he smiled to himself several times.

Then, as if shaking off pleasant daydreams and getting back to business, he frowned at the woman sitting opposite him.

"Now, Mrs. Twite—let us have no more prevarication, if you please."

"I never prevaricate," said Ruth.

He ignored that. "It is plain, by the evidence of the necklace and those silver coins, that you and your son know where Charles's treasure lies hidden. Listen to me, dear Mrs. Twite, I am prepared to make a bargain with you. Pay attention, if you please! You know that my deepest wish is —ahem!—to provide the Silent Sect with the means to set sail and buy land in the New World, to establish their own settlement there."

"Is that really so?"

Ruth's voice was quiet, not skeptical, but Twite shot her a sharp look. "Of course! Indeed it is! So: there is the treasure, hidden away, underground, of no use to *anybody*. Why not fetch it out and devote it to this excellent purpose? Listen, Mrs. Twite, if you will only conduct me to where it lies, I will make a pact with you. *I* have the use of the treasure, *you* may keep the Handsel Child (why you

220

should wish to do so, I cannot imagine, a most pestilential child, but it seems that you must, or you would not have been at such pains to remove the creature and keep it in concealment). Well? What do you say? Is it a bargain? Do we shake hands?"

"No," said Ruth.

De la Twite began to grow angry. He remained quiet, but seemed to swell and kindle inside his clothes.

"No? And why not, pray?"

"Firstly," said Ruth, "because I have no idea in the world where the treasure is buried. Oh, somewhere in this neighborhood, perhaps—or perhaps not. My son did not tell me where he found the treasure, nor did I ask him. I am not *interested* in the treasure, Mr. Twite. Secondly, you have no right to use the child as a bargaining counter. She is not a piece of property, she is a human being—though you have not used her as such. So you may just as well stop the carriage and put me out in the road, for I am no use to you whatsoever."

De la Twite exploded with fury.

Ruth was reminded of Pye as his face darkened and his breath came in surges.

"No use to me, madam! But I'll see that you *are* of use to me—if you won't help me yourself, you shall be made the means of putting pressure on your son, who is back in Seagate with my sister at this time."

Ruth turned a little pale.

"And as for the child," Twite went on furiously, "since it seems that you have so little value for her, I may as well tell you that your charming establishment, your cozy home in the tree—is not in existence anymore, but has been blown to Jericho! My colleague—ah—my colleagues have contrived to drop a packet of highly explosive hop manure—which is made from wool refuse, you may know!—onto the *Throstle*, and that, combined with the gunpowder stored in the ship's hold, was quite sufficient to send the vessel sky-high!"

Ruth stared at him. Then she said slowly, "So you lied, when you offered to let me keep the child. Since she was already dead."

After a pause she added, "In any case, how do I know that you are not lying to me now?"

A few lights began to show on either side of the road.

They were entering Folkestone.

Arun lay tossing and twisting on the dusty floor of the loft. It is hard to sleep with your hands tied behind you; harder still if your teeth ache, and you are still painfully thirsty, and worried to death, besides, about what is happening to your mother, and have been told that you yourself are to be sent off on a slave ship to the plantations in the Tornado Islands.

Down below there was complete silence. He wondered if Miss Merlwyn Twite had gone to bed. Or was she sitting, bolt upright, with her big-knuckled hands in her lap, waiting for her brother to come home?

And where was her brother? In Folkestone, trying to extract directions from Ruth as to the whereabouts of King

Charles's treasure? Although he felt so miserable and frightened, Arun could not help a faint grin at the thought. First of all, she doesn't *know* where it is, he told himself, and second of all, even if she did know, she wouldn't tell Twite, not if the Queen of England was his aunt.

Arun was obliged to admit to himself that, aggravating and difficult though she might be in some respects, Ruth had plenty of grit in her; it was absolutely impossible to imagine that she would ever in any circumstances knuckle under to a tyrant.

Well, look at the way she took and pinched the Handsel Kid, just because she thought it was right. And a plaguey lot of trouble *that* led to. But still, he might do the same himself. Or at least he hoped he would.

When he considered his own danger, and the unpleasant prospects that lay ahead, Arun shrank, and ached, and wished he could think himself back into being a cat instead of a boy, as he had been used to do. But now, when he thought about Ruth subject to similar dangers and despairs, he had not the heart to retreat into cathood. Besides, cats can't sing. Cats don't fight battles, either, he thought. (Well, perhaps Figgin might, but then, Figgin's no common cat.)

What had been the meaning of that confused message from Is about the ship being smashed? Had Twite done that? Was Figgin all right? Were Is, Penny, and Pye all right? Where were they?

Why was he lying here immersed in rambling, miserable thoughts, when he ought to be sitting up and singing his head off—if that was what Dominic de la Twite particularly disliked?

He sat up and began to sing:

"Dance the Barnaby Prance
dance the Paddington Frisk
gambol as you advance
take no thought of the risk . . .
Boys and girls, come out to dance
Take your partner, take your chance
Dance your way to the coast of France
Along with your playfellows, all night through
Dance your way to a *parlez-vous* . . ."

Pretty fair nonsense, but it kept up his heart.

To his amazement, his song was answered by a number of voices outside on the beach.

First in thought-speech.

"So that's where you are! Jen told us that you had gone to the dentist's house, but we never saw you come out . . ."

Then they all burst into song:

"Sing, sing, everybody sing
Speech is the queen, and music is the king!"

One of the voices out there, a girl's, high and ringing, he recognized as that of Jen Braburn, the girl in the red dress.

"Hello, boy! What are you doing up there?" she called.

"I'm shut in!" he called back. "My hands are tied and the trap is bolted."

"Hold on, mate, we'll just fetch a beam and break down the door. Don't you fret. They burned up some of us, but they haven't got us all! Not by a long chalk! And there's more on the way—they'll *never* get us all!"

He heard the sound of many scampering feet.

But now, also, Arun heard the voice of Merlwyn Twite, and her rapid, angry footsteps on the stair below his trapdoor. The bolt slammed back, the trap shot open, her furious face came into view.

"What do you think you are up to, boy? You will please stop that disgusting noise immediately!"

Much worse, he heard horses' hoofs and carriage wheels on the landward side of the building. A shout went up: "Miss Twite! We've come to fetch the boy! The Leader wants him in a hurry."

"He's here," she called. "Come and get him."

Three men—from the sound—tramped up to the first floor; two came onto the second. Arun was grabbed, unceremoniously dropped through the trap, caught down below; then the same speedy process was repeated on the lower flight of stairs; he was half hauled, half carried across the empty ground floor and bundled swiftly and roughly into a waiting carriage.

"The Leader wants you too," one of the men called to Miss Twite.

"Well, you can tell him it's not convenient," she grated. "I've had my rest disturbed quite enough for one night. I'll come tomorrow, in my own good time, tell him. And I'll thank you to leave me in peace now."

She banged the outer door and bolted it just as Jen and her friends came running back with a tree trunk they had taken from a builder's shipyard farther along the beach.

"I'm in the coach. They are taking me to Folkestone!" Arun called in thought-language as the carriage sped past the hurrying group; but he could not tell if they heard him. His head had been tied inside a sack and he was thrown roughly onto the floor as the horses accelerated into a gallop.

Above his head the men in the carriage were talking casually.

"What's to become of the *Gentian* now? If more and more goods are to be carried by train?"

"She ain't the Nob's ship. She belongs to His Fish. And he don't want to part with her, I've heard."

"A ship's allus handy, in case of trouble."

"A fly card he is, that owd Admiral, with his contraptions and his kites; dang me if I'd ever a beleft he could shift that frigate out of that tree where she was perched so snug!"

"A right shame, *I* call it," pronounced another voice. "The owd *Throstle* made a rare handy nest for any cove as wanted to lay low for a while."

"Still, 'twas clever. That you can't deny. His Fish has got more brains than the Nob."

"Ah. But what about smashing up Pook's Pantry? Knocked to blazes, so they do say, a place what had been a refuge for poor folks for dunnamany thousand year. *That* ain't pound dealing."

"Ah! That's so," they all agreed thoughtfully. One voice

asked, "Were there folks a-refuging in the Cold Harbor when it was strook? Is that known?"

"If there were," somebody said, "their own dearest wouldn't know them now. You get a ten-ton hunk of rock atop of you, *and* a little owd Majesty's frigate on top of that, you ain't going to be so handsome."

Arun shivered, listening, curled on the coach floor among the feet. Oddly enough, he had no wish to turn into a cat.

Nine

Penny suddenly exclaimed, "I remembered about the tortoise!"

"What *do* you mean, Pen?" Is asked, rather crossly, combing her hair with her fingers.

They had passed a most miserable night, under the great yew tree at the Cold Harbor, having piled themselves damp, lumpy beds from all the debris that lay scattered thickly about.

It is dreadful to see a place that has been your comfortable home utterly smashed up and reduced to pieces no bigger than shoes. The arrival of daylight only made this scene more depressing, as a thin, cold rain had begun to fall. Penny found some bits of her dolls strewn about; Is found the blue headscarf that Window Swannett had given her, wet and torn. Pye actually came across the remains of the loaf she had baked, and was furious that Is and Pen would not allow her to eat it.

"*Why not?*"

"Because it's all full of broken glass, Pye, that'd cut your stomach to ribbons."

Worse still was the unspoken question—which neither Is

nor Pen dared put into words—as to whether there might have been any wayfarers taking refuge in the Cold Harbor when the ship fell on it like a meteor and knocked over the great sarsen stones. If there had been anybody inside, no human hand could help them now.

"Reckon Mrs. Nefertiti didn't give us very good advice that time," Is was remarking glumly, when Penny made her unexpected statement about the tortoise.

Is, who had found a few squashed turnips in a muddy sack, had been trying to persuade Pye that they would do for breakfast.

"I *know* you ain't partial to turnips, Pye—but, honest, there ain't anything else."

"Mrs. Nefertiti didn't mean for us to come here," Penny went on excitedly. "Now I remember what it was about Diggory. The tortoise. He used to eat wood lice. They were a big treat for him. Like strawberries 'ud be for us. Or chocolate cake."

"Well," snapped Is, "Pye and I ain't a-going to eat *wood lice* for our breakfast. Nohow! And there *aren't* any strawberries."

"What made me think of him," Pen went on, without paying heed to this, "one time Diggory was just going to munch up a wood louse when it nipped right up to him and hid in his armpit, where he couldn't find it."

"What are you getting at, Pen?"

"Mrs. Nefertiti meant for us to go back to Cold Shoulder Road. In Folkestone. *That's* her cold pillow. Folkestone's where the Merry Gentry have their main center, you may lay; that's where the Channel Tunnel comes out. And where the Admiral lives. And that's just where they won't be looking for us."

"You ain't so clung-headed, Pen," said Is, after a moment's pondering. "I reckon you may be on to something there. But how are we going to get back to Folkestone? It ain't far, I reckon—not as the rook flies—but it's all open country close around the town. We're likely to be spotted."

"We'll have to wait till after dark."

Accordingly, they spent a dismal day.

Arun was flung out of the coach and landed on rough ground. The sky was still dark, but there were lanterns round about, and a number of men busily at work. He had no trouble in recognizing the place. It was the valley, the entrance to the Channel Tunnel, and members of the Gentry, all hooded, were bustling about with crates and bales and barrels, taking them from the goods wagons and piling them into the carrying-panniers of a line of ponies.

Just up above, in the thickety hillside, Arun realized, was the gully from which he and Is had looked down the last time they'd watched this scene. And in behind, deep in that hill . . . Arun almost choked at the sudden realization that the treasure Dominic de la Twite was so urgently seeking lay less than half a mile from here, behind a pile of rubble and sand.

"We brought the boy," said a voice over his head.

"Good, Fobbing. Take him into the station."

Arun was dragged over to the neat little rail station with

its tarred platform and flint buildings. He was thrust through a doorway, under a sign that said LADIES' WAITING ROOM, and left on the floor, half propped against a wall.

Facing him, to his horror and dismay, he discovered his mother, sitting on a wooden bench. Her hands and feet were tied, and she looked dusty, pale, and tired. But she smiled at him and remarked in a matter-of-fact tone, "There you are, my dear! I hope you have your new teeth?"

Arun smiled back, in order to display them. "All I need," he said, "is something to bite with them. I haven't tried that yet. Folk aren't too free with their vittles around here."

Dominic de la Twite strode into the small room, making it seem smaller. Arun noticed at once that he was wearing the chain of brown diamonds, twined among the folds of his high white neckcloth. He seemed angry and somewhat distracted.

"Now!" he snapped. "I've no time to waste. In a few moments I must travel to France on urgent business. Let us have no nonsense, pray!"

A voice called, "Sir? Only one third of the tusks have come."

"I know that!" he called back impatiently. "This time I am going to look into it myself. Now: You boy! I want you to tell me where these came from." He tapped the chain of stones round his neck.

Arun stared at him without replying. De la Twite called, "Fobbing! Come in here! Bring a pitchfork!"

At this command, Ruth looked up sharply. One of the men came in; like the rest, he wore a black hood with slits for eye holes. He carried a long-handled farm fork with three steel tines, tapered and shining and sharp.

"Push them against the boy's throat and chest—yes, so."

Fobbing stood stolidly as directed, holding the fork handle level, so that all three points of the prongs pressed against Arun. The point against his throat felt as if it had pierced his skin. The cold bite of it made him cough.

"Now then, boy. Let's have no foolishness. If you don't tell me at once where these stones came from, Fobbing is going to spit you through."

Arun's eyes met those of Ruth. I wish I could talk to her in thought-language. Just to pass the time of day. Just to say, hullo, Ma. That would have been nice.

He tried. He poured out a series of messages. He could tell they did not reach Ruth. But, strangely enough, Dominic de la Twite shook his head angrily, rubbed it, and looked discomposed, as if loud noises were distracting him, noises that he disliked but could not understand.

Anyway, thought Arun, I don't really *need* to talk to Ma in thought-language. I know well enough what's in her mind.

Don't give in to them. Never mind what happens. Never give in to them.

On his first encounter with de la Twite, Arun had felt completely cowed and overpowered. But now—perhaps because he had had time to prepare himself, or because he knew more about the man, or because Ruth was there—the situation was quite different. Arun felt collected—ready— like a boxer balanced on his two feet.

As the steel tine sank a little deeper into his neck, he said politely to Dominic de la Twite, "I think the stones come from High Brazil."

"Not that, idiot! Where did *you* find them?"

"I didn't find them."

"Stop quibbling and paltering. I'm in a hurry. My patience is wearing very thin. Where did the necklace come from?"

"My cousin found them," said Arun in a tone of mild surprise, as if only now he grasped what Twite was getting at. "My cousin Is, she found the necklace. She never told me exactly where. . . . But, when we were on the ship coming from France, I remember she did say something about diamonds . . ."

He tried to look vague and willing, as if he were being asked a question in a school test.

"Ship coming from France?" Dominic de la Twite looked utterly taken aback.

Now, in the background, not too far away, but not too close either, Arun began to hear a number of thought-voices. Were they speaking to him? Or to each other? Was it because of the spike sticking into his neck that he heard them?

"Who are you?" he called urgently. "Where are you?"

And again, he noticed Dominic de la Twite wincing and shaking his head, then scrubbing at his forehead with impatient fingers as if trying to rub away a cloud of midges.

"Why yes," Arun slowly answered Dominic's question with an innocent air. "My cousin and I came here on a ship, the *Dark Diamond*—she often puts in at Calais before crossing to Folkestone—"

Ruth now entered the game. "In Calais," she remarked thoughtfully, "there are many stories of King Charles's treasure. Le Trésor du Roi Charlot, they call it. Queen Henrietta was bringing it on the H.M.S. *Victory*—but some say it sank off Cap Gris Nez. The treasure may just as easily be on that side of the Channel."

Dominic stared furiously from mother to son and back again.

"*Where* were you and your cousin in France?" he asked Arun.

"I don't know the names of French places," Arun replied simply. "I don't speak French."

"Aha!" cried a lot of voices inside his head. "Thought-language needs no translation!"

"Did you do any digging? Go into any caves? Did your cousin?"

If it were not for the steel prongs jammed against his neck and ribcage, Arun could have burst out laughing; and also if it were not for the frightening and sinister memory of the men's talk in the carriage coming to Folkestone. For, so far as he could make out, the frigate *Throstle* had been blown up into the sky by some diabolical contrivance of the Admiral's, had smashed the Cold Harbor refuge when it fell to earth again, and, for all he knew, his cousins and Pye had been in one or the other place when this happened.

In which case, as Twite must very well know, any knowledge that Is might have as to the whereabouts of the treasure had been blown to smithereens along with her.

He's going to get nothing more from *me*, resolved Arun, and received an approving glance from Ruth.

The voices in his head sounded louder and louder.

"Where are you?" he called again.

At this moment there came an urgent voice from outside.

"Sir, Sir! The train is ready to start. We daren't delay any longer."

"Oh, Devil take it!" De la Twite moved restlessly forward. He made a half-gesture toward Fobbing with the pitchfork, then restrained himself.

Coming to a sudden resolve, "We shall finish this talk in France!" he said with menace, and touched the brown jewels in his neckcloth as if to reassure himself. He called, "Niland! See that both prisoners are put on the train. In separate wagons. I will travel in the parlor coach. It is a *deuced* nuisance about those tusks. Fobbing, you may go in the tender with the fireman."

Fobbing nodded without speaking—he did not seem particularly enthusiastic about this permission—then picked up Arun under one arm and carried him with ease out of the station and down to the track. Arun was hoisted up and flung into a wagon, which was otherwise empty. A few minutes later a thump near at hand suggested that Ruth had received the same treatment.

The rain never let up all day. In one way that was useful, for it meant that fewer people were about, and the misty drizzle cut visibility down to little more than a bowshot's length. Pen, Is, and Pye made their way by cautious stages from one patch of woodland to the next.

Pye grumbled a great deal, and asked why they could not go through villages and buy food.

"Because we'd be nabbed for sure," Penny told her. "We can't risk it, we don't know who'd cry rope on us to the Gentry. You don't want to go back to the Twites, do you?"

"No."

"Well then!"

Pye was silenced. She trudged along after them doggedly enough, but was plainly very miserable. Every now and then a tear slipped down her face. At dinnertime Penny produced a small supply of hard cheese and ship's biscuit from her pack and said, "Here, little 'un. Have a bit o' this."

But Pye could not be comforted by food. "Want Figgin," she whispered dolefully.

Privately, both Is and Penny feared that Figgin had probably returned to the *Throstle* after the human inhabitants had left it, and had been blown to atoms in the explosion. They did not say so aloud, but Pye caught the picture that Is had in her mind, and shouted, "No, *no*! Figgin's not dead! No, he *isn't*! I won't *have* him dead."

"Well, we certainly hope not, Pye," Is said, trying to sound cheerful and encouraging. "We just have to wait and see."

Is noticed that Pye's ability to catch other people's thought-patterns appeared to have been sharpened and strengthened to a surprising degree by all the sad and worrying things that had been happening. All night Pye had been restless, calling out, sometimes aloud, sometimes in her head, to unseen people. And Is had to be very careful not to think gloomy or anxious thoughts, especially about Ruth or Arun, for Pye picked them up with lightning speed. "When are we going to see them? Where are they?" she repeated, over and over, and all Is and Penny could answer was, "We're looking for them. We're trying our best to find them."

"I've thought of the name of a chap who might help us," Penny said, as they sat shivering in Biggins Wood, near Folkestone, waiting for dusk to fall. "Ruth spoke of him, said he was the new Lord Lieutenant of the county, was spoken of as a decent cove that wants to put an end to free trading and crime and rascality."

"He'll be a clever one if he can do that! What's his name?"

"Sir David Greenaway."

"Hey!" said Is. "I've met him, when I lived in Wapping. I know his brother Sam. Sam's all right. So maybe this David feller *might* be some use. Where's he hang out?"

"In Dover Castle, I reckon."

"What we need," said Is, "is some *proof* of who's doing what's being done. No use just telling him what we think." She thought of the burnt cottage at Birketland and shivered.

"Who all burned up?" said Pye at once.

"Never mind it, Pye . . . why don't you make up another piece of your song?"

"Yes—I see what you mean," Penny agreed with Is. "Maybe what we need to do is for one of us to creep into the old Admiral's house after dark and do some snooping around there. Then we might find something that would fix him in the picture."

"Ah . . . that's not a bad notion." But Is quailed at the thought of Rosamund. "Ugh! Spiders! I hate 'em!"

"Rosamund?" said Pye unexpectedly. "Is Rosamund a spider? Big spider? Pye don't mind spiders. Pye likes spiders!"

"Good heavens, Pye! But this spider's as big as a cockerel."

"Pye wouldn't mind. Nice! Furry, like Figgin!"

"Croopus . . . You tend to your song, Pye."

Instantly Pye recited:

"Mums, kids, hold together
  fin to fin, feather to feather
  claw to claw, toe to toe,
  goose to gosling, fawn to doe."

"Well I'll be hammered, Pye! You fairly take the cake!"

Pye looked smug. Is softly sang her verse to Arun's "Whales and Snails" tune, which it fitted quite well.

"I reckon you'll be putting Arun out of business, Pye, at this rate."

Having said which words, Is felt a dreadful qualm, and heartily wished the words unsaid again. Pye, perhaps picking this up, remained silent for many minutes. Then, stumbling, faltering, and hesitating, as if images were coming into her mind one by one, from a long way off, she slowly announced, "Arun's in a train. He tells me to tell you that. Tied up. Arun's going under the water. He says Ruth too. In train. Can't see Ruth. Arun got new teeth. Under water with new teeth. Arun going to France. Where is France?"

"Pye! Is that really, really so?"

Pye nodded solemnly, looking puzzled at her own vision. Is hugged her. "Pye! If you're right, that's the cleverest thing you ever did. Is the train a whole row of wagons, going along *clonkey-clonk*, in the Tunnel?"

Pye nodded again. "Arun sick with toothache. Lying down. Very thirsty and sick."

Suddenly she began to cry. Overstretched from her poems and visions, she fairly howled. "Very sorry about poor Arun's teeth," she sobbed. "I won't knock his teeth out, not ever anymore."

"Shush! Shush! No, no, of course you won't," Penny said soothingly. "But do keep quiet now, like a good girl, or folk will grab us."

"Don't want Arun and Ruth to be so far away," wept Pye.

"Is that you, Ma?" called Arun softly. "In the next wagon?"

"Yes it is!" Ruth called back in the same tone. "What a pity we are not traveling in the same wagon. We could have enjoyed the trip so much more! And I wish it was daylight. I've never been to France, I should like to be able to look about."

"You forget," pointed out Arun, "we are going through the Tunnel. It will be dark."

Indeed, in a moment, with no more than a gentle jerk, the train crept quietly out of the station and down the incline to the Tunnel entrance. The gate whined up—Arun well remembered the sound—and then they were through, and gliding along in a tubular, dimly lit cavern. Every now and then there would be a blue disk overhead. (These were activated by electromagnetic currents, Arun learned later.) Once inside the Tunnel the noise of the train grew too loud to permit conversation from one truck to the next.

Arun concentrated on sending out thought-patterns. *Somebody* might hear these, after all, he thought, if I keep calling for help loudly enough.

If only he could make contact with Is! If only she were still there, *somewhere*! And Penny, and Pye. And Figgin. He could hardly endure the thought that the wicked old Admiral had, in one callous, wholesale act of destruction, demolished not only the *Throstle*—that happy home—but also the Cold Harbor, welcome refuge of travelers since inconceivably long-ago times.

Thud-thud, thud, went the train. *Click-click-click.*

Arun was thirsty—he could hardly seem to remember a time when he had *not* been thirsty—and his teeth ached and throbbed. But despite this, and the worry about Ruth, and the fear and uncertainty regarding Is and Penny and Pye— not to mention Figgin—he began to feel a faint, unreasonable hope. It was something to do with the man Twite. He had suddenly begun to seem beleaguered, fidgety, unsure,

240

much less powerful than he had been on that first nightmare carriage ride into the wood.

Was it something to do, also, with those voices?

"Is—are you there?" Arun called in thought-patterns, over and over.

Oddly enough the Tunnel—despite being underground, undersea—helped to provide a good background for thought-patterns. Presently Arun began to pick up more and more voices—voices from farther and farther off—transmitting messages of hope and goodwill. They arrived in all kinds of unfamiliar forms, new shapes, new keys—but he was sure they were friendly.

And then, suddenly, much stronger, making his brain buzz and tingle with its unexpected force, came a call from another direction, a childish, familiar, peremptory voice:

"Arun! Is that you? Where are you? Have you got new teeth? Arun, where are you?"

"Pye! Is that you? Are you there?"

He poured himself through to her as clearly as he could and, in return, received a confused impression that she, Is, and Penny were in a wood somewhere, hungry and wet.

Then the connection faded and the new, unfamiliar voices resumed their soothing murmur.

As he lay back on the jolting wagon floor, tired, but hugely relieved, it suddenly occurred to Arun that these might be *French* voices.

Ten

The rain was still falling, later that night, as Penny, Is, and Pye made their cautious approach along the beach to the eastern end of Cold Shoulder Road. Not a light showed in the little row of identical houses.

"Looks like everybody took and cleared out from the neighborhood," whispered Is.

The tide was low. The sea whispered to itself far away down across the flat sand. Nobody was stirring in the dark street, and piles of driftwood and seaweed left lying about suggested that the town authorities had given up bothering to clean the street anymore.

When they reached the end house—the one that had once been occupied by Dominic de la Twite and his sister—they saw that there was a burnt-out gap next to it. Is was reminded of Arun's missing teeth after Pye threw the grommet.

And she fancied that Pye suddenly had a similar thought, for she gave a little whimper and muttered, "Don't *like* this place."

"We might use Twite's house, I suppose," Penny murmured doubtfully, but Pye whispered, "No! No! *Horrible* house!", and you could hardly blame the poor kid, Is thought, since she had been shut up in a box in it, every night.

Mrs. Boles's house, beyond Ruth's, had also suffered somewhat from the burning, and was plainly uninhabited, with open door and smashed windows. And serve the woman right, thought Is, I shouldn't wonder but what she had a hand in the burning. I don't think she liked Ruth, and she was certainly scared of the paintings. I wonder where she has moved to? Just as well if she ain't anywhere nearby. She was an untrustworthy piece of goods, if ever there was one.

The house next to Mrs. Boles's was empty also, and seemed in reasonably good repair.

"Shall we lodge ourselves in this one?" whispered Penny. "I remember it belonged to a weaver, Matthew Penge. He was a good friend to Ruth. But he died of the lung-rot. I bought some wool off him once."

They found that one of Matthew's rooms was still almost entirely taken up by the enormous wooden loom, which nobody had bothered to remove. And upstairs there remained several piles of uncarded wool, which served handsomely for beds. They were all three dead tired and thought of nothing but flopping down on the soft mass and instantly going to sleep.

Next morning Penny said, "It's best I'm the one to go out and buy the prog, for I haven't been to Folkestone in some long while; folk won't remember me. Is, you and Pye better stay close."

This made obvious sense, though it was tiresome. Is said,

"Buy a bit of paper and writing things, Pen, while you're out; we'll send a letter to that Greenaway. And while you're gone, Pye can work on trying to pick up another message from Arun."

Pye would have liked to go out and run on the beach (a thing she had never been permitted to do while she lived with Twite and his sister), but even she could see that this was far too dangerous; people in Folkestone would remember her as the Handsel Child at whom they used to go and stare fearfully in the days when she hung in her cage over the railway.

"But we might sneak along the back gardens and into some of the other houses," Is said, to pacify her, and this they did, finding a good deal of rubbish and a few interesting relics in the little deserted dwellings: a whole roomful of wigs left behind by the master wigmaker Amos Furze; some cups, plates, and stools, which they took back for their own use; an umbrella; a musical instrument made of clay and shaped like a fish; a book, *Snake-Charming Without Tears*; and, to the delight of Is, four paintings by Ruth, which she must have presented to neighbors and they had ungratefully left behind.

Pye had never seen Ruth's paintings and was spellbound; after they had been brought back to Matthew's house she lay curled up on the wool, gazing at them in a trance of pleasure for a long time, while Is made a cautious survey of the overgrown little kitchen gardens, finding some leaves of spinach and a few old carrots and parsnips, which she made into soup.

Penny arrived with news, as well as provisions.

"What do you think! I came across Mrs. Nefertiti at the market with one of her daughters. They've a stall, selling goats' cheese. Oh, she was so angry about the *Throstle*! Lucky they weren't hurt by the explosion at the farm; only shook. But I told her we'd seen the Admiral, with his kite. She knew it was his doing. Dunno how, she just knew. And she's terrible angry about the Cold Harbor, too. She said it won't be long before the Admiral's time is up. She'd not say how. She just feels it coming. No news of Ruth. I told her we've a notion Ruth's in France. And she said yes, that made sense, for she could feel that a new kind of wave was going to roll across the Channel very soon."

"A tidal wave?" said Is anxiously. "Like the one that hit Blastburn?"

"No I don't think so. . . . A wave of people, it seemed to be."

Pye came downstairs, playing a breathy tune on her clay pipe.

"That's an ocarina," said Penny. "I've seen Italian peddlers with 'em at fairs. I will say, Pye, you soon got the hang of it."

Pye was playing the tune of "Whales and Snails Make Merry in Gales."

"Maybe Arun can hear music," she said hopefully. "Some people can—I can hear them—times—they pick it up and sing. Like Ruth's pictures! I tell people about those. I tell them lots of things."

Penny had bought apples and mutton pies and a pinch of

tea, for which she had a passion, done up in a paper twist; she set water to boil, over a driftwood fire, in an old iron pot Is had found outside.

Pye took a mutton pie and an apple and retired upstairs again. The others were soon glad that she was out of sight, for just as Penny was about to raise the longed-for cup of tea to her lips, there came a tap at the front door, and the unpleasing head of Mrs. Boles poked round it, lumpy with curlpapers.

"Well, I never!" she said, stepping inside and closing the door behind her. "I *fancied* it might be you that I saw in the High Street," with a nod at Penny. " 'Well,' I says to my-self, 'if that ain't the young lady as used to come and stop once in a way with Ruth Twite! Well,' thinks I to myself, 'what a shock it will be for her if she goes along to Cold Shoulder Road and finds the house all burned up.' So, I thinks, I'll just step along and see. And what do I find? Made yourselves real snug in here, haven't you? Very sen-sible, too, for poor old Matthew long ago handed in his cards, and poor Ruth's house, as you can see, suffered a fatality. Oh, ever so shocking, it was! And my poor little home suffered too—I was obliged to move in with my sis-ter, who has premises in Eccleston Road. It's a disgrace, I tell the Council, over and over, but not a bit of notice do they take."

All the while she was talking, Mrs. Boles's little red-rimmed eyes were running round the room like cock-roaches, taking note of everything that was there, or was not there.

"And how *is* Mrs. Ruth?" she asked chattily, "do you have good news of her? And that poor little Handsel Child, what they used to hang over the track with her head in a bag—what Mrs. Ruth made off with? Are they well, the both of them?"

"We reckon Aunt Ruth is in France," said Is stolidly. "That's all the news we have of her. And that ain't definite, no way."

"In *France*? Well, now, fancy that! Who'd ha' thought it? That's a long step for her to have taken the kinchin. Though, mind you, France ain't so far as it was, not now they've got this Chunnel Tannel! And will *you* be stopping here long?"

She wiped her hands on her apron—which was just as damp and grimy as the last time Is had seen her—and looked hopefully at the pot of boiling water and the paper of tea.

"That depends," said Penny. "Would you like a cup of tea?"

"Thank you, dear, I wouldn't say no. Most acceptable, that would be. Now, I remember when you were here before, with the young lad"—nodding at Is—"you carried all Mrs. Ruth's pictures up to the Admiral's place. How *is* the young lad?"

Her eyes wandered to the stair.

"He's well, thank you," Penny said, passing her the tea in a broken mug. "Is, I reckon there's a cat upstairs, you better go and chase it out."

Is took the hint and vanished upstairs.

"And will you be *seeing* the Admiral, like?" inquired Mrs. Boles, blowing the steam off her tea. "To take a look at Mrs. Ruth's pictures, like?"

"Well . . . ," began Penny.

"Why I ask," went on Mrs. Boles, "round here it's getting to be a known thing that the Admiral's the gaffer of those"—she whipped her eyes round the room and sank her voice to a murmur—"those Gentry. And it's a known thing that, quite soon, he and that other feller, that Deller Twite, and that sister of his, are all a-going to scarper off to the Ay-zores, to live on toasted larks and sherry wine forever after. While the rest of us shiver and starve and all the poor devils they done away with are gone and forgotten."

"Oh, really? Is that so? How do you know?" said Penny.

"Sure as you're born! There's the Admiral's own schooner, the *Merry Gentian*, anchored out there in the offing, ready to take 'em, whenever they decide to flit."

I lay they want to find the treasure first, though, thought Is, coming downstairs.

Mrs. Boles said hopefully, "If you went up to call on the Admiral, friendly like, as you *might*, being wishful to see the pictures, you might notice summat in his house, to, well, to tie him in with the Gentry. So he'd get put away. So they couldn't go to the Ay-zores."

"What sort of a thing, Mrs. Boles?"

"Like, maybe, those hoods they all wear. Or the white hat."

"But, you see, we've no reason to go and see the Admiral. He's no friend of ours."

Mrs. Boles said, "Tomorrow night he's to go off to Do-ver. He's been ast to a grand dinner, what's being given for what'shisname, the new Lord Left-thingummy. Seems unfair, dunnit, that the Admiral gets to drink wine with the nobs when all the time he's as wicked as they make 'em?"

"But how do you know he's so wicked, Mrs. Boles?"

"Ah," said Mrs. Boles darkly, "I know what I know."

"And how do you know he's going to Dover Castle?"

"Ah! My cousin's boy Alf, he's one of the gardeners in that-ar fancy high-footling garden of the Admiral that sticks out from the top o' the cliff. It'd serve him well, the old wretch, if the whole shevoo was to fall off into the sea, and him with it. That's what *I* say! My cousin's boy Alf, he's to drive the Admiral to Dover in his barouche, in style; for once he ain't a-going on his two-wheeler."

"Is that so?" said Penny thoughtfully, pouring more tea for Mrs. Boles. "But of course we wouldn't dream of going to a person's house when they weren't at home."

Mrs. Boles made a most peculiar grimace, laying her fin-ger alongside her nose and squinting horribly.

"D'you reckon that woman's telling the truth?" Is said to Penny later, when Mrs. Boles, after a good deal more in-quisitive peering about, had finally taken her way back along Cold Shoulder Road toward the center of town.

"I don't think the truth comes naturally to her," said Penny. "She's certainly out for Number One. But maybe it is so about the dinner at Dover. That *might* be a time for us to go and take a look at his place."

"You don't think it's a take-in? A trap? That he might have sent her? The Admiral hisself?"

"Well," said Penny, "I suppose we could go and skulk around in his garden, to see if he goes off in a barouche."

"Ye-es," agreed Is without noticeable enthusiasm. "We could do that . . ."

"Now we'd better write that letter to Greenaway," Penny said. "The baker's boy said he'd take it. They deliver bread to Dover Castle."

Arun supposed that he must have fallen into a catnap. And it had done him good. Although he was still thirsty, the new teeth seemed to have settled into their places, and felt more as if they belonged in his mouth. He would have liked to tell Pye that—and, as the idea came into his head, he could have sworn that he heard Pye singing his "Whales and Snails" song. Or rather, to the same tune, she was singing different words:

". . . Hold in a chain for the future's sake
    hold in a chain that man can't break
    hold till the world is wide awake . . ."

But that can't be Pye singing, he thought, I must have dreamed it. Now she was playing the same tune on a soft, wheezy instrument that sounded like the wind blown through a crockery drainpipe.

Arun became aware that the train was slowing down.

Thud—thud—thud. Click—click—clickety click. Click.

250

He called softly, "Mum! Are you there? Are you all right?"

"Yes, I'm here!" Ruth called back. "And right enough. Though I'd not say no to a plate of buttered eggs!"

The train crept to a stop. There was an immensely long pause. In the distance, Arun could hear people talking. But what they said was mostly incomprehensible. French, he supposed.

Then footsteps approached his wagon. A voice ordered, "Stand up." Arun stood, obediently, finding himself hungry, stiff, and weak. He saw the tall, bulky figure of Niland, who had now left off his black hood and revealed himself as grizzle-bearded, gray-haired, and worried-looking. As he hauled Arun out of the truck, Niland whispered in his ear, "When I undoes yer hands, *don't let on!* Keep holding them behind yer back. Then, when you gets the chance, scarper!"

Very much astonished, Arun nodded. He saw that Ruth had already been taken out of her truck, and was sitting quietly on yet another wooden bench. He wondered if her hands, too, had been undone. He certainly wasn't going anywhere without her.

They were—Arun assumed—in the French Channel Tunnel station, a neat little structure, identical to the English one, except that the signs said DAMES and MESSIEURS, and that from somewhere came a heart-rending smell of fresh coffee.

Arun looked about him carefully. The station was tucked into a green, chalky dent in the hillside, which was not at all unlike the country around Folkestone. To the north lay level, marshy land, intersected by dykes and canals, and beyond the marshes extended a long, flat, glistening beach, tapering away to the distant horizon. A glimmer on the left of the hill behind the station showed where the sun would presently rise into the pale, empty sky. And, southward, over the hill, a few trails of smoke suggested the whereabouts of a town, Calais perhaps.

Close at hand was a house—a large house, a mansion really, Arun supposed. It was built of brownish stone and had several turrets, each of them crowned with a little slate-capped cone.

"C'mon." Niland gave Arun a prod and a wink. "The Gaffer's going to that house. Chatto, it's called."

He gestured to Arun and Ruth to walk toward the mansion. There was a stone wall, a pair of iron gates, a gravel path. Not far ahead strolled a group of three or four people, including Dominic de la Twite, Fobbing, and a couple of strangers.

"I wonder why Niland's so friendly?" Arun murmured to Ruth as they walked.

"I nursed his daughter through measles," she murmured back.

"You an' yer ma 'll just have to watch for your chance," whispered Niland in Arun's ear. "Maybe when they've all gone inside."

Niland's kindness was welcome, of course, thought Arun, but the chances for escape just at present seemed fairly slender. The mansion stood on its own, with a group of outbuildings to one side and, around the other side, a large formal garden with paths and pools and fountains. There seemed no cover, no trees, bushes, shrubberies, or hedges. Where could they hide? The outbuildings would be searched at once. . . .

The group ahead turned aside from the front door of the mansion, and walked under an arch into a cobbled stable-yard. And then through a wide doorway into a great vaulted chamber which had perhaps once been a storeroom or granary. Now it seemed to have been furnished as an office, with long, scrubbed tables and piles of paper and account books.

"Stand over there!" Dominic de la Twite ordered his prisoners sharply, and gestured toward a corner. Arun caught his mother's eye; she shrugged. Niland jerked his head resignedly. Ruth and Arun moved to the corner. Now they were cut off from the entrance by a long table.

Dominic was involved in a long, acerbic discussion with a thin, elderly Frenchman, who wore a white wig (his own gray hair showed under it) and seemed, Arun thought, both terribly anxious to be polite and as if he deeply disliked the whole conversation. He kept gesturing with his hands as if they were fishes' gills, opening and closing them to let in badly needed air.

"But, monsieur, I assure you, I absolutely guarantee—" he kept saying.

Arun caught the eye of a dark-haired girl, thin and worried-looking, who stood beside the elderly man and seemed to be giving him support. She resembled him—perhaps she was his daughter. Every now and then she would confirm what the older man said, nodding and frowning at Twite. "It is so, monsieur. It is just as he says. Ask our steward, also."

She doesn't like Dominic, thought Arun. In fact, she detests him.

He cast a sideways glance at Ruth, who flicked him a wry grin and then slipped a hand under his arm, giving it a friendly, conspiratorial squeeze. Not much chance to escape, I fear, but isn't this interesting! was what she conveyed by the look and the touch. Arun grinned back at her, wonderfully cheered and sustained by her presence.

Then he suddenly realized that he was receiving a powerful thought-message from the dark-haired girl.

"Who are you? Why are you here?"

"My mother and I were brought here by Twite. We had no choice," Arun sent back. "Who are you?"

"I am Annette de Puy. I live here. My father is the Comte de Puy."

Evidently the white-wigged man.

"What are they arguing about?" Arun asked.

"That hateful man"—evidently she referred to Twite— "says that my father cheated him out of three loads of mammoth tusks. My father is a man of honor—he would never do such a thing!"

Arun wondered why a man of honor should be involved in a smuggler's trade of mammoth tusks.

He had not particularly intended this thought to reach

the girl, but it did. She flashed back indignantly, "We are very poor! My father is the last of his line, and he had the château to keep up, and all our people on the estate to look after. Times are hard."

Now the Comte de Puy was saying, "But, monsieur, I can readily prove the fact to you. Here, only see —" and he moved to open a massive ledger on one of the tables. Its pages were all covered with figures in columns, and were interleaved with other papers, presumably bills of lading, invoices, and receipts. Even the smuggling of mammoth tusks, it seemed, was here carried on in a very efficient and businesslike way.

"Look, monsieur!" the Comte announced triumphantly, producing a sheet of paper and flourishing it under Dominic de la Twite's nose. "Your own sister's signature! Instructing us that the three consignments were to be diverted to Zeebrugge and would not come to the Château de Puy or cross the Channel. We were sorry about it, naturally . . . but of course in affairs of this kind one must accept the inevitable."

The sight of the paper handed to him by the Comte de Puy plainly came as a shattering shock to Dominic. He was already pale — he now turned whiter than the paper he held, and stared at it with starting eyes. It shook in his hand.

Arun suddenly started to hear his thoughts, which went round and round in a frantic spiral.

"My own sister cheated me! How could she? What has she done with all those tusks? What is she planning to do with them? My own sister! How could she? Somebody must have suggested it—helped her. She would never be able to arrange such a fraud by herself. She is not clever enough for that. She is a stupid woman. Who could have helped her? Who?"

And then, in a kind of scorching fury: "It was Fishskin! The cunning, calculating rat! Now I see it all. He wanted us out of Folkestone so that he could load up the *Gentian* and be off to the Azores without me. But I will catch up with them. I will—"

He said to the Comte de Puy, "That my own sister could put the double on me—I would not have believed it possible! But it is certainly her hand—no question of that. I regret, monsieur, very much, that I should have questioned your word."

"Doubtless it is some family misunderstanding that will soon be cleared up," said the Comte graciously. "But you are ill, sir! You are suffering. My daughter will procure you a stimulant."

Dominic de la Twite did look deathly ill. His color had worsened from white to a kind of glazed green; his cheeks shone with perspiration.

"No—no," he said hoarsely. "No, I thank you. But there was something else that I wish to ask—to find out—"

His gaze roamed round the vaulted chamber as if, almost unbalanced by this proof of his sister's cheating, he could hardly command his own wits. But the sight of Ruth and Arun reminded him.

"Ah, yes. The treasure. King Charles's treasure."

The de Puys, father and daughter, looked at one another

in total bewilderment. Twite went on hoarsely, "Brought by Queen Henrietta on the ship *Victory* to help her husband, King Charles the First—sunk in the Channel. Thought to be hidden somewhere in this area—"

The de Puys still looked at him blankly. "Non, monsieur. We have not heard of any such treasure. Never!"

"Look!" screamed Twite hysterically, pulling his neck-cloth so as to loosen it. "This necklace of brown diamonds —The Living River—this piece was part of the *Victory*'s cargo—where this came from, there must the rest be!"

"But truly we know nothing about it, sir," said Annette de Puy pityingly. "Indeed we have no knowledge of any such a treasure ever, at any time, having been deposited hereabouts."

Her father was frowning. "But I do have some knowl-edge of that necklace," he said. "I have read about it in a history book. Brown diamonds are not natural. They ac-quire their color from exposure to powerful rays which are transmitted through the rock in one especial region of Bra-zil. I recollect now. I would most strongly advise you *not* to wear that chain for too long, Monsieur de la Twite. For I have heard that another name given to that necklace was The River of D—"

But Dominic de la Twite was not listening to the Comte de Puy. He seemed to be choking, or unable to catch his breath. He gasped and gasped, grabbing at his own throat, dragging off the white neckcloth, snapping the chain of brown stones, which bounced and flashed all over the cob-bled floor.

"Air!" he gasped. "I must have more air!"

Tearing open his white ruffled shirt, he rushed out into the stableyard.

"What is it? What can we do for him, Papa?" cried Annette, aghast.

"Very little, I fear," her father said ominously. His eye lit on Ruth. "Would you, madame, know, by any chance, how long has monsieur been wearing the chain?"

"Twelve hours at least, monsieur."

"Then I fear there is no hope for him. He is done for," said the Comte de Puy, who did not seem unduly distressed by the fact.

And indeed, when Niland and Will Fobbing ran outside to help Dominic de la Twite, he had already fallen to the ground; his breath came slower and slower. In another couple of minutes it stopped altogether.

"I suppose," said Annette thoughtfully, "the poisonous effect of the stones, coming just after the news of his sister's double-dealing —"

"The necklace itself must in any case have killed him within twenty-four hours," her father pronounced.

Croopus, thought Arun, it was lucky for Is that she never put it on, only carried it in her breeches pocket.

"Is? Who is she?" flashed Annette's question in his mind's ear.

"She's my cousin . . ." Telling Annette the whole story of the Gentry, the Handsel Child, the Silent Sect, Admiral Fishskin, the treasure, was far quicker and easier in thought-language than it would have been in plain speech.

She listened absorbedly; meanwhile the body of Dominic de la Twite was wrapped in a piece of tapestry, placed on a stretcher, and carried by Fobbing and Niland to the Tunnel train.

"But this is wonderful—amazing!" Annette cried at the end of Arun's story. She gave Ruth and Arun warm hugs. "Listen—I have much—much—much! to tell you both, about the man Micah Swannett, about children we have here—but first, you poor things, you must come into the château and have some *déjeuner.* You must be fainting! Papa disliked Monsieur de la Twite so much that he would never ask him inside, but you, you are different—"

She poured out a flood of rapid French explanation to her father, who bowed at once, most graciously, to Ruth, and offered her his arm, to lead her into the château.

"We have here a countryman of yours," Arun heard him telling Ruth in polite but halting English. "He was rescued from a small boat—very sick, starving. For days he knew not even his own name—would not speak to us when we questioned him—but my daughter, who is very sympathetic, she found out that his name is Micah—so, by degrees we find out what place he is from. And there are children also. They were thrown from the train—they were hurt, but they lived—"

"The Handsel Children!" cried Ruth.

"Quoi? You can, perhaps, help us to discover where they belong . . ."

Eleven

The next day passed very slowly in Cold Shoulder Road.

Overnight they had written the letter to Sir David Greenaway.

"Dere Podge," Is wrote, her spelling here and there corrected by Penny, "do you remember me, Dido's sister Is Twite. Well in fokston now things is turble bad. The mery gentry what smugles mamoth tusks is makin fokes lives a Mizry. Two many fokes getin kild. Too meny fokes scared to speke. An the 2 heds of the hole show is Admiril Fishkin an Dominik della Twite. Fishkin blew up the Throssle an Twite had mike Swanet drownded what was a Decint fella. They are a pare of Raskils. Tis time you shood do sumat about them Podge. Yours respecfly from Is Twite an my sister Peny Twite who sends her kind regards."

The baker's boy promised that it should reach Dover Castle by noon.

Pye spent the day playing the ocarina, reading *Snake-Charming Without Tears*—it was the first book she had encountered, so she was quite absorbed by it—and, a large part of the time, doing something she vaguely described as "sending off messages."

"Messages to who, Pye?" Is asked her.

"I dunno, exacly. Some are kids right here, in Folke-stone. Some a lot farther off."

It seemed plain that Pye's ability to send and receive thought-talk was increasing almost hourly.

"I gotta boy, now, in Blastburn. Name of Coppy. He sends love to you, Is."

"Oh, yes, little Coppy! He was a right decent little char-acter."

And, later in the day, "*I got Dido!* I got Dido, way off in Whale Island! She sends love to you and Penny and com-ing home soon."

"Good heavens, Pye! Are you *sure*?"

"Course I'm sure," said Pye, rather offended.

Halfway through the day, Penny went out for provisions. She came back only after so long a time that Is and even Pye had begun to grow deeply anxious. When Penny did turn up, it was from the wrong direction, down the brambly hill, and she had a cut and bleeding cheek and a black eye coming.

"Pen! What *happened*?"

"Two chaps recognized me. They must have seen me, long ago, with Ruth. I think they were Gentry fellows. They shouted 'Witch, witch!' and chased after me and threw stones. I managed to give them the slip, but it took hours of dodging, and I had to go all round the houses."

Penny flopped crossly down onto a heap of wool, while Is carefully swabbed her cut cheek and anointed it with some of Ruth's feverfew ointment.

"The nuisance of it is, that means we dassn't stay much longer in Folkestone," Penny said. "Not if we're that liable to be spotted."

Toward evening Penny's eye swelled up, and her head began to ache badly. It was plain that she would not be able to come on the spying expedition to the Admiral's house.

"Don't you stay there too long, now," she warned. "For I'll be in a terrible worriment about ye till I see you back. In case he's left a charley on the lookout."

"No, we'll be as careful as King Solomon's cat," Is promised. "We won't even go near the place till we've seen old Fishskin off the premises. And then we'll lurk around a whole lot longer till we're sure it's all rug."

"What'll I do if you don't come back?" demanded Penny, thrown off her usual brisk competence by headache, pain, and weakness.

"Wait till dawn and then send the baker's boy to Dover Castle with a message," Is suggested, though rather doubtfully, since that would mean Penny had to go into town.

Then Pye unexpectedly said, "A girl called Jen says she's coming to Folkestone. Tomorrow morning early. With a whole lot of friends. I'll ask her to come round by Cold Shoulder Road. Then they can take a message for you. If you want."

"That sounds all right," said Penny, somewhat relieved. "Now—will you please *watch out*!"

Dusk was falling and light was thickening as Pye and Is climbed up the chalky path that led to the East Cliff. The weather was cloudy and windy.

"Blowing up a gale, feels like," said Is. "That ain't a bad thing. It ain't so easy to hear boards creaking and doors shoved open in a house if the wind's wuthering outside."

They found a good vantage point, a thick clump of laurustinus not far from the front door of East Cliff House, and settled down to watch and wait. Pye had brought her ocarina, but Is firmly forbade her even to *think* of playing on it. Pye therefore went back to her message-game, sitting cross-legged on the damp ground with a look of immense concentration on her face, like a cat collecting spit for washing.

Three quarters of an hour passed. Then a carriage driven by (presumably) Mrs. Boles's cousin's boy Alf drew up at the front door, which opened, letting out a pool of light. Out came the Admiral, dressed up to the nines—white silk stockings, diamond buckled shoes, blue velvet jacket, gold lace, cocked hat, and gold-hilted sword. He looked like an inn sign, Is thought, or something off a wedding cake. Surprisingly, he had a lady with him: he led her out of the door and politely helped her into the coach.

"Who's that?" muttered Is, and heard Pye, beside her, give a little hiss of horror.

"Miss Twite! Twite's sister!"

Merlwyn Twite, too, was dressed very grandly, in a stiff dress of yellow Tribute Silk, some large diamonds, and feathers in her gray hair.

The coach door slammed; the horses broke into a trot.

"Give 'em fifteen minutes," said Is. "Just in case Miss Twite forgot her fan."

They made it twenty minutes. The house was all dark, not a light to be seen anywhere, and not a sound to be heard.

"Now we'll go round to the back," breathed Is, who remembered the way into the garden room where they had taken Ruth's pictures. By now their eyes were well accustomed to the dark. Is had remembered that the door to the conservatory had a broken pane in it. Sure enough, there was not the least trouble in slipping a hand through the hole and pushing back the bolt. The door opened with a gentle *scrunch* and they tiptoed into the warm interior, which smelt of earth and geraniums.

"Shut the door behind you, Pye, but don't bolt it. We may need to scarper fast. Now we'll wait again till our eyes is used."

When they had done this they went next door into the garden room, where, Is remembered, there had been candles, matches, and small oil lamps on a shelf. Is lit a couple of lamps.

"Now we go into the kitchen," she whispered, and opened the door at the back of the garden room.

The kitchen seemed exactly as Is remembered: cozy, stuffy, and unbelievably untidy, musty with the smell, almost a taste, of many potatoes that had boiled dry, and many slices of bread fried in rancid lard.

"Now, keep your eyes peeled for Rosamund."

They had not long to wait.

Down her silver thread, silent as shade, large as a black and eight-legged cushion, shot Rosamund, her brilliant little eyes fixed on the visitors in a very unwelcoming manner. She began to advance toward them.

"Oh, flame it," muttered Is. "I really hate spiders."

The fact that Rosamund was followed by two friends or sisters did not improve the moment. Is looked round for a rolling pin or a fish slice.

"Don't do that," said Pye. "It'll only aggravate 'em. I can fix 'em."

She pulled the ocarina from her pocket and played a gentle tune.

To the huge relief of Is, this had exactly the required effect. The spiders, lulled and charmed, sank together into a sooty, hairy, shaggy heap with eyes like diamonds gazing sleepily in every direction.

"Nice!" said Pye. "Cozy! Ain't they?"

She seemed inclined to give them a pat.

"Never mind that, Pye, how long will they stay that way?"

"I dunno," said Pye. "The book don't say. But I can always play some more."

"Well, let's have a lookabout quick while they are dozing."

Is and Pye went down the long passage that Is remembered, and she noticed with interest that a large number of Ruth's pictures had been brought in from the cave and had replaced the engravings of ships on the walls. On the floor were the same piles of books and papers. Open doors showed rooms filled with rusty machines, rolls of carpets, moldy and blistered furniture, whole sets of chinaware.

"How the plague are we going to find anything in this clutteration?" said Is. "Let alone we don't rightly know what we are looking for."

By the front door they found twenty black cloaks and twenty black hoods hanging on pegs.

"But that," Is pointed out, "don't prove a thing. Old Fishskin 'ud say he likes to have plenty of extras in case it rains. Let's try upstairs. Maybe we'll find a white hat."

At the top of the stairs, unfortunately, they were faced by another group of spiders, which advanced in a menacing semicircular formation, waving legs, champing jaws. It took Pye longer, this time, to charm them to sleep with her music.

"Maybe we should call it a night," said Is, drawing several deep, unhappy breaths as the spiders collapsed into a whiskery heap. "But I'll just take a look in one or two bedrooms—"

She opened a door, and discovered a bedroom that was packed right up to the ceiling with large, buff-colored, smoothish, pointed objects. They were about the size of double basses. There appeared to be hundreds of them. Perhaps thousands.

"What the blue blazes are these?"

"Oh, I know," said Pye. "I've seen lots of those taken on and off trains. Mammoths' tusks, they are. They get made into sneeze-boxes."

"Ah hah! That really shows he's a queer cove then— scaly as an old alligator! If we can get one of those out and take it away with us, we have him on toast."

Is braced herself, put her arms round one of the tusks—
which were packed together tight as sausages in a packet—
and gave it a tug.

The result was disastrous.

The whole stack of carefully piled tusks, once disar-
ranged, came crashing and tumbling out of the doorway.
They started a domino effect. More and more tusks cascaded down. They bowled over Pye and Is. They went
thundering from step to step down the staircase.

Worse: the collapse started up some kind of alarm mechanism that must have been cunningly set up by the Admiral. Bells rang. Gongs clanged. And a huge rusty cage,
which had been suspended above the stairwell, came creaking out of the ceiling and locked itself into four slots in the
floor.

Pye was caught inside the cage. Also, she had been hit on
the back of the head by a falling tusk, and looked not a little
dazed. She crouched in a nest of tusks, rubbing her head in
a bewildered manner.

"Pye! Are you all right? Are you hurt bad?"

"I'll havta see," mumbled Pye after a moment. "Dunno
yet."

Is tugged and wrestled frantically with the bars of the
cage. But, though rusty, they were strong and solid, locked
firmly into place. And they were set too close together for
Pye to escape between them, small though she was.

"Like old times, eh," she said vaguely. "Shut in a cage."

"Oh, *Pye!*"

For a moment—no more—Is felt real despair.

Then she set her lamp on the floor—Pye's had gone out but mercifully hers had not—and carefully inspected the cage.

"There's a keyhole here. So there's gotta be a key."

"Oh, aye?" muttered Pye, still dazed.

"Don't you fret, Pye. I'll find that key."

But *where?* Is thought, in this rabshackle house? Perhaps in the Admiral's bedroom?

But all the rooms on the upper floor were now inaccessible, barred off by the cage, which fitted across the head of the staircase.

The kitchen seemed the likeliest place. Practically everything was kept in the kitchen.

But what about the spiders there? Might they have livened up again by now?

Is really hated the idea of hunting for a key through the chaos of the kitchen, hampered in her search by half a dozen spiders the size of terriers.

"Pye: lend us the ocarina."

It took three of four minutes for Pye to comprehend what Is wanted. Then she pushed her hand into her pocket and brought out a broken earthenware mouthpiece.

"Oh, *frizzle* it," said Is. "Musta been smashed by a tusk. Or by the cage."

Pye looked stricken—much more upset by this than by the previous mishaps. "My pipe," she said forlornly. "Busted."

"Never mind it, Pye. Very likely Penny can fix it. Penny's extra good at mending things."

Anyway, Is thought, most like I couldn't fix the spiders the way Pye can. I don't have the gift.

Fortunately she remembered seeing a brass-hilted sword in the hall umbrella stand (the Admiral's second best, no doubt); armed with this, feeling more confidence, she returned to the kitchen.

Here the spiders were still piled up in a furry, drowsy heap. Sword in hand, Is skirted round them warily, hunting in all the places where a key might be kept; behind the clock on the mantelpiece, in the knife-and-fork drawer, in a bowl of coins, razors, and thimbles on the kitchen table, in a flowerpot, in a jug, in the soap container by the sink. She had almost reached the point of giving up when she lifted the lid of an earthenware crock that had once held Mrs. MacBeavor's Superior Potted Highland Grouse, and found that it contained a whole mass of keys, rusty and shining, large and small.

In the middle of her joy over this find, she heard a skittering on the floor, and spun round with horror to see that Rosamund and family were awake again and hurrying toward her.

Not wasting a second, Is leapt out of the kitchen, sword clutched in one hand, lamp and pot in the other, and kicked the door to behind her.

She was close to the main hall when—to her utter dismay—she heard the front door open and, worse still, the voices of the Admiral and Miss Twite in the hall.

So early! What could possibly have happened?

"Very vexatious indeed!" the Admiral was saying angrily. "Cannot understand it—how could they have made a mistake over our admission tickets? The whole thing seems deucedly queer to me—all that way for nothing—and in our best clothes—and in the rain—"

"I did not observe anyone *else* being turned away. Our tickets were the only ones they rejected, so far as I could see. You should certainly write to the *Times* about it," Miss Twite remarked in her grating tone. "But stay, Percival— something is surely amiss here? You had not left a light burning in the house?"

"Damme no, certainly I didn't—"

Then the Admiral saw Is in the passageway, with her lamp, and let out a hiss like a cobra. He snatched a blunderbuss from the umbrella stand.

"So, miss! I find you here, poking and prying! What explanation have you for this?"

Now that's a foolish question, thought Is. What explanation *could* I have, except to find out some of his havey-cavey secrets? Specially considering all the tusks that are lying about.

She did not trouble to reply—her mind was too occupied with wondering how she and Pye could possibly extricate themselves from this unpromising situation.

"Who is this girl, Percival?" Miss Twite was inquiring. "She looks somewhat familiar, but I—"

The Admiral, however, had noticed the cage at the top of the stair.

"Ho! I see that my little antitheft device has caught another intruder!"

He stumped up the stairs and peered through the bars at Pye, who was still crouching among scattered tusks and squashed spiders, looking sleepy and bemused. "And who are *you*, might I inquire?"

"Why, anybody can see who *she* is," said Merlwyn, now following him up. "That is the Handsel Child, the brat who resided in the care of myself and my brother, until abducted by Ruth Twite."

Indeed, at the sight of Miss Merlwyn, Pye let out a faint, pitiful wail. Is, who, temporarily forgotten at the foot of the stair, had been wondering if the most sensible course would not be to nip out through the open front door and yell for help, now changed her mind.

She ran up the stairs and said rapidly, "Admiral, I dunno why I should do you any good turn, considering you left me and my cousin shut up in your cave, but I'll tell you summat you don't seem to know: there's three huge crocks of cash and joolry and silver fal-lals stashed away down in your cave. Look"—and she rummaged in her pocket and brought out the last two of her Charles the First sixpences and tossed them on the stairs.

"A likely tale!" said the Admiral, but the speed with which he snatched up the coins contradicted the chilly incredulity of his tone.

"Is that coin genuine?" grated Miss Twite. "If it is, Percival, do you not think we should delay our departure while we investigate—?"

"First we have to rid ourselves of these intruders. Over the cliff, perhaps—"

"But if the girl knows where the cache is situated—"

"Oh, we can soon extract *that* information from her," said the Admiral, directing his blunderbuss toward Is in a very menacing manner.

Can you, though? she thought, just as another voice entered the conversation.

"Well, I never did! The Admiral, his own self. And Miss Twite! Back home early from the party, ain't ye? Did you come over poorly, then? Or wasn't the vittles up to your taste?"

The newcomer was Mrs. Boles, who, to the amazement of Is, now came through the front door. She wore a crocheted scarf over her head, and a shabby shawl over her shoulders. Her red-rimmed eyes gleamed and her long nose twitched interestedly as she peered about. Then she looked up the stairs and saw Pye in the cage. She let out a loud cry of real astonishment.

"My little Abandella! What the Gentry took, ever so long ago. And handed over to those Twites. Well, I will be jiggered. What have you got her buckled up in there for, you old monster? You make haste, right away, and let out the poor little precious, afore I call the Watch!"

"What the deuce are you talking about, woman?" snapped the Admiral, pale with fury. "Pray walk your chalks out of my house, before I lose my temper and set Rosamund on you."

"And I'll tell you summat else you don't know, you nasty old man," pursued Mrs. Boles (though she did flinch a bit at the mention of Rosamund), "my little Abandella is your own grandchild, for her dad was your good-for-nothing son Horatio. O' course I never said nothing when she turned up at the Twites. Least said's soonest mended, is my motter."

"*Wh-What* s-spiteful nonsense are you talking?" stammered the Admiral, even more startled.

"Well! If you don't believe me—*look* at her! Isn't she the spitting likeness of you, close as one halfpenny is to another? That my own daughter Meena should ever go off with such a capsy fellow I never could understand, and a lucky chance it was he got killed in a smugglers' fray afore she had cause to repent it—but there! done is done. They called her Twite—just like their toffee-nosed bossy ways—but properly she's Abandella Fishskin—bless her liddle heart."

Now, for the first time, Is realized why, when she looked at Pye, she always absentmindedly fitted her with a pair of imaginary rimless spectacles.

Put them on her nose, and she was the identical image (only smaller) of the Admiral. Mercy, what a horrible grandpa to have, thought Is.

Though I daresay mine was a right skellum too, for that matter.

All this time, Is had been almost unconsciously combing through the boxful of keys, hunting for one that looked as if it might fit the small keyhole in the metal cage. Now, having found a likely key, she edged up the stair, past the Admiral, who had come down to engage in heated dispute with Mrs. Boles.

"Your daughter Meena, madam, was no better than a slattern. And where is she now, pray? My son Horatio was at least killed fighting bravely—"

"Ay! In a smugglers' scuffle!" Mrs. Boles spat out venomously.

"But your daughter Meena, where is she? Went off and abandoned her defenseless infant."

"Not a bit of it! The Gentry took the babby from her, for their Handsel Child. Cried my eyes out, I did. So then Meena cut her losses and went to New York, where she's doing nicely in the hotel business—"

"Hah! That I can *well* imagine!"

Is went quietly up the stairs and tried her key in the lock. It fitted, but refused to turn.

Pye's lamp had been broken by tusks and lay inside the cage, leaking oil on the stair carpet.

"Pass the lamp through, Pye!" Is whispered. Pye did so with a nod of comprehension. She was beginning to look more pulled together. Is wondered, dribbling oil onto the lock, if she had heard and taken in what Mrs. Boles and the Admiral were saying to each other.

"That's the dandy! Now it turns."

The key turned, the lock clicked.

"Now let's give the cage a shove, Pye."

Remarkably, the cage, when shoved, glided silently and easily back into the cobwebby ceiling. This old Admiral, Is had to admit, is no fool when it comes to making machines work. Perhaps that was where Pye got some of her unusual abilities.

"C'mon, Pye, let's get us outa here. Penny'll be worrying."

But Miss Merlwyn barred the way, large and threatening in her inappropriately gorgeous dress of pale yellow silk. Her face, above it, was exactly the same shade of yellow; her eyes had turned to angry slits. She had helped herself to another blunderbuss from the umbrella stand.

"Wait a moment, my fine pair! Stand still where you are, until you have told us where the treasure is to be found. Otherwise the smaller one gets a breakfast of lead shot."

"I wouldn't advise that, ma'am," said Is.

"Oh? And why not?"

"Because there seems to be a whole caucus of folk outside the front door. And somebody might see you do it."

Miss Twite turned and looked down the stair, through the open door. Her jaw dropped, her eyes widened.

By a slow, unnoticed process, while these events had been taking place, the dark of the night had faded to gray. The hall windows had turned from squares of black to squares of pale blue. And a distant sound, which Is had at first taken for the *shush*ing of the sea at the foot of the cliff, was now recognizable as something else.

It was people singing.

Without giving any more thought to Miss Twite and her blunderbuss, Is ran outside the front door.

"Come on, Pye. Come and take a look at this!"

The Admiral's house, set on the slope of land between the cliff edge and the hilltop, faced in two directions, uphill and downhill.

275

To the south lay the sea, faintly silver now, with the black shape of the ship *Gentian* bobbing gently at anchor down by the foot of the cliff. And to the right the white chalk track that led down the steep slope to the town gleamed faintly in the predawn light.

There were dozens of people coming up the slope and gathering steadily in front of the house. There were more people—many, many more people—winding down from the top of the northerly hill behind, in a long, black, snake-like procession.

"Croopus!" murmured Is. "What a lot of folk. Where the pize have they all come from?"

"Some here, some from France," Pye told her matter-of-factly. "That lot up there from France." And she pointed to the procession winding down the hill. "I called 'em. Where is France?"

"Over the water," said Is absently. She was listening. "Pye, they're all singing 'Whales and Snails.'"

Or, if not, it was something very like.

"Mums and kids better stick together
Hang in there whatever the weather
Hold in a chain that none can break
Hold together for the future's sake . . ."

At the head of the file of people coming down the hill, Is—hardly able to believe her eyes—saw Ruth and Arun. And a black-haired girl whom she did not know. And Micah Swannett. A voice shouted, "Look, *look*, there's our kids! Back from France! There's little Sam Ringwould."

"Pye, look who's there!"

With a shriek of joy, Pye raced toward Ruth and Arun. She was hugged, passed from one to the other.

Now suddenly there came an outbreak of shots and angry shouting in the town below. There were puffs of smoke. Heads turned that way. The crowd on the hillside was momentarily hushed. But it was only for a moment. More and more people came pouring from both directions. Up the hill from the town. Down the hill from the Channel Tunnel entrance that lay beyond. And all of them assembled in front of the house.

They were all singing. Some in one language, some in another. But the words they sang seemed to dovetail well enough.

Is ran to Arun. "What happened to Dominic? How did you get here? Were you in France?"

"He's dead," said Arun, answering her questions in order. "The diamonds killed him. They gave off poisonous rays. Yes, we were in France. We walked back."

"*Walked* from France?"

"Through the Tunnel. It took all night."

"Why not on the train?"

"Held up by French customs officers. Is, this is Annette de Puy. She helped Ma and me. And she saved Micah. Where's Penny?"

"There she comes now," said Is, who saw Penny, still with a black eye and swollen cheek, coming up the hill from Folkestone. She looked angry and sad, but hugely relieved at the sight of Is and Pye, Arun and Ruth.

"They shot that poor girl," she told Is bitterly, when she was within speech range.

"Who?"

"Jen Braburn, she was called. From Seagate. She came to the house in Cold Shoulder Road to fetch me. Those two coves who followed me were lurking outside and shot her. But then the crowd just took them and threw them off the pier."

"Oh, poor Jen, how dreadful. How *wicked*. Why should *she* have to die?"

"Why should any?" said Pen, staring at the huge crowd.

The Admiral came out of his front door and looked about him in a bewildered manner.

At sight of the Admiral a tremendous communal groan of hate and disapproval went up from the crowd, followed by another, equally angry, at the sight of Miss Twite, who followed close behind. The pair glanced nervously this way and that, then made their way at speed across the lawn and into the cantilevered triangle of garden beyond, which hung on its platform right over the sea. Nobody tried to stop them. Everybody watched. Down below, the ship *Gentian* rocked gently. Now it could be seen that sailors were very busy about her, unfurling sails, undoing ropes, fastening hatches, testing the anchor windlass, stowing cargo, shutting portholes, making all fast.

"Getting ready to make sail," said Arun.

"But will folk just let them go? After all the harm they've done?"

"We'll see."

With shoulders hunched and heads bent forward, as if they expected showers of missiles to be launched at them, the Admiral and Miss Twite made their hurried way to the very tip of the cantilevered garden, where a ladder hung down by which the ship could be reached.

"I'd simply hate to climb down that," muttered Ruth.

"But it's good they are going," said Pye. And then, with tremendous emphasis, in thought-speech:

"Sing louder, everybody. *Sing!*"

The crowd burst into a roar of song:

"Hold in a chain around the earth
  Life to death and death to birth
  Hold for whatever your soul is worth—
  Hold—hold—hold—"

The sudden shattering roar of so many voices had a formidable effect. The Admiral and Miss Twite, at the edge of the garden, stopped in fright and looked behind them. Then they both shrieked and started to run back, for a gap had opened between the artificial garden and the true cliff edge.

They were too late. The crack widened with startling speed, the whole quarter acre of man-made garden peeled away from its support and fell—carrying the man and woman with it—straight down onto the ship, which vanished under the water. A dull boom came up later from the foot of the cliff, and the shock of huge waves could be felt.

"So they got their deserts," remarked Mrs. Nefertiti, who

had been walking slowly up the cliff path and now reached Ruth and Is. "Not before time. Things'll be better from now on. You done well, child!" she said approvingly to Pye. "You fetched a lot of folk from long ways off. And now I reckon everybody can enjoy a big hop-about. The Gentry's finished. There'll be no more of them."

Indeed, the hop-about was already beginning. People were dancing in rings, they were laughing and forming sets, waltzing and weaving.

Into this scene of festivity rolled a carriage from along the Dover Road. And out of it stepped a tall, plump, cheerful man in white breeches and a green velvet jacket.

"Where is Miss Is Twite?" he was asking.

"Podge! It's Podge Greenaway!"

"Well, there you are, little Is! You haven't growed much!" he said. "But how's this?" His pleasant face wore a look of mild surprise. "In your note you said that things were mighty terrible round here. But this looks to me more like a jollification!"

"Well," said Is, "things has turned out better than expected. But we're mighty pleased to see you, Podge, just the same. This here's my cousin Arun Twite, this is his mum, Mrs. Ruth Twite, here's my sis, Penny, and this is little Pye." With a grin she added, "Her name's really Pye Fishskin, but I reckon she ain't too keen on that moniker."

"What happened to the Admiral?" Podge asked, looking round. "When I got your note I decided that it would be quite unsuitable for him to attend the dinner at Dover Castle. So I had him denied at the door. Until his name should be cleared of the suspicion of running the Merry Gentry."

"I reckon his name never will be cleared now," said Is, "for he's dead, drownded, along with his ship—but if you step into his house you'll find it's just chockablock with mammoths' tusks all ready to be carved into sneeze-coffers."

"Oh well," said Podge cheerfully, "if that's so, that saves a deal of trouble."

"And, Podge—you know King Charles's treasure? Well, we found it. Three great king-sized crocks of gold and stuff —it's all hid away over yonder. Or under yonder." Is nodded to the Admiral's conservatory and the hillside beyond. "But it'll take a deal of digging out, for the ground's very sliddery thereabouts."

"Bless my soul!" said Podge. "Who found it?"

"Me and Arun."

"Well, then, young 'uns, I reckon it's yours—if it was lost, that is; if it was hidden for safekeeping, then it belongs to the Crown. There'll have to be an inquest about it."

"It *was* lost," said Is, "for first of all it was on the sloop *Victory*, and she sank. And then someone found it on the Goodwins and stowed it in the cave; but they weren't the owners, the folk who stowed it away."

"I reckon that'll be for the Crowner to sort out," said Podge. "But if it's yours, what would you want to do with it?"

"Oh, me and Arun don't *want* it," said Is hastily. Arun shook his head in agreement. "But what we thought—those poor Silent Secters might like a lump of it, to help 'em buy themselves a passage to the New World and a plot of land there."

"You'd think there would be plenty for that," said Podge. "The Silent Sect—which are they?"

"Umn," said Is, looking about. "They're the ones in black hats. But they seem to have taken a day off from being silent."

Down the hill she could see a number of the Silent Sect in their black-and-blue costumes, laughing and dancing just as freely as everybody else. Window and Micah had found each other and were dancing hand in hand.

"I think I'll go with them," said Ruth suddenly. "With Micah. And Window. To the New World."

"But—*Ma!*" Arun was tremendously shaken. "Just when you got into the way of talking? You're going back into Silence?"

Ruth gave him a hug. "We'll see! But I find that silence suits me very well. There's a lot to be said for it. You get time to listen. And paint pictures. I'll go to the New World for a trial. A year, perhaps. Just to see . . ."

"Not for always, Mum, please! And what about Pye?"

"Pye's going to have plenty of friends," said Ruth affectionately. "She could live with Penny and Is. Or with Dido. Or with her grandma."

"No thank you!" said Pye firmly.

"So you are Arun Twite?" said Podge. "I have a message for you from His Majesty. From King Simon."

"From the *King*?" Arun was startled to death.

"You were a great friend, I believe, of the last Prince of Wales—of Prince David?"

Arun nodded.

"And you make up songs?"

"You can hear 'em!" said Is. "Listen."

The crowd were singing:

"Whales and snails aren't bothered by thunder
Snails and whales play hooky in gales
Snails slip over and whales dive under
Weather's a pleasure to whales and snails . . ."

"The king," said Podge, "wants to appoint a Court Musician and Song Writer. And he would like you to apply for the post."

"M-M-Me?" said Arun, stammering.

Mrs. Nefertiti said to Is, "You and your sis and little Pye are welcome to come and stay at Womenswold, dearie, until you've got your home built again. And—I didn't bring him, for I reckon he wouldn't enjoy the crowds—but I've a friend of yours back at the farm."

"Not Figgin?"

"*Figgin?*" cried Pye, her cheeks scarlet with joy. "Let's start now!" And then she added, sliding her hand into her pocket, "Penny! Can you mend my ocarina?"

BOOKS BY JOAN AIKEN

The Haunting of Lamb House

Morningquest

Jane Fairfax

Blackground

If I Were You

Mansfield Revisited

Foul Matter

The Girl from Paris

The Weeping Ash

The Smile of the Stranger

Castle Barebane

The Five-Minute Marriage

Last Movement

The Silence of Herondale

Voices in an Empty House

A Cluster of Separate Sparks

The Embroidered Sunset

The Crystal Crow

Dark Interval

Beware of the Bouquet

The Fortune Hunters

JUVENILES

A Creepy Company

A Fit of Shivers

Return to Harken House

Give Yourself a Fright

A Touch of Chill

The Shadow Guests

Midnight Is a Place

A Whisper in the Night

The Wolves of Willoughby Chase

Black Hearts in Battersea

Nightbirds on Nantucket

The Cuckoo Tree

The Stolen Lake

Dido and Pa

Is Underground

The Skin Spinners: Poems

The Green Flash and Other Tales

The Far Forests: Tales of
    Romance, Fantasy and Suspense

The Angel Inn by the Comtesse de
    Segur, translated by Joan Aiken

Bridle the Wind

Go Saddle the Sea

The Teeth of the Gale

The Faithless Lollybird

Not What You Expected

Arabel's Raven

Arabel and Mortimer

The Mooncusser's Daughter: A
    Play for Children

Winterthing: A Children's Play

Street: A Play for Children

Died on a Rainy Sunday

Night Fall

Smoke from Cromwell's Time and
    Other Stories

The Whispering Mountain

A Necklace of Raindrops

Armitage, Armitage, Fly Away
    Home

The Moon's Revenge